"There is something in every one of you that waits and listens for the sound of the genuine in yourself. It is the only true guide you will ever have. And if you cannot hear it, you will all of your life spend your days on the ends of strings that somebody else pulls."

– Howard Thurman

For Our Readers

Go to <u>www. Friends-N-Neighbors.info</u> to get first hand news, and to read of upcoming books.

Please feel free to email us at friendsnneighbors.info@yahoo. com.

Like our Facebook page: https://www.facebook.com/ friendsnneighbors/

We would love to hear from you.

BROKEN ARROW WAR

Book 1 ... The Beginning

Authors:

Teresa Sewell & Rob LE

We want to thank Shawn S. for believing in us and
the book.

To Charles, and Marc.

For all the times you were there no matter the
time, day or night for being friend, sounding board,
cheering squad or anything else when needed.

Special Thanks, to Nicki S., Mark M. for all the hard
work and dedication you put into us to help us
become better writers.

You guys are the best, Thank you.

Dedicated to all our friends in the
Immortal Night and Immortal Day.

Join us in a mystical time where lycans and vampires rule, and where magic, cruelty, and blood are part of everyday life.

Where good battles evil on a daily basis trying to protect the innocent.

If good fails, the world is lost to an evil that seeks to destroy it all.

****

The king of the vampires wants an heir. The prophecy states that the princess's child would have powers that have not been seen before.

Teera was being hunted so she could be used to breed a powerful child that all factions want to control.

The red cloaks captured Brenat for his betrayal, and turned him over to the upper echelon. The witch Keres decided she wanted Brenat for her own plans. She has Brenat sent to Arena City and placed in the slave pens. Brenat's mysterious escape from the inescapable pens have Silfer's army, Keres, the red cloaks, as well as the broken arrows all searching for him.

Sid and Elsie escaped the massacre with their grandson Joel and are pursued by those seeking to kill them. Joel gets captured and sent to Arena City, the very center of those that seek to control him.

Broken Arrows prepare for battle....

The Legend

In the early days, Lucifer was the first archangel, God's first creation. He loved his father unconditionally, following his every order, until the human race was created. He, along with the other angels, were ordered to love these flawed creations by his father. Lucifer hated humans because they were favored by his father over the angels and it started a terrible war in heaven. The war raged on for a thousand years until Lucifer and the other angels that sided with him were beaten and cast down into hell.

In revenge Lucifer created immortal beings called Vampires. God watched from the heavens as these immortals took the lives of many humans. He then created beings of his own to protect the humans, shape-shifting werewolves he called lycans to destroy the Vampires. Along with the lycans, he secretly created special shifters he named Royals to push the balance more to his side. The Royals consisted of Tigers, Bears, Wolves, Jaguars, Panthers, Dragons and Lions. They were bigger, stronger, and deadlier than regular lycans.

When the royals were discovered by Lucifer, he made many attempts to kill them with vampires, demons, and witches. Their attempts were thwarted until one lowly witch figured a way to help her master Lucifer succeed.

The witch found a young royal hungry for power. She

promised him unlimited power if he obeyed her completely, he immediately agreed. She then had him kill and feast on his own father, thus corrupting the young royal forever. His hunger to eat all life steadily grew stronger. Hate and malice made him powerful, while love, hope and happiness were painful and weakened him. His journey of corruption was so successful that before long the royals were hunted to extinction. A few managed to escape and live as humans striving to remain undetected, soon the tale of the mighty royals passed into myth and legend. The witch was rewarded by becoming Lucifer's mistress, and was given powerful magic to do his bidding.

The legend also told of a princess with this royal blood that would one day set the righteous path into motion. Her child would have powers never seen before and would restore the balance of good and evil.

Lucifer created an elite group to find and kill this princess, thus ensuring the destruction of her child. Unknown to Lucifer, God had created from one of these special assassins, the other half of his plan...

The Beginning

Two powerful kings had been at war for many years. Asslam of the vampires and James of the lycans had been battling in a give and take fight for land, both sides losing many in the daily skirmishes, in which the sound of weapons on shields could be heard. Often the fights would continue until the warriors were down to fighting with teeth and claws.

In many battles the lycan war generals, Dukut, Silfer, and Kenny had proven themselves by defeating many vampires as well as holding and gaining ground. These triumphs were becoming more difficult with the vampires easily refilling their ranks from the human population.

Many vampires had started converting pimps and small gangs to grab more territory, so they could get more humans to convert as fodder in the war for control against the lycans. The converted pimps and gangs control the humans instead of vampires controlling them.

Meanwhile, with the war going on for thousands of years, the purebred and bonded mates among the lycans were becoming fewer and fewer, as the lycans could not refill their ranks as easily as the vampires. Worse, with so many losing their mates, very few new lycan births had happened in the last hundred years.

The Blood moon sat low in the sky as the vampires attacked the small town, they hoped to capture more humans for their army against the lycans. Not knowing that an earlier scouting report had the lycans ready and waiting. All but a few of the humans had been silently spirited away to safety. A small handful had stayed behind to aid the lycans in the defense of their village.

Fourteen days and nights the battle raged, with the dust of hundreds of dead vampires blowing in the breeze. Among the dead, the heads of six high ranking vampires were counted. The humans and lycans had also lost several in the battle, but the town and its people had been saved.

Many of the tired and wounded took the day to heal and celebrate their hard won victory. With the peaking of the blood moon, many lovers paired off feeling its heightened lustful effects, for even in the height of the day the blood moon could be seen brightly.

King James and Queen Rizalle, the leaders of the lycans feeling the moon's pulled, as well as weariness from the long battle, decided to relax. To take time from battle planning and spend some much needed time together.

As they retired to their tent, James wraps his arms around Rizalle then lightly bit at the back of her neck as he ran his hand under her shirt to grab her breasts rubbing his thumbs over her erect nipples. Smiling, James pressed his hardness against her while listening to the moans of pleasure that he elicited from his wife. He whispered, *"I need you Rizalle, it's been so long since we have been able to enjoy the pleasure of the moon's passionate effects on us."*

Rizalle turned and begun undressing teasingly before James, smiling as she watched him adjust himself as he hardened more with her display. Rizalle, with her heightened senses, picked up on James's arousal, before he suddenly tore off his clothes. Licking her lips as she saw the pearls gathering at his tip, she knelt and ran her tongue over it. James gasped as he felt the warm moist heat of Rizalle mouth engulf his swollen member as she worked her magic on him, she made him harder than ever before.

When they reached the bed, James turns Rizalle towards him, and gently pushed her into a sitting position on the bed. He dropped to his knees before her and started kissing her from her feet all the way up her hip. He reached her other hip, he gently laid her back onto the bed and kissed from her stomach towards her neck. Rizalle sighed and squirmed with his kisses. As he reached her neck, she grabbed him, and brought his lips to hers. Their kiss quickly deepened as their tongues danced with each other.

He again begun to kiss down her body. When he reached her breasts, he took each one into his mouth and lightly sucked on them, causing her to moan. James growled low in his throat as the scent of Rizalle's arousal filled the air.

He continued to kiss down her stomach towards her center. Once there, he slowly flicked his tongue tasting her. At her sweetness he instantly needed more of her. He found her swollen bud and sucked it into his mouth while rolling it with his tongue.

"James!" she cried as her hips bucked from the motion of his tongue. Using his arms to steady her, he continued suckling her until she peaked. Moving quickly, he covered her body with his. Rizalle caresses James's cheek tenderly, *"I Love You, James,"* she whispered just as he encased his shaft in her heat.

Slowly moving himself in and out of her, he reveled in the feeling of her muscles clenching around him. She lifted her hips up to meet his thrusts and he obliged by holding them up supporting her. She was his mate and his wolf side was more than ready to show it. He felt the knot starting to swell up in his shaft and had the insatiable urge to bite her and claim her. He needed it.

He suddenly flipped her over, onto her hands and knees. James quickly entered her and mercilessly began to pound into her deeply.   She felt him getting bigger as he plunged deeper into her. He leaned his body forward and positioned himself so that he was on his hands and knees on top of her. *"Mine,"* he growls in her ear. Her body felt aflame as she becomes even more aroused from the possessiveness in his tone.

Suddenly, she felt James shift above her.   Instead of the man, she was being taken by the wolf. She felt even fuller now that the wolf was there and the thrusting seemed to be shorter in length. She felt herself shift into her hell hound / wolf hybrid and knew that she was again going to reach an earth shattering release. Their mating grew wilder as their wolves took over. Right before she peaks, James bit her at the base of the neck, causing her to growl out him. A couple of thrusts later, James howled above her and as he spilled his seed deep inside her, her own unique howl answered his.

Weeks later, Rizalle had a special meal prepared for James and herself in their private suite. The news she was about to tell him was to be a fabulous surprise.

Entering the room, James noticed the aromas from the food and candles. Suddenly worried he had forgotten an important date, he thought hard knowing their anniversary was months off as was Rizalle's birthing date, as he had her presents already arranged. Nervously he asked, *"Rizalle, Did I forget an important date?"*

She arched her brow and wondered if she should tease him. Deciding to let him off the hook, she smiled and laughed, *"No James, you did not forget anything, I have some wonderful news to tell you after our meal."*

As they ate, Rizalle watched James as they finished and sat together, *"James you're going to be a father,"* Rizalle blurted out just as James took a drink of his blood brandy. The brandy spewed as James sat up straight, *"WHAT? HOW? WHEN?"* he shouted in disbelief.

James pulled Rizalle into his arms, placing her on his lap his hands running over her still slim form finding the ever slow slight bulge where their child lay as she laughingly replied, *"We are having a baby. As to how, I would have thought at your age you would've known how it's done. It happened the regular way it does when a couple make love. As to when it happened, the best I could figure was at the peak of the blood moon."*

James kissed her gently, *"Oh Sweetheart, this is the greatest news."* He suddenly grew protective and concerned, *"Are you feeling OK? Are you sure you should be up? Maybe you should be in bed resting. Is there anything I could get you?"* James asked.

Rizalle kissed him softly and stroked her hand along his firm cheek, *"I'm fine love, I'm not a china doll to be wrapped in cloth. I am healthy and strong. Though I am still in shock that we are going to have a baby after so long trying without any success."*

James pulls her closer deepening their kiss, *"I am in a bit of a shock myself but very happy. This requires a very special gift."* James grows serious, *"We will need to take precautions and make special arrangements for you and the baby our enemies will not like this nor I fear will a few others that hope to gain control upon our deaths."*

Resting her head against his as she allows herself to enjoy the warmth and safety of his arms her love for him seemed to grow stronger every day since they had bonded all those long years ago. She still marveled at how he had literally swept her off her feet in battle when his half-brothers and him had came to aid her people against vampires that had set out to destroy her family. James had not only saved her that day but defeated the vampire coven and their lycan lapdog allies as well.

Many had told her upon learning of her feelings for the dark haired lycan that he was blackhearted totally without feeling and a loner but she had known different, from the moment their eyes had met she knew he was the one for her. Their courtship had been short and swift, their bonding had been wild, passionate and powerful under the full moonlight. To others he appeared cold and aloft but every time she entered the room his dark eyes always lite up in happiness and passion.

"James, we will not be able to hide it for long once they notice me increasing and us preparing for the birth, trouble is sure to start."

"Yes, I know and the worst part is that the ones I should be able to fully trust in this I don't. But don't worry nothing will harm you or our baby, not the living or the dead blood sucking ticks." James picks Rizalle up and carries her to their room instructing the guards that they are not to be disturbed not even if the castle were on fire.

Over the next few months, James saw to it that Rizalle was treated with kid gloves, until he almost drove her crazy, not wanting her to do anything. She secretly enjoyed the special care James lavished on her, especially when her back ached or her feet were swollen.

Keres was summoned before her master, entered the chamber and knelt, awaiting her master's arrival. Suddenly the room filled with a red glow and a smell of sulfur, for a brief moment, Keres heard the wales of the damned and felt the heat that always heralded her master's appearance from his domain. Keres bowed lower, her forehead nearly touching the floor in submission, as the tall figure appeared.

"Keres my lovely, your obedience and submissive nature always pleases me." Lucifer smiled as he walked around, looking

over his servant, admiring the strips just starting to fade from their last play session. He felt himself stir at the memory. *"Keres, a royal princess is to be born soon. She is the one foretold it the ancient legend. She and her future offspring must be ours. The one that controls them shall rule the world."*

Keres after leaving her master was deep in thought upon the news that her master had given her, barely noticing someone lurking in the shadows as she approached her rooms. She recognized Morley, once of the human gang leaders that Asslam had had converted to fight in the war.

Smiling her deadly sweet smile, she decided here is the perfect pawn to use to capture the princess. *"Morley, you were just the one I was seeking for a very important mission. The lycan rulers are going to have a baby. I want you to bring me the baby, alive and unharmed. I plan to convert her for our use against the lycans. If you succeed, you will be richly rewarded and strike a blow against the ones that have killed your brothers."*

"Yes, mistress, I'll not fail you," Morley replied.

Keres's smile grew bigger just before she said, *"Failure is NOT an option, if you want to keep your fangs."*

Morley left with his slave Arris and proceeded to shadow the queen, following her and waiting for the birth, making sure they could not detect him in the shadows.

Months later during an intense battle, Queen Rizalle, heavy with child, was fighting beside King James and their warriors. She was fighting to protect her people when she went into labor. Shifting into her wolf form, she crawled into a small den in a hollowed out tree to give birth and hide her pup. After the birthing, Rizalle felt James became over whelmed by a wave of vampires, and rushed to his side after instructing her newborn to stay hid and be quiet until she returned. With fire and blood everywhere the tiny pup, Teera shivered and hides.

From the shadows, a vampire watched as Queen Rizalle

crawled from the den and rejoined the battle, before he went to investigate. Morley decided to see what the Queen had hidden. Crawling inside, he found the newborn hiding in the corner. He quickly formed a plan that would get him in good with his king and protect him from Keres while possibly raising his status in the vampire hierarchy.

Teera saw the stranger as he reached for her. She felt the hatred pouring from him combined with the smelled and noises coming from outside. As he grabbed hold of her, she quickly attacked, sinking her tiny teeth into his hand. Morley cursed and slung the pup against the wall, knocking her unconscious. Cursing the pup and her parents he grabbed her limp form, stuffing her in his carry sack, tossing the sack to Arris to carry. Glanced to make sure they were not spotted, Morley quickly slipped away from the battle scene to take his prize back to his dilapidated castle's dungeon.

Teera came to, collared, and chained in a cold dark room; lying shivering in cold and hunger, crying for her momma. Suddenly she smelled the evil one that had hurt her coming closer. Her eyes blazing in hate, she shifts into a white tiger cub and waited for his approach. Morley stared in shock at the cub that snarled in hatred, where once a wolf pup had been. He quickly realized that his prize had just gotten better.

Morley thought of a new plan, that if he converted the cub to be more vampire then lycan and trained it to hunt lycans for the vampires, then his king would reward him greatly without that witch Keres getting the credit. He thought that if he force fed it his vampire venom, with it being so young, it would convert easily. He did not know that she was not a regular lycan, but a hybrid like her mother, who was a hell hound mix, that survived on vampire venom.

Although Teera survived on the venom, being newborn, it was still very painful being fed it directly instead of mixed in her mother's milk. Her cries of pain tore at the heart of the young human slave, who snuck the pup milk to ease her suffering. Arris promised Teera he would free her and return her to her family.

❂ ❂ ❂ ❂ ❂ ❂ ❂ ❂ ❂ ❂ ❂

After the battle ended a battle weary Rizalle and James went to retrieve their daughter from the den. Smelling the vampire's scent, they rushed in only to find Teera gone, her blood splattered about and the smell of death heavy in the den. Frantically, they searched for their daughter, only to rightly suspect she had been taken by their enemy. Their howls of rage and sorrow filled the air at the loss of their daughter. Both vowed to destroy the vampires completely.

Rizalle and James spent the next few weeks, seeking warriors to join their ranks. Humans were recruited, and trained to help the lycans destroy the vampires for the upcoming battles. These new forces once trained went on the offensive and attacked with a vengeance, killing mass numbers of vampires; destroying their villages and castles.

❂ ❂ ❂ ❂ ❂ ❂ ❂ ❂ ❂ ❂ ❂

Asslam wondered at the sudden extreme viciousness of these new attacks and sent out spies to find out why the lycans, as well as humans, had suddenly grown more vicious. The spies soon returned having learned of the disappearance and suspected murder of the lycan king and queen's first born. Along with this news, he learned of Morley's new pet that he had acquired at the same time as the princess's disappearance. Asslam set out for Morley's castle to acquire this special pet for himself, with a plan to not only finally win the war, but to gain control of the lycans and their lands as well.

❈ ❈ ❈ ❈ ❈ ❈ ❈ ❈ ❈ ❈ ❈ ❈

Meanwhile, Arris managed to get the keys to Teera's collar and to an unused passage that led from the dungeon. Waiting until Morley was away, Arris quickly freed Teera. With the tiny pup wrapped in a blanket tied to his side, Arris headed towards Teera's parents' castle and what he hoped would be safety from the vampires.

Arris noticed an increase in vampire patrols and assumed correctly that they were hunting for them. He took to hiding at any sign of others and sneaking only into towns or farms to try to steal food for himself and the pup. Finally, after many long, frightening days of travel, Arris and Teera reached Castle Black.

The castle guards stopped him, *"You, boy, what's your business here? We've never seen you here before"* the large guard growled.

Arris swallowed in fear before stating, *"I have important business with the king and queen. I'm returning something that was stolen from them by my former master."*

Kenny appears from the guardhouse and saw one of Silfer's men start to grab a sack from a young human boy who was ready to fight to protect it. *"What's going on here? Why were you two assaulting that boy?"*

The guards paled and released the boy. Kenny watched the boy reach into the sack and remove a tiny white cub. He paled when the boy said, *"It's okay Princess, I'll not let them hurt you we are at your home now."*

Kneeling and looking from the cub to the boy, he hoped that his suspicions were correct. *"So you say you have something stolen from the king and queen. I suppose that this is the stolen item?"* Kenny pointed to the cub.

Arris looked up at Kenny and said, *"Yes, Sir."*

Kenny ushered the pair into the throne room, Teera smelled the familiar scent of her momma. Crawling from the blanket Arris had wrapped her in, she stumbled crying, *"MOMMA".*

Rizalle, seeing her lost daughter, grabbed her up, looking at Arris and Kenny, *"Explain how you have my daughter!"* Rizalle growled.

Arris explained. *"My old master, Morley, captured your daughter and tried to convert her so he could train her to hunt lycans once grown. He fed her pure vampire venom and it hurt her, so I feed her milk and freed her, bringing her to you, to save her. May I stay here? My life is forfeit if Morley, or his gang of vampires, catches me?"*

James and Rizalle agreed, *"You'll remain as Teera's caregiver. James's most trusted personal guard, Kenny will be assigned to protect both you and her."*

Meanwhile Asslam, accompanied by his witch mistress Keres, arrived to find that Morley's captured princess had been stolen by the young slave Arris and Morley had disappeared. Keres told Asslam that the princess was the one foretold in the ancient legend and was a key to Asslam ruling the world. He must sire an heir by her.

Asslam started making plans on how to gain control of the princess and the power she contained. He sent an emissary to James with a message requesting a meeting between them. He notified James in the message that he had learned of the kidnapping of the princess and that the vampire, Morley, had fled and was being sought with a bounty of a thousand gold on his head.   The bounty was payable to vampires, lycans, and humans alike. It was to be doubled if he was brought in alive. Asslam told James that he had thought of a way that would bring peace and prosperity between their two kingdoms. The details could be discussed and worked out at the meeting. Until then, he suggested a truce between their kingdoms.

James talked to Rizalle about the message and they agreed. The emissary was given a reply with the meeting set in three months' time, at a central location on the border of both kingdoms. No one was truly happy with the meeting, but if there was a way for their people to have peace, then it must be done. Too many had died in the war, many shape shifting species had been lost until only a few remained. Only the lycans still existed in any number. The royals, the mightiest of the shape shifters, no longer existed except a few rumored to be living in hiding.

The time went by slowly, while everyone prepares for the meeting.

Teera's parents noticed that she had strong empathy; feeling others passions, emotions, and pain. As she grew, her empathy grew stronger until she withdrew into herself, trying to block out the pain from the constant onslaught of others feelings.

To help her until she learned to block her empathy from castle day to day life, her parents took her to a nearby walled valley in the Obsidian Mountains that had been formed from a long extinct volcano. Only her personal guards, and servants were allowed to join her during her weekly reprieves from castle life.

With the help of friendly powerful witches, her parents had the valley protected from outsiders and built a magnificent cave house with all of the amenities for their daughter. The house was large enough to support an army and their families for years. It was a castle in its own right. Its walls and archery towers were made of mountain peaks, while the treasury consisted of veins of gold and gem stones one could pick right off the walls. Teera's cave was the envy of many and protected by powerful magic.

The day of the meeting arrived, and Asslam was accompanied by his witch Keres. Both sides were surrounded by their security teams and troops. The kings greeted each other peacefully before sitting to discuss the terms of the peace agreement.

James looked from Keres to Asslam barely able to hide his hatred of the two before he said, *"Asslam, you wrote that you had a plan that would end the war."*

Asslam answered, *"Yes, this war has gone on since the beginning of time. Many have been lost on both sides. I propose a marriage between myself and the princess Teera. It would bring peace between our two kingdoms and prosperity for our people. She is the first royal born in a millennium as well as your only heir. When she is my queen, it would bind our two kingdoms together. I propose we agree to a betrothal with the marriage to take place upon her coming of age. I will supply a teacher to instruct her in royal etiquette .... for vampire royal court."*

James and Rizalle looked at each other in shocked disbelief at Asslam's words, and they began speaking through their mental bond.

Rizalle thought, *"We want peace, and a chance to allow our people to once again grow and have children."*

James responded, *"But to give our only baby girl to the blood sucking tick, and not just any vampire, but our long time enemy. Is the safety of our people worth Teera's happiness? She is only a baby, not even a year old."*

Rizalle replied, *"If we do this, we have to insure her safety in the contract. None of our people have had a child in a long time, our bonded pairs are losing their mates in battle. If we do not gain peace soon our people will go extinct like the royals and the leech's will control everything."*

James sighed, *"If we do this we must insure her safety in the contract."*

They nodded in silent agreement.

Then returned their attention back to Asslam to work out the details for both the safety of their people and their daughter.

Asslam, hid a smirk as he watched the flea infested mutts work out between them that his offer was their only choice at survival. He sat thinking to himself, *"Once he got a child from the mangy mutt then he could be rid of his bride."* He barely suppressed the shutter of distaste at having to bed the freak. *"He could raise his heir to help him control the lycans, humans and the rest of the succulent world. The rest will either bow down to him or die."*

Another Beginning

During that time, in another part of the world, a young lycan was born; also in war. The victors, after capturing the young lycan's village, set out to destroy any future resistance by having all surviving males sterilized and sold off as slaves.

A newborn baby called Brenat, whose parents were killed in the siege, was left in the care of an older female captive by the victors. Both were soon sold to slavers, along with the other captives, and sent across the sea to be sold into servitude. Brenat was dismissed from the slavers mind and left in the young girl's care. She cared for him. He beat the odds and survived. Later after an arduous journey the pair of children were sold to a childless couple.

He grew to learn about the land and it's beauty as a farmer under the love and guidance of his new mother Elsie, father Sid and sister Rose. They became a small, close knit family of lycans.

Years passed, and his sister Rose married and left with her husband. Brenat missed her greatly, but was soon busy in his own new career. For at that same time, even as young as he was, he was recruited into the militia because his strength and speed were noteworthy.

His testing showed little affinity to active magic, but strong natural lycan abilities. His strength, agility, speed, and endurance passed that of older lycans. Even his trainers found him hard to track and were often surprised by Brenat and his uncanny stealth. Though he was tested time and again at a young age to see if he was a royal, as more than once he bested all the older royal boys and excelled through the red cloak trainers, his results always came back to him being a regular lycan.

His parents, Sid and Elsie, had taught him from a very early age to hide his true nature from all, including themselves. Confused and unsure, but always trusting his parents even over his red cloak monk teachers, he followed their instructions. He soon went into advanced training that focused on how to identify and then kill exceptional vampires, powerful magic users, and royal lycans. It was at that time he understood why he needed to hide his true self.

Brenat's aptitude became so apparent that he was recommended by the red cloaked monks for killer status. The Elites took over his training to which he also excelled.

Secret Friends

One full moon, after a hard day of training, his body was badly beaten and bruised. He laid near death in the infirmary. His soul wandered, led by the moonlight, to a young girl. They could see and sense each other, but neither could hear or touch the other because the mystic veil blocked sound and feeling, over time they developed their own type of communication.

The same full moon Teera's mind was bombarded by the castle inhabitants and it guests. Barely restrained in the tenuous truce and feeling the hate from and towards Asslam, her husband to be. Teera retreated to her garden, hoping the head ache would subside. The boy's spirit shielded the girl's mind from the turmoil of her empathy with others pain, sorrow, and passions. With the appearance of the boy's spirit, her mind became shielded from all others.

As the years went by, every evening that he could, Brenat visited. They played "Hide and Seek", or sat among the trees and flowers just spending time together. Every morning he awoke after visiting his ghostly friend with his breaks and bruises from the previous days training healed; his mind cleansed of the atrocities of war. Her compassion healed his damaged soul. They sat together, becoming forever linked, yet separate, and always healing one another.

Every blood moon, they battered at the mystic veil separating them, needing to be physically together. To observers, it appeared that Teera tore at the sky and wind as if fighting demons. Her body shifted and fought. No one dare approach her during that time after one servant and a guard were torn apart when they angered her by trying to restrain her. Her parents ordered that on the blood moons, she was to left alone, with her unseen ghost, in the garden and undisturbed.

The following morning both Teera and Brenat would wake, after the setting of the blood moon with their fingers bleeding, as if they had been digging at a rocky cliff face; bodies bruised and sore and their minds exhausted. Brenat would wake deep in a strange forest, far away from his bed and home. He would have to find his way home, sometimes covered in the blood of anyone unfortunate enough to have came across him during that time.

Apart

At Teera's coming of age ceremony, she was married to Asslam. Teera could sense that Asslam had a hidden hatred for her and her kind. She hid her fears from her parents as she knew that her marriage would save the peace between their people. Because of Teera's empathy, her coming of age ceremony and wedding was kept simple, with only Teera's parents, Arris, Kenny, Asslam, Keres, Kapral, and a scribe from each castle to record this monumental peace treaty between vampires and lycan's.

Asslam, on his trip home with his new wife, looked at Teera and snarled, *"At least you're not a flea bitten mongrel like most of your kind. Your job is to bare me a son; the sooner you accomplish this, the sooner you will have your own room in my castle as far away from me as possible."*

Asslam looked at his witch Keres, *"Your job is to prepare her with properly scented oils to remove the lycan stink from her and a potion to enhance her fertility so I can finish this as quickly as possible."*

Keres bowed her head, *"Yes, my king, your wish will be done. I did not foresee her needing the fertility potions with my lord's virility so it will be some time before I could complete the potions. She will be rubbed down with the oils until her body aches with want of you and she smells of scents that you will find to your liking, my king."*

Even with Asslam's magic, it took weeks to travel back to

his castle. During this time Asslam chose to ride his horse for the duration of the trip, as soon as they were out of sight of Castle Black. Teera was left alone, with only her thoughts to keep her company. Keres who had returned to her private carriage had it brought alongside Teera's just long enough to give her the scented oils with instructions that she was to comb them through her hair and rub them on her body for the duration of the trip, so as to prepare herself for her wedding night that would happen once they reach the castle.

Arriving at the castle, Teera stared at its forbidding appearance. Unlike the beauty of her parents' castle, this one was built of dull gray stone that seemed to chase all hope and sunlight away, no happiness could be felt; only fear could be felt coming from it and its people.

Upon arriving, Teera was quickly taken to Asslam's bed chamber where she was bathed by a pair of ladies-in-waiting while being over seen by Keres. Who gave Teera instructions on how she was to act and present herself to her new husband upon his entrance into the bed chambers. While Keres watched the oils were rubbed all over Teera's body again until her body started moving on its own to the caressing hands. They left Teera frustrated and wanting, her virgin body aching to be touched.

Soon Asslam entered and Teera's pulse quickened with both a fear and a need she did not understand. Asslam eyes glazed with passion as the aroma's assaulted his senses. Teera knelt in front of her king and husband as she had been instructed to. Asslam without thought to her innocence snatched her up and threw her to the bed, tearing the sleek lacy nightgown from her body. His fangs pierced the flesh of her bared breasts, suckling on the richness of her blood as he thrust into her without warning. Her screams of pain ignored in his potion fueled lust. Her young body protested to the intrusion yet slowly learned to take his hard rough thrusts as she lost her virginity on her wedding night. With a final grunt he released, rolling off of her. His eyes lost their glaze as he called to the guards to take her to her own room without saying a word to his new bride that he had used so violently. Hurting and naked, they escorted her down the halls, blood dripping from the bite marks on her breasts while his seed mixed her virgin blood ran down her legs.

Keres, in her room next to Asslam's, pleasured herself as she listened with glee to Teera's torment and screams of pain. Smiled knowing that she had specifically designed the scented oils to enhance Teera's fertility and to bring about Asslam's lust, but she had done nothing to lower his hatred for lycans but in fact had made it so it increased his hatred for Teera especially.

Within the castle bounds, Asslam's magic was strong causing Teera's ghostly visitations with her friend to stop, making her believe that her ghostly friend had finally moved on, leaving her truly alone. Yet even with Asslam and Keres's power, they could not override the feral power of the blood moon. So on those nights, he stripped Teera, before chaining and locking her away in the dungeon.

Asslam tried again and again, for five years, to get a son from Teera. At one point even risking life and limb as he strapped Teera down just before the blood moon then proceeded to take her several times in the dungeon during the night.

With the coming and passing of every Blood moon, Teera became more vicious and feral as she tried to kill all that came near her. Teera's viciousness became such that even Asslam avoided going near her on Blood moons.

In frustration, Asslam used magic to lock Teera in her wolf form for months while he took her and treated her like a pet. When that failed he locked her in the form of her royal tigress, viciously filling her with his seed and locking her in a cage like an untamed animal for months. When that too failed, he kept her from shifting, so her human form suffered the worst of the abuse as his hatred and anger grew.

Even with the help of Keres, all her witches, and their potions; Teera still did not become pregnant. Asslam, night after night in a drunken rage, chained, whipped and took Teera roughly in his frustrated effort to get a son, leaving her chained to the end of his bed on the floor after.

One morning he awoke, and found Teera unconscious and near death in her silver collar. The large bloody welts standing out sharply upon her pale back, his dried seed, mixed with her blood, coagulated upon her legs and the floor.

Asslam realized that her death at his hand would kill the hard fought for, bountiful peace between him and her father. That peace had stopped many a skirmish from becoming all-out war and soothed hateful feelings on both the vampire and lycan sides. Both sides had been able to expand their territory even more than the red cloaks.

After much thought Asslam came up with a plan to banish Teera from both his sight and castle while allowing the peace to remain. He sent a message to James requesting a meeting to discuss Teera's health to which James agreed and quickly met with Asslam.

"James, thank you for agreeing to meet me. Teera is infertile and castle life is proving too hard on her. I thought that it is best that she be sent to the valley you had built for her, where she would remain secluded from all others. I would see to it that it's protected for her safety," Asslam said, not wanting her parents or others to learn of the abuse at his hand. He watched the play of emotions as they ran across James's face before he spoke.

"Asslam, I do not like the idea of locking Teera away. Her mother and I would want to spend time with her especially as we have not seen her these last five years. We do not want her completely abandoned and alone plus she will need supplies that her mother and I will provide for her."

During the luncheon break, Keres accompanies Asslam to

his private room. *"Asslam, that mutt Teera must bear no children by another if you are to gain and keep the power we seek."*

His anger built with her words. *"Why did she not get pregnant we did everything even your damned potions had no effect. Why should I believe another could breed the bitch when I couldn't?"*

Keres felt a moment of fear before answering, *"I have no idea my lord, but I can assure you that she is the one spoken of in the legend."*

Growling in frustration, Asslam slammed his fist down on the table, *"Fine then have your witches ready to seal that valley from everything. I want nothing and no one getting in or out once I convince those mutts that locking her away is for her own good. They'll do anything for their precious daughter."* Gulping down the blood in the goblet and snarling at its taste he said, *"Who dared to serve me this swill it's not even fresh. See that I have fresh blood upon my return while I deal with this mess with Teera and her parents."*

Asslam returned to the meeting room where James and Rizalle waited, after much debate they consented to Teera being sent to the ancient valley where her cave palace was. Her parents believed that it was for the benefit of their people and the kingdom, to agree to Asslam's plan for Teera. Thus Asslam removed Teera from his presence and maintained the peace between the kingdoms.

Using the blood of the ancients, Asslam had the valley mystically sealed so that even griffins, and wyverns had to adjust their flight paths around the mystic barrier. The valley became Teera's prison; even the entrance was closed, having been turned into a mystic portal, locking all out. The only reprieve was when the mystic portal opened in the light of the full moon, allowing Teera to bring in the supplies left for her. There was a penalty of death if she failed to be in the valley when the portal resealed at dawn's first light.

James, still full of distrust, gathered his witches adding,

unbeknown to Asslam, an additional reprieve every new moon for Teera and an escape tunnel leading to the ocean in case the seal was ever broken. Although still mystically bound to the valley at dawn's first light for only if the seal was broken could the death curse be broken.

Teera remained silent regarding the abuse at her husband's hands knowing the resulting war would harm many lycans, magical beings, as well as many innocent humans and town people.

During that time, Brenat after he lost his ghostly contact with Teera, became a solitary, cold, calculating, and exceptionally efficient assassin he was promoted faster than any of his predecessors. He had been part of three wars and executed a score of assassinations, his leaders brought him into the fold and gave him the title of Elite.

Because he never failed or faltered in his assignments, they gave him a cloak made from the flesh of his enemies, soaked in the blood of the tormented and damned. Those that met the Elite, whether they were a warrior, a noble, or a peasant, never lived long enough to even utter his name, which was a blessing. For those that did live long enough to utter the name Elite, ended up screaming and begging for death for weeks.

Reunion

One full moon as Teera escaped her prison to go visit her parents Brenat, after a long day of helping Sid on the farm, laid resting. His soul wandered, guided by the light of the same full moon until he found Teera alive and well. They rejoiced, just walking together and feeling whole once more. Still unable to verbally communicate, they used their own personal way of communicating and spent their time just enjoying that they had found each other again. The trip to get her supplies interrupted part of their time together but they still managed to enjoy their time together as they walked.

As they approached the valley Teera noticed the first light of the sunrise and bolted, racing the light to get back inside the valley before it was too late. As the sun sealed Teera away Brenat watched as she disappeared then with a hand touched the mystic barrier, unable to follow or find a way in, his spirit went back into his body.

Every night Teera hoped for a visit from her ghostly friend while imprisoned but her friend did not show, alone she rightfully guessed that he could not pass through the barrier that kept her prisoner. When duty did not call Brenat sent his soul in search of his friend for days, to no avail.

The next full moon rose and hope was renewed for both once more. Teera once again escaped and Brenat's soul was drawn to her, Brenat was oblivious of all others, even while Teera visited her family to get more supplies. Teera and her friend comforted each other, just knowing the other was near, until Teera retreated once again into her prison. Brenat, losing his contact with her, retreated to his body again.

Brenat continued completing assignments with cold efficiency, so he could spend his off days with ease and contentment, farming, and at night dreaming of seeing his friend again on the next full moon. Teera spent her valley existence keeping busy by hunting and leather working, awaiting her reprieve and her visit with her ghostly friend. The visits went on through winter, spring, and summer aiding both to survive their lonely existences.

The Blood Moon Awaking

As the Blood moon neared Brenat was again given his space, for many had died and been found half eaten after trying to follow him during his feral reclusive time on previous blood moons. No one knew why or what had attacked and killed the followers, because none had returned alive. None dared challenge Brenat, as he was the best of the Elite Assassins and had never lost a fight no matter how many challenged him at one time.

Both Teera and Brenat felt pulled by the upcoming blood moon; the edginess of every nerve on fire as their need to be together strengthened.

Teera paced back and forth in front of the stone wall that would soon open, freeing her for a night of wild abandonment and reveling in the feral glory of its red glow.

Brenat secluded and free, spent the day resting in the shade of a big cedar, its thick trunk supporting his back while he smelled the patch of gardenias wafting to him on the light breeze.

With the blood moon came the feral energy, passion, and hunger followed by an uncontrolled shift that seized them both. Brenat paced the clearing, his true royal wolf form revealed. Teera, in the full glory of her royal tigress, burst from the mountainside like a flash of pure white lightening.

The trees whipped by as she was drawn to the hot scent of a future battle mixed with adrenaline fueled rage. The massive wolf and tiger viewed each other from opposite sides of the clearing. They entered the clearing like two opposing gladiators facing off in competition as the blood moon's light gave the grass a bloody, killing field appearance. The two shifters roar a challenge at each other before circling and sizing each other up, looking for their opponent's weakness and their opportunity to attack.

The tigress sprang from the field into the forest, adjusted her body in midair, her claws catching and leaving long gashes in a tree. As her whole body did a one eighty, from fleeing the field to flying back at the wolf, all four paws claws were outstretched to rake the chasing wolf's face. The wolf flattened to the ground, his body slid on the dew covered grass, as the tigress flew over top, narrowly missing her target with her slashing claws. The wolf spun his body around, sliding backwards as he faced the tigress, landing in the middle of the clearing. The wolf sped towards the cat, his huge canines gnashing the air as he snarled. The tigress easily avoided the seemingly clumsy attack by leaping straight up into the air, ready to land and rake at the wolf's back. The wolf, missing his target, leapt to the side watching as the tigress landed where he was only moments before. Once again they circled, the speed of which left gouge marks in the grass as if turned over like a farmer's plow. The tigress charged and swiped as the wolf dodged and countered with a bite, catching nothing but air as the tigress had quickly moved.

Panting from the exertion of the give and take as they, circled again, sizing each other up. The wolf charged and the tigress jumped up again. The wolf flew past where the she was. The wolf planted his paws on the opposite tree and threw himself back up to where the she cat hung seemingly in midair, twelve feet above the grass below. They collided in midair, paw upon paw, saber sized canines gnashing at each other. Neither the wolf nor tigress scored a bloody mark with tooth or claw.

Falling back to the ground before springing apart again, the tigress seemed to limp as she landed at the edge of the clearing. The wolf, seeing weakness, charged again. The tigress swiped a tree, her claws cleaving through the bark and trunk with ease. The tree fell towards the wolf, its slow motion crash easy to dodge. The branches blocked his view of her as she moved to ride the tree down. She leapt from the falling tree, swiping at him, her claws touching nothing but a tuft of fur as he rolled away. The tree continued to crash around them, branches and leaves fluttering about them.

He leapt at her, her body twisting to avoid his claws. His teeth clamped shut, only managing to grab some hair from her tail. Her rear claws raked backwards, just missing both sides of his head. Separating again, their tails slowly swished back and forth. They tensed and circled each other again, awaiting their moment to spring, they each snarled lethal threats that was also filled with admiration of their skillful opponent, as they prepared to attack again.

Their speed and aggression increased made their movements a mere blur. Their attacks, retreats, and chases became white and black blurs in a reddish background. Flying dirt, grass, bark, and leaves the only visual evidence of their battle. The colors of their coats became so entwined that an observer could not have distinguished one from the another.

Her agility surpassed his yet he wore her down with his superior skill from years of battle training. Teera's agility waned as she tired and his superior endurance started to show. She leapt as he slid right, her agility paying off as she twisted in midair, swiping out with her claws cleaving a bloody mark into his jawline, howling in her triumph at being the first to draw blood. Her triumphant howl was cut short as the wolf's momentum carried him past her. His body spun with the swipe and he clamped his jaws onto the scruff of her neck. His body momentum pulled the tigress off of her feet with him landing, pinning her beneath him.

The tigress laid tired, and dazed, she knew she had been bested, and awaited the killing bite. The tigress, acknowledging his strength and power, submitted to her worthy opponent. The wolf at once sensed his adversary submitting as he moved in for the kill. His bite was halted, his rage quickly turned into an unbelievable passion as her heat and sweet smell assaulted his senses. His arousal grew as he pressed against her. She encouraged him by rubbing against his swelling need. His musky scent filled her nostrils and her own need intensified.

Submitting to his dominance, the mighty cat stretched out her front paws while raising her hindquarters, presenting herself. The wolf mounted, gripping her hips his shaft pushed hard into her. Her body hot, wanting, and moist resisted slightly as she stretched to accommodate his size. He slid deeper her body pulling, stretching, and gripping him, he swelled even more. The great cat pushed back onto him hard and fast as he drove himself into her again and again; his knot swelling, pressing, and filling her tight tunnel. The cat shivering pleasure, her body stretched even more. The knot throbbed, her body clenched down on the fullness inside her. He growled and bit her neck marking her as his, just as with a unified howl they released, his seed filling her the tigress' body milked his shaft. Her body reacted upon waves of pleasure. They laid flat on the soft grass, locked together. He tenderly licked his mark, healing it as his tongue caressed her neck.

The blood moon's light down shone on the lovers, their passions quickly rebuilding as his gentle thrusts being met as she slowly pushed back on him with equal want, their bodies quivering with every movement. She rolled her hips slowly while her body gripped, teasing him for more. With a pleasurable growl his thrusts grew more vigorous and deepened. They continued before the knot had even settled. He swelled inside of her with slow strokes, meeting her rising hips. Their heartbeats sped up, unified and strong. Their bodies danced together in the rhythmic beat, moving apart, but never separated. As they clashed together again and again, their passions built as the electric waves once again flowed through them. She felt him fill her once again, pushing her to her own release. They howled their release under the moons blessing. Her body clenched his throbbing shaft in time to their heartbeats.

Passions spent once again, they rested; his weight a comforting presence. Looking back, the tigress licked at the wolf's jaws, healing as she cleaned her mate's wound. The knot still locked them together as they moved until they laid facing each other. The moon's glow brightened the blessing as he again bit her neck at the shoulder, and remarked her as his. Her smell and taste were strong as he drank of her, he raised his head to howl of his bond with the tigress to the blood moon. The moon shone upon the marks with glowing intensity. The tigress took her cue and sank her teeth into his neck, close to his shoulder, taking his blood, smell, and taste in before she too howled, and claimed her bonded mate. With the blood moon glowing upon the marks, the union was blessed by its powers and a new life started. They licked each other's wounds until they were healed, leaving the blessed scars of their bonding.

They separated from each other's embrace with a little disappointment just as the scent of a wild pig came to them on the wind. With stomachs growling, they started the hunt. The wolf flushed the razor back from hiding and it ran in fear. At the last minute, seeing the tigress suddenly appear in front, it swiped at the great cat with its razor sharp tusks. With an easy jump, the attack missed and the tusks embedded into a tree, pinning the pig. The tigress' jaws clamped down on its neck; snapping its spine. With a single claw she opened the pig throat to stomach. Tigress and wolf shared the still beating heart of the wild beast as their bloody lips touched as half a heart disappeared down each of their throats.

The tigress, with her belly full, with loving tenderness, groomed the wolf, cleaning the blood from his fur before biting his jaw in playful needed. The wolf licked the blood from her face, his tongue stroked down her body. The tigress shivered in pleasure as his tongue traveled closer towards her seductive core. She lifted her hindquarters and tail, allowing him better access.

He lapped at her sweetness, savoring the taste. His tongue moved up and down, each trip sending waves of pleasure through her. Over and over again his tongue penetrated, tasting and lapping up her readiness. She purred and rocked her hips against his face, moving her tail, clearly ready for more. With slow deliberation he penetrated her his hardness slipping deeper into her velvety warmth. Her body stretched with ease, accommodating him once more, as it clenched and pulled him deeper. Their growls of pleasure resounded around the clearing as they felt God's blessing, their bonding marks glowing. With loving tenderness their passion built again. Their rhythm increased with the beating of their hearts, their bodies locked together. Their souls, hearts and essence intertwined until dawn's approach forced their separation as the moon's pull started to wane.

The tigress saw the moon had begun to set, leaped up and raced into the forest, leaving the wolf to look after her in silence. Teera just made it into the valley before the portal once again sealed her away.

As she shifted, feeling sore and a little sad at their separation her hands unconsciously caressed her stomach. She laid back in the warm bathing pool to clean and relax, reminiscing about the beautiful passion they had shared. For the first time she had felt the need, want, and pleasure at someone's touch; not the pain, humiliation, nor the fear of being forced and beaten into submitting.

His scent was still in her nostrils, and the taste of his blood still on her tongue his warm seed sitting inside her. Smiling, she rested as their shared essence grew inside of her. She looked forward to the next full moon when she could look for her mate again and share him with her ghostly friend. She wondered if her mate would be able to see her ghostly friend.

Contracts

Brenat went back to the farm, hoping to finally get some rest, when a message arrived for him to see his commander immediately. Commander Rivek's visage clearly identified his demonic heritage, as he gave Brenat his next assignments. Brenat thought *about how he would miss seeing his ghostly friend and searching for his mate would have to wait. Five assassinations meant three months of killing and travel, but the gold would help his family's farm and shop.*

While on assignment, Brenat dreamed of sharing the experience of his tigress with his ghostly friend, all the while reminiscing on how the tigress tasted and smelled. He wondered when and if he would see her again, and if his tigress and friend would be able to see each other.

❈ ❈ ❈ ❈ ❈ ❈ ❈ ❈ ❈ ❈ ❈

When the new moon arrived Teera made her way to the clearing, searching and marking, hoping her mate would find her. She waited through the night, but he did not show. *Would he find my scent and wait for my return?* She wondered *if had something had happened to him. Had he given up at founding her? Had he left for something better?* Yet even as doubts plagued her she waited until the very last minute. When she could wait no more she rushed back through the barrier, her mind whirled with doubts and questions that were left unanswered.

❋ ❋ ❋ ❋ ❋ ❋ ❋ ❋ ❋ ❋ ❋

Brenat traveled speedily northward until he came to the town of his first target. His target, a young noble who liked his drink and the entertainment of the ladies. With the day still young, he checked out the general store, unsurprised that there are no books for sale, as they were a rarity. The store was also waiting on its delivery of sugar candy. He bought a big sack of salt and pouch of rice then went to the pub to eat and rest out the day.

The evening arrived and the noble appeared with his entourage friends and guards. Brenat noticed them all partook in the drink. He waited until the noble picked out the lady of his choice. Brenat left with a staggered gate and hid, the alley shadows covered him. He poured out a third of the salt in the alley, drew his sword, and waited deep in the shadows.

The noble, with some jeering from his friends, left the pub for the local inn. He staggered with an equally intoxicated lady under his arm. As they passed the alley where Brenat was waiting he stepped from the alley, his silver katana slicing the air with ease took off the foolish noble's head. Brenat put the head in the bag of salt, disappearing into the shadows before the lady even realized she was walking with a headless corpse. Traveling south to his next target he heard the lady scream as she realized she was holding hands with a headless corpse that slowly fell to the ground. He spent his spare time thinking of his tigress and how he planned to find her when he returned, while he continued southward to complete his next task.

On the next full moon found, Teera traveled to the clearing again, searching for signs and waiting for her ghostly friend and her mate until just before sunrise. As the month progressed she noticed her monthly cycle was late and her stomach started bothering her.

Brenat, with his first assignment bagged in salt which kept the head from rotting and the stink from giving him away, turned southwest. After many days' travel, he came to the crossroads where a decapitated head was displayed on a stake in the ground, draped in a red cloak, sat as a warning. Brenat folded his cloak, put it into his bag, and rolled in the dirt before continuing on to the small village. With no horse to stable, he headed straight for the brothel where massive guards stood at the door. Disguised as a weary traveler, he was shown in. The buxom merchandise advertised their assets until the mature madam approached, inquiring as to his needs with a skeptical look. He asked for a bath, mead, and hot food. Checking out the ladies, he looked at her and said, *"Well I'm partial to red heads, but I notice you have none available. Maybe you could find one that could serve me while I rest up here for a couple of days."*

The madam replied, *"That is a pricey order, none of my ladies work for the meager money of a warrior."*

Brenat tossed a gold coin to the madam, in sight of the well-off patrons and ladies. *"If she is a red head, well trained, and good at what she does, I'll have another coin for you."* He replaced the heavy, obviously full pouch back under his tunic.

The madam's eyes glittered with greed as she directed

two ladies to run his bath and get him a drink and food while she escorted him to a private room. *"Your food and companion will join you soon."*

As Brenat stripped down and climbed into the tub, he drew a small metal flask and added a drop of liquid to each eye before closing his eyes and resting in the hot steamy water that smelled faintly of vanilla.

Soon he heard the door open and faint chatting was coming from below, accompanied by the tinkling of little bells. As he listened to his companion sway her hips with a clink, he heard the mead and food placed on the table. He opened his eyes that appeared bloodshot from long travel. Thanks to the potion of true sight in his eyes, Brenat saw the lavish room he had entered revealed to truly be a loft. He saw that the buxom lady was in fact a withered hag covered in warts. She had talons for feet and predatory teeth that would make a lycan jealous.

Her voice had a musical, sing-song quality that had a lulling effect. With her surprising soft hands, she started washing him, a shiver of revulsion was passed off as pleasure. His bath completed, Brenat closed his eyes and thought of his mate. His arousal sprang to life as he climbed from the tub. She guided him to the bed, her hands wrapped around his manhood, stroking him more to life. He sat on the bed as she lowered her head, her lips peeling back. She purred in a sweet sing song lilt about how tasty he would be.

Brenat opened his eyes, grabbed the glass of mead and smashed it against her head. Grabbing the knife from the plate, he impaled her right eye. The hag screeched in pain, trying to claw him with her talons, she tried to focus on him with her one good eye. Brenat moved behind her and pushed her face first into the bale of hay that, a moment before, had appeared as a lush bed. Pinning her, he took the knife and sliced her throat. The sing-song voice became a gurgle as she drowned in her own blood, her scaly tail whipping his back. When she finally stilled, he cut off the tail, wrapped it around the head, and put both back into the bag of salt.

Getting dressed, he climbed down from the loft. He looked towards the door and two oxen stood where the guards had been when he first arrived. He then looked over to the trough where pigs fed, that had been the bar. He shrugged as he walked from the barn, the tail still twitching in the bag.

Brenat thought "How *disgusting and dangerous Ferlairns were. Why a demon would breed with a harpy baffled him.*"

Hours from the Ferlairn's den he stopped to build a fire and added a concoction from his belt that sizzled and smelled of rotten feet. He pulled out the scroll he had been given. Brenat read and was very specific as to get the pronunciation correct, as he was instructed, before adding the scroll to the fire. The fire flared and then extinguished itself, leaving a thin green smoke. Brenat walked around in a circle, the vein of smoke always proceeding him by a foot. When Brenat turned, the smoke stayed east ahead by a foot distance, even if he turned his back on it. With the spell working right, he followed the smoke through the dense trees and came to a burrow big enough for a bear. Brenat stopped as the smoke bellowed and flowed away from him into the den where he soon heard rattling and sneezing.

"*I tassste a lycan, come in and visssit lycan,*" said a voice with a lisp from deep inside.

Brenat replied, "*No, Naga, I will not enter your domain. You come out and we shall converse and discuss your terms of trade for your knowledge.*"

With a hiss, Naga said, "*You are a sssmart lycan. Before I come from my home, who and what do you ssseek?*"

Brenat said with a sigh, "*Meridth's spinner cut from her corpse.*"

With a hiss and a laugh, Naga said, *"Even if I give you the knowledge you ssseek your oddsss of sssurviving that tassk are ssslim and what do you have to trade?"*

"I have gold and knowledge to trade." replied Brenat in an impatient voice.

"I have no need of gold and asss for the Ferlairn, I already know. But I would trade a ssservice for the information you ssseek. Do you agree to my termsss?"

Brenat hesitated before replying, *"Yes, as long as it will not interfere in my completing my duties in a timely matter. Come on out so we can complete the deal."*

With a rattle, Naga said, *"I tassste truth, I ssshall not harm you and you will not harm me. You will do me the ssservice firssst or you can go and find her on your own, deal?"*

"Yes," Brenat stepped back two paces as he heard movement inside.

A lovely, lithe naked woman appeared. She had cat like eyes, a smile with two large fangs, and a forked tongue that she tasted the air with as she came from the den. Her bottom half was legs that looked like serpents' tails, thick and scaly. Each one was ten feet long and had rattles on the end.

"What's the task?" Brenat asked.

Naga replied, *"I have been alone a long time. The time isss now that your ssseed may bring about my offsssspring. My need to be ssserviced by a man hasss been a long time coming. In one hoursss time you ssshall continue on your quessst. Time to ssshow me your sssnake."*

Brenat removed his armor. Her eyes glint with lust as she looked upon his member. She lowered her body and her forked tongue slid out to tickle and taste his well hung jewels before wrapping around his member pulling and squeezing with the strength of a python but the gentleness of a lover. Under the caress he swelled and pearls appear at the tip as she licked them off, her eyes blazed with passion. Her serpentine legs slid around him lifting him to her as she laid upon her back. His body positioned by her legs that had him in a pythons' grip. Her hands grabbed and guided him into her moist center core. He pumped into her as she withered and slithered under and around him, pulling on him with a strength best described as uncomfortably powerful yet erotic. She was not encouraging his release as much as she was squeezing the release from him. Even after he released, her body pulled and squeezed, not allowing a single drop to be left behind.

With her passion sated she released him, tired, drained, and feeling very used. *"When your tasssk isss complete come back if you wisssh and I will sssshow you how I can ssswallow you."* She smiled as she slithered back into her den. She said, *"Head wessst through the foressst until you come to a mound of corpsssesss. Watch for sssilk threadsss along your path and you will know you are near."*

Brenat walked west through the trees, the forest steadily becoming denser and darker; evidence of life's struggle everywhere he looked. A centipede the size of Brenat's forearm was eating a rat of equal size. While a bright plumage bird watched a snake with hungry, weary eyes, the snake in return watched it, as if they were trying to figure out which was the prey and which was the predator. Soon there seemed to be less creatures, big and small and the occasional fine silk line brushed and stuck in Brenat's hair.

Brenat, constantly feeling the need to slap the back of his neck, felt something crawling through his hair and around his neck on more than one occasion. He suddenly stopped in mid step, his hackles raised as he looked around before looking down. A glint of moonlight was sneaking through the dense foliage above, showing the forest floor covered with sticky silvery webs that held creatures from as small as a mouse to as big as a pig. Everyone were wrapped in silvery cocoons with leaves stuck, here and there, to the carefully wrapped corpses. With slow, carefully placed steps, he walked so as not to step on one of the lines laid carefully just above the ground. He made his way to the mound where the tunnel of silk led into the darkness.

Brenat, drawing his katana, looked around found a line the size of two of his fingers put together. As he cuts it, there was the sound of a taut support cable snapping back upon itself. Brenat waited, watching and wary the almost imperceptible movement of some of the silk lines pulled Brenat's attention.

If he had blinked at that moment, he would have missed the spider lowering herself to the top of the mound. Each of her eight legs was as tall as Brenat. Her bulbous abdomen glinted with the shape of an hour glass. She had two mandibles, the tips glistening green, on either side of her head, each was about the size of his chest.

With a sweet voice that made him think of his mother's lullaby, Meridth whispered, *"My food does not usually take such care to sneak up to my cave then knock as you did. The last one to do that was a good mate and even now my baby eats her way out of her very alive, yet paralyzed, father's stomach. So human, wait your too big, correction, so lycan did you come to mate and be food to your child or is there another reason you knock upon my home?"*

"I am here to collect you as a bounty," replied Brenat.

With the same sweet voice, she replied, *"Ah, I was hoping your seed would produce one of my children. Your body would be your one-time support for our child. You lycans have it rough with your children coming to you crying for food. Mine run as soon as they are able before they become food."*

Brenat watched as Meridth spun a sticky net behind her with all the stealth she could muster. With a flick of her abdomen, the net flew with the accuracy of an arrow.

Brenat threw a dagger through the web lines at her eye while side stepping three feet to avoid the net. Meridth seeing the dagger, moved her head and the dagger bounced harmlessly off of her mandible.

With her sweet motherly voice, she said, *"Ah my food wishes to play. It's been a while, let the game begin."* She stomped her fore legs and hairs the size of daggers flew at Brenat, who leapt out of the way. His sword deflected a few, while his leg was caught on a sticky line. He brought his sword down to cut his leg free just as another web flew, pinning his sword and arm to a tree. Meridth moved in, singing a sweet lullaby, *"I would wrap you in a swaddle and rock you to sleep. My love would cocoon you while my venom digests your meat, then I shall drink you as you sleep."*

Brenat was ready as she lowered her fangs and the green venom dripped like drool as they started to close upon his chest. At the last second he pulled his last dagger, shoving it through her nose into her brain. Then managed to pull back just in time as the poisoned mandibles closed on empty air, Meridth's eyes flare with rage. With a swipe of the dagger along the mandibles, Brenat pierced her eye with her own flesh eating venom. As she rears back in rage, he cut himself free and jumped upon her back, as he sent his sword through her back again and again. He was beginning to wonder if she would ever die when suddenly she fell dead, her legs twitching. Withdrawing his sword from her body, Brenat went to her palm sized spinner and cut it from Meridth's corpse.

Brenat turned as he heard a scream of pure rage, just as a creature a quarter the size of her mother, but almost identical in appearance, half emerged from her father's cocoon. Brenat, with all haste beats a retreat, muttering, *"One creepy spider a day is enough"* as he adds the spinner to the bag of salt.

He headed south for two weeks, coming to a town he had previously passed. With a room rented, he rested at the inn, his window overlooking the street, ever watchful for his target.

His mind wandered to his beautiful tigress while he ate

some roasted pork. He wondered if he would ever be able to quit killing and just farm and love, maybe even adopt a child or two, for he would never have any of his own.

Two days passed, and he still sat at the window, wondering what his tigress was doing and how he would find her. Tracing the mark, she had left with his fingers, he asked himself the many questions that haunted him *"Is she alive? Had she moved on? When he found her would she still want him? With how clean she smelled she must be a soap maker by trade."* He smiled to himself. *"Between farming and a ready supply of soap, maybe I would finally be able to forget and wash the stink of death from me."* He scoffed, *"It's been two months, she is probably gone forever."* His mind went to his friend that he visited with every full moon when he wasn't too far away.

It was noon the following day when a fancy carriage arrived and the noble lady, with her ladies in waiting, headed to the store. Brenat left his room, payed his bill, and walked over to the store.

While walking in, he noticed the ladies chatting excitedly over the new lace and silks the store keeper had. While waiting his turn, he smelled the soaps and perfumes, looking for a hint of his mate's scent, but none seem to match hers. He picked up a bottle of perfume for his mother that smelled of strawberries, his parents' favorite dessert. The store keeper asked what he could do for Brenat. Brenat set down the small bottle of perfume on the counter, then ordered some sword oil and a whetstone. Noticing some rare imported sugary treats his mother would love, he bought a small bag. A rare book his dad would like grabbed his eye, so he purchased that as well.

Buying the book and perfume, which was strange for someone of his class, piqued the interest of the noble lady. She noticed his strong hands, handsome face, and bright blue eyes.

Brenat stepped from the store and leaned against the pillar absently thumbing and reading the book as he sucked on one of the sugary treats. The noble lady soon followed him out with her ladies, approaching Brenat with an inquiry about the book he just bought. He smiled, dropping the book into his bag and stated it tells the legend of the shape shifters as he plunged his dagger into her chest. He cut out her still beating heart and dropped the heart into the sack of salt beside the other gory trophies. The noble crumpled on the wooden walk, her blood staining the wood. He escaped into the northern forest minutes ahead of the cry of alarm, as the ladies in waiting came out of their stunned silence.

Brenat had miles of forest between him and his last target. He turned south again towards one more target. Thoughts on his targets running through his mind, "*The nobles he understood, they made many enemies, but why would someone want a peasant farmer's eyes?*" With a shrug, his thoughts cleared as he knew the noble's people had started their hunt. He was secure in the fact that they were following the trail he had left, he continued on, knowing it would take them a day to realize they were on a false trail.

❈ ❈ ❈ ❈ ❈ ❈ ❈ ❈ ❈ ❈ ❈

Teera, with each passing of the new and full moons, wondered why she could not feel her mate. She rubbed her bonding mark, not understanding why it was not working. "*Bonded mates could always feel each other and find each other through their blood bonds. They are mentally linked only death could break the bond. She would have known if he was dead and bonded mates would not take another mate. Once bonded, they remain together for life, unless he is behind a magical barrier like me. Is he hurt somewhere that I cannot feel him? That would explain why I cannot feel him. Maybe he is too far away. She did not know what he did for a living, but she remembered smelling fresh turned earth, horses, and cedar on him. Surely he must have been royalty from far away or possibly a knight because he fought so skillfully.*" Many possibilities ran through her mind.

She felt the new life growing and moving like butterflies playing in her stomach. "*Maybe her ghostly friend had finally moved on to be born again. Was her friend the soul that allowed her to have a baby?*" Finally, after several moon cycles, the growth of the baby was evident. Teera planned for her next reprieve to go to the castle. "*She would need to start gathering the supplies she would need for the baby and to tell her parents they were going to finally get a grandchild.*"

Sadly, she wondered "*If her mate would want their baby or her.*" She laughed at herself, "*Of course he would, they were bonded. What if he had been killed after their mating and would never know of the gift they had? She would have felt his death through their bond; unless her being pregnant was blocking that part of their bond.*" Placing her hands on her rounded belly, she told her son that his parents loved him.

⊠ ⊠ ⊠ ⊠ ⊠ ⊠ ⊠ ⊠ ⊠ ⊠ ⊠

Meanwhile Brenat, after many weeks of travel, came to the farmer's land. The young man hailed him, as his wife and children worked nearby. Brenat replied then sipped from his water bag. The farmer was strong with callused hands and a friendly demeanor. He offered the guest to his land an evening meal.

Brenat declined with a nod saying, "*I bring bad news.*"

The farmer, suddenly suspicious, had his wife usher the children inside. Brenat had a hushed conversation with the farmer while his wife and children watched from the door way.

With quiet indifference, Brenat said, "*I'm here to kill you. Why does not matter. There are two options. I can take your eyes and you can move on from here, forever dead in this land, or you can try to defeat me and if you succeed, you can then run before another comes hunting you. I will wait as you decide. You are the only one I have ever given a choice to."*

The farmer looked at Brenat in stunned disbelief, then grabbed a nearby axe, and charged at Brenat. With a glint, the farmer faltered then fell to his knees, the axe forgotten as he clutched his throat, blood seeping between his fingers. Brenat walked over, and plucked the dagger from the farmer's throat then plunged it into his heart for the instant kill, to end the farmer's suffering. He then popped out the farmer's eyes, adding them to his bag. He dropped two pennies and a gold coin on the corpse before he continued on his way, the wife and children cries falling on deaf ears.

Brenat remembered his first kill and how bad it had felt. He wondered when he had lost all feeling. Even hurting was better than feeling nothing at all. *"With the next moon I should be home and my friend may be able to heal my deadness. I could find my mate then stop killing to just farm and help things grow."*   On his trip home, he wondered *"If his next assignment would finally end his life and he would be free at last."* Thinking of the tigress, he acknowledged to himself that *"She was better off without him, so he would not search for her. He would farm, visit his ghostly friend, and do his assignments until he finally reached his own demise."*

After months of travel, through mist, rain and sun he arrived at Commander Rivek's camp and dropped off his bloody proofs. Brenat then collected his gold, before he headed home to his parent's farm and shop.

The Confession

Teera knew that she would soon have to tell her parents that she was to have a baby. She could not believe she was finally going to have a baby. After five years of having been forced to endure pain and humiliation at Asslam's hands, only to have the breeding's fail to produce a baby, then being banished and alone for months, her tigress had found her a worthy mate.

She wondered *"If her ghostly friend would finally appear during this reprieve."* Teera sat and stared out over the valley, dreaming *that her mate lived in the valley too. She dreamt about how they would raise their children together and grow old together. She could finally be happy.*

With the moon's arrival, Teera headed to the castle, happy about her news. When she arrived at the gate she was told that Asslam was due to arrive for a visit. She rushed to deliver her news so she could avoid encountering Asslam.

Teera headed towards her parents' office, failing to notice the shocked looks from those she passed. As she entered the great hall, she met Kenny and Arris, *"Princess, congratulations on your pregnancy,"* a shocked Kenny stammered.

Smiling, she hugged their necks, *"Thank You both, I'm very excited and happy. I'm on my way to tell my parents the great news."*

Entering the hall leading to her parents' office, Teera ran

into Eve, the young omega she had rescued years before from the former dungeon keeper. Eve had been taken and made a slave by the former dungeon keeper after he had killed her parents and burned their farm when they refused to sell her to him. He had collared her in a silver collar, not allowing her to shift, instead treating her as a pet. Teera had felt her pain and told her parents who then confronted the keeper. When the collar was removed and Eve shifted to human the truth of his crimes was revealed. Teera's father had the former keeper tossed to the hell hounds that had torn him to pieces. Teera walked on, reminiscing of the good she had done before Asslam, as she looked for her parents.

James and Rizalle stared at Teera as she entered, noticing her condition. *"Your pregnant!"* exclaimed an excited Rizalle.

James hugged Teera and ordered his scribe, *"Quickly, sent out the announcement to all of the castles inhabitants that the Teera and Asslam are to have a baby,"* before Teera could even get a word in.

Teera repeatedly tried to get her parents attention to explain that it was not as they thought, but in their happiness at finally getting a grandchild they started making plans and Teera was seemingly forgotten. Shaking her head, she sighed thinking *"That they would soon slow down and remember her."*

Asslam arrived at that moment and Teera's fear rose knowing his temper and what he would do to her and the baby once he found out. Without a word, Teera fled in tearful panic, wanting to grab her supplies and return to the valley before he could catch her.

Rizalle apologized *"I'm sorry Asslam, pregnancy makes for emotional women, I'll go calm her while you and James talk."* Rizalle promptly chased after her daughter.

James said, *"Congratulations Asslam on your heir."* He turned to a servant nearby and said, *"Fetch us some warmed blood wine to celebrate the new babe that will forever link our two kingdoms together."*

Asslam sat in stunned, seething rage, barely keeping himself in check. Smiling he accepted the congratulations. The wine turned to vinegar as it touched his hate filled tongue. Asslam's mind whirled with the news. *"That mutt of a wife of his had finally gotten bred not by him but by another. He was inwardly raging that the bitch had come in heat and bred with another. He never should have agreed when her parents had wanted her to be allowed to visit them monthly. He should have forced the dogs to go to her in the valley. That way she would not have been able to breed."*

Silently, he asked himself, *"Who was the father? Where was he? One thing for sure, he would find out. Once he did, he would kill him, his cheating wife, and her child. How could she breed with another? She had not produced with him and his mistresses had proven he was fertile as he had many illegitimate sons with them. It had to be something those damn mutts had done. Maybe she had not been ready yet. Maybe she was just coming into the age where these mutts breed, especially with her being a rare mixture. One of her type had not been born in a millennium. It was possible that she was even more different than he initially had thought. He thought about the fits she had on the blood moons. Even his witch, Keres, with her potions, had not been able to control her during those times."*

Asslam calmed his mind recalled the reason for his visit. *"James, I have another reason for my visit, besides the good news of our future heir. It had been brought to my attention that raiders are making things dangerous of late and there have been assassinations of many of our noble allies, yours to the north and mine to the south, everyone must take extra caution."*

Asslam formed a plan, and the wine tasted like sweet revenge. With a genuine smile, Asslam cuts his visit short. *"We will truly celebrate on my return. I will go so you can enjoy the remainder of the night with your daughter."* Asslam thought, *"It will be the last time you see her alive."*

Asslam left through the main gate after having a hushed

conversation with one of his guards. A rider soon separated and disappeared down the north road in haste. Once out of sight of the castle Asslam lashed his horse to a deadly pace. On the way home, the head guard handed over his reins to Asslam, and silently wondering *"How many guards would be walking and how many dead horses he would find on his way home."*

Teera gathered supplies with tears in her eyes when she felt a hand on her shoulder, and heard her mother say, *"Teera, everything will be OK."*

Teera looked at her mother tearfully and stuttered, *"Mom, I must get to the safety of the valley, it's not Asslam's baby my tigress chose a wolf as her mate. I felt Asslam's hatred and anger earlier when he found out I was pregnant."*

Rizalle, was stunned by the news quickly recovering, she tenderly hugged and kissed her daughter's cheek, making a mental note to report this news to James at once. *"We will miss you until your return. We'll have baby supplies delivered to your supply cave."*

Teera hugged her mother tightly. *"I really must go before Asslam finds me."*

Just as she started to leave a guard approached Rizalle, reporting, as requested, that Asslam had left. Rizalle ordered the guard to fetch Walt, the fastest scout, and Kenny to her at once. Rizalle sent mental message to James that she and their daughter needed him at once. Rizalle turned to Teera, *"It seemed we have time to talk after all,"* as they headed to Rizalle's private sitting room after ordering the kitchen to send up some tea.

Teera blurted out, *"Mom, it was during the blood moon. My tigress chose a royal wolf as her mate whom I haven't seen since, and my ghostly friend has been absent for months. Oh Momma, it's so lonely in the valley."*

Walt, Kenny, and James appeared and Rizalle ordered Walt to take the scouts and secure the path to the cave entrance. She then told Kenny to arrange an escort for Teera to the barrier and told them both to protect her from everyone even her husband, Asslam. Both without a word bow and turn to make the necessary arrangements for the princess's safety.

James poured himself a cup of tea and looked at his wife after hearing her orders and said, *"Why do I think I'm going to need something stronger then this tea soon?"*

Teera looked nervously at her mother. Rizalle said, *"Tell him."*

Sighing, Teera looked at her Dad. *"Dad, the baby is not Asslam's. His father is a royal wolf that my tigress choose on the Blood moon, I have not seen or heard from him since."*

James silently pushed the tea to one side and reached for the bottle of blood whiskey and a glass he had hidden behind the cookie jar. He only shrugged at Rizalle's exclamation, *"SO, that's where you have been hiding it,"* as she gave James a look. *"A man needs a drink from time to time and this is one of those times,"* he replied.

James looked at Teera, *"Well, that is better news than it being half LEECH. I never did like that blood sucker anyway. Tell me about this wolf. Who is he? Where is he from? Did you bond? How many men can he field in the alliance for the upcoming war with the LEECHES?"*

Teera looked at her parents, sipped her tea, and took a deep breath. *"He is a royal wolf of at least black knight in standing, for he has great fighting skills. His scent hints of horse and expensive cedar. My Tigress chose him on the blood moon. Yes, we bonded but I have not seen him since. Well, you know I'm locked away except on the moons and how demanding royal life is. To make matters worse, the valley stops all from entering, so he is either far away or behind a mystic barrier himself. Maybe the baby interferes with my bond with him. I have noticed that the castle's emotions were muted too when I arrived,"* Teera said in a rush of what seemed to be a single breath.

James sat thinking as he downed his drink before pouring

another. He replied, *"Well there are several good things coming from this. You found your mate, he is a lycan, we get to be grandparents, and you're not bonded to that blood sucking leech, Asslam. I'd prefer diseased ticks and infected mosquito's over that vampire and his coven. Even a flea infested, peasant lycan farmer would be better than that conniving vampire and his whores that pass as witches."*

Rizalle and James hugged Teera goodbye. They watched as Teera prepared to leave the castle with her escort. As Teera started to leave the castle, Ryan, one of the lycans that handled the castle supplies, handed Teera her pack and congratulated her on the new heir. On her way out through the gate, Tom, who worked in the gardens ran up handing her a pouch to add to her pack. *"My mother, who tends the herb garden, sent me to give you this tea. It is made with ginger to help when you feel nausea. Mother said it helped when she had me and to tell you she would have more ready for you on your next trip."* Teera smiled and told him to thank his mother for her. Then she hurried on out through the gate to return to the valley.

James looked at Rizalle with love and passion dancing in his eyes. *"If I could not feel you it would kill me. Maybe he died when he lost the bond connection as she entered the valley?"*

Rizalle replied, *"I hope it is the baby blocking and the block affects him as well."* Rizalle wondered with trepidation about the changes the news would bring as she looked at James. *"We need to talk about what we're going to do this will cause trouble and break the peace agreement."*

"I know but I cannot help feeling happy that it happened, especially if the rumors are true that we recently heard. I feel that we had best act for now like its Asslam's baby," James replied with a sigh.

James and Rizalle sent out news of Asslam and Teera's pregnancy to all the nobles, and then sat back to contemplate their next move while wondering about what Asslam's next move would be. They wondered if Asslam would stay silent, allowing the peace to continue, or would war once again consume both kingdoms. They wondered, also, if all of the recent assassinations were Asslam's doing or had another player, like the red cloaks, entered the field.

Outside of the gate, Teera walked slowly with her escort, looking around hoping her ghostly friend would show before she had to rush to the barrier. To slow progress, Teera often stopped to smell the flowers on the way or admire the beauty of the natural back drop to the castle. Teera's escort patiently allowed her all of the time she needed while wondering why she delayed so.

New Life Brings New Hope

Brenat missed the last full moon by weeks, so after delivering his bloody proofs to his commander and collecting his gold, Brenat headed home to the apothecary shop to drop off the gold and book to his father. He gave the sugary treats and perfume to his mother with a hug. Elsie fed him a warm meal of roast beast and fresh bread before rushing off to tend another customer. Brenat ate with no real appetite before leaving for the farm. Elsie sadly watched Brenat leave.

Sid came and hugged her closely. As he told her, *"If he gets time the farm will bring him back to life."*

Elsie commented, *"He needs a purpose other than gold and death. If only he could find where his heart belongs."*

Nodding, Sid kissed Elsie. *"I will go to the barn after we close and check on him and the horses."* Then he walked away to attend yet another customer as he placed his newest book behind the counter.

Heading to the barn, Brenat looked at the fields noticing the green crops. He sighed, *"Well at least something grows."* While checking on the animals he noticed that his favorite mare was heavy with a colt and gave her a sugar cube. While petting her, he felt some of his tension leave his tired body.

He filled the tub that was in the barn with fresh stream water and hung his sword and armor close by in the stall. Climbing into the tub and soaking the journey from his bones, the cold water felt warmer to his flesh than his soul did.

He thought, *"Why do I only feel when I am with my friend. The rest of the time my body moves but there is no life."*

Climbing from the tub, the dust, the trip, and the death having been washed from his body. Exhausted, but too tired to care, he decided to forgo going to the house to rest and climbed to the loft instead. The smell of fresh hay and horses was his lullaby as he laid in the straw to sleep. Brenat was finally able to rest, the muscles in his legs relaxed after months of constantly moving. He awoke hours later from a dreamless, death like sleep.

His stomach growled with hunger as he awoke to the smell of food cooking from the house. His father patted him on the shoulder as Brenat passed him on way to the house. Sid told him to return to the barn once he was done eating because his mare was soon to foal.

His mother smiled as he came into the house and motioned to the food on the table. She gave him a kiss on the cheek and a loving hug for the thoughtful gifts of the book, perfume, and treats then added, *"Should I ask about the last trip or would you just say the same old thing about how you don't talk about your assignments?"*

Brenat looked at her and between mouthfuls, *"You don't want to know, even if I wanted to tell you, the red cloaks would do horrible things to us if they found out I was sharing any information with you."*

Brenat, full and relaxed, went to the barn and helped his dad with the new colt that had arrived just moments before. With a smile, the two watched as the mare cleaned her colt, as the little miracle quickly learned to stand on its wobbly legs.

A passing thought of sadness ran past Brenat's lips, *"I will never be a father,"* before he laughed at the antics of the lively colt as it finally fed.

Sid looked at his son and replied, *"With every new life comes new hope, if you're rested, there are a lot of things that need to be done. The wagon needs greasing and the stallion threw a shoe. Your mother is planning a big meal tonight with your favorite pie, so work up an appetite."*

Brenat smiled and went to do the chores as his father continued to observe the colt and mare. Brenat thought of his mate, smiled and started making plans. *"A couple of days here and I can go find my Tigress. Maybe at the next moon I can introduce her to my ghostly friend, if the red cloaks leave me alone long enough."*

✵ ✵ ✵ ✵ ✵ ✵ ✵ ✵ ✵ ✵

With the new moon, Teera picked up the baby items and supplies that her parents had delivered hours before to her supply cave. She smiled as she dropped the old cart off and hauled the new cart with her supplies to her cave before spending the rest of the moon in the clearing.

Suddenly her thoughts turned to her missing mate and her ghostly friend. *"She wondered if she would ever see them again. Was her wolf dead? What would her mate say about her being pregnant? Would he have even care? Had her ghostly friend left her or was he the baby she carried, being reborn as her son?"* She sat crying in the clearing, missing both her ghostly friend and her mate.

With sunrise, she found herself back in the valley checking out the supplies. A soft, knitted baby blanket sat on top and covered the mobile she had as baby. She ran her fingers over it reminiscing while snacking on the chocolates her father had slipped into her supplies. She smiled and noticed the tin of sweets her mother knew she liked in the supplies as well.

With the supplies put away, Teera continued working on the rabbit skin jumper for her baby. While running her fingers over the soft fur she wondered "Would *her son have her father's strong chin, her mother's fiery hell hound eyes, or be more like his father. Would he be a white tiger like her or a black wolf like his father? Would he be a royal lycan or something totally different?*" Rubbing her belly, she hoped he would be able to escape the valley and discover the world, without war dogging his every step.

Her stomach growled in reply, reminding her more nourishment then sweet treats was needed.

Another Contract

renat was summoned by his commander to get instructions about his next assignment. His target, another of royal rank, was one that only came out during full moons. He was instructed that the next full moon would be the only time it could be done and he was given the path he was to take.

Rivek instructed Brenat, saying, *"Your target will be found between the Obsidian Mountains and Castle Black on the full moons. The princess can only escape the Obsidian Mountains on full moons and she is Lycan so will have more than just her human form. Kill her, then carve out the unborn child, and bring back the fetus, the client wants that as proof. You will get pay for two kills and double the risk pay as its time specific."*

Brenat with the cold demeanor of a seasoned killer asked *"Any defining traits?"*

Rivek gave him a description of her human form before dismissing Brenat.

With sadness, Brenat realized he would not see his friend for yet another moon. The extra gold would help his parents for quite a while. Brenat smiled, *"If I time it well I may be able to start my search for my Tigress, since it will take several days to get there and scout things. Our clearing is not far from my target's path. I just hope the months of being gone have not destroyed any trace of my wonderful Tigress."*

Leaving immediately, he arrived days before moon rise. Scouting, he found the path to the castle from the mountains. The rocky cliffs strangely hid the princess' path inside the mountain. He found her cave where the supplies are left with little effort, but how they got into the mountain was still a mystery.

With days to spare before the moon rise, he expanded his search into the forest and found the clearing. The downed tree was still there, the bones of the pig had been picked clean by scavengers and the bones were the only evidence left of his time there with the tigress. He found her scent and markings to be only a few weeks old.

Brenat smiled up at a raven staying well out of reach. *"Well, my winged friend, she has been here of recent. I should be able to find her when my task is done."*

He rested and reminisced, his mind wandering and for the first time he wondered, *"What did the princess do to cause the contract? Why do I fill the contracts like I do? Why don't I just leave and search for my mate?"* He knew that he would kill the princess as he was ordered to do, yet he surprised himself with his treasonous thoughts.

With his mind occupied, Brenat surprised himself by missing the moon rise. Rushing to pick up his targets path, he searched for evidence of his target's passing.

Brenat watched as a white wolf seemingly appeared out thin air, admiring its beauty and grace as it ran into the forest and down the path. Brenat was drawn to follow the white wolf as if his body was not his own until it entered the castle. Hidden in the deep shadows of the forest, he continued observing the castle gate through which the wolf entered. Hours passed until the princess left with a pack on her shoulders, walking along the exterior of the castle walls as if waiting for someone.

Before she turned and left the safety of the watch towers and headed to the forest path.

Teera's thoughts once again wondered to where her ghostly friend was or does she carry him with her.

Brenat watched as she stopped and stripped, adding her cloths to pack she carried. Her beautiful flesh was lit by the moon as she slid on the pack, her flowing platinum blonde hair falling like silk down her back. He saw the round fullness of her breasts and the bump of her belly where the child grew. With ease, she shifted to that of the white wolf now noticeably with child. He followed as she detoured from the path to his clearing.

Teera scented the smell of her mate close by and followed it towards the clearing, her thoughts centered on the excitement of seeing her mate and sharing the news with him that they were soon to be parents.

Brenat edged around so the scent of the pines masked his smell as he moved closer to his target. He sprang forth, his silvery sword in a downward swing, the blade's cutting edge slicing through the air. He stopped a hair's breadth from severing the head from the body of the wolf, the sword stopped as if by a mystical hand. His mind was flooded by an image of his tigress, and the feeling of his friend's closeness.

Confused, he stood frozen. Teera stunned, wondered, *"Am I dead?"* Minutes passed with neither moving or speaking. Brenat lowered his sword in absolute confusion.

The scent of her mate in her clearing forgotten, Teera realized she had been saved from certain death. She felt her ghost but could not see him as she bolted for the safety of the barrier.

Brenat watched as she disappeared into the forest before shaking off his trance like state. Realizing he had missed his opportunity, he would have to attempt it again on the next moon.

Teera, inside the protection of the barrier, weary and shaken from her near death experience, felt a touch of sadness, for her ghost had left again.

Brenat headed back to the red cloak camp confused and disorientated, his friend's aura was absent once again.

When Brenat fails to drop off the bloody proof, his commander asked, *"Is there a problem getting the job done?"*

Brenat said, *"No, I did not find her."* He uttered his first treasonous lie.

Leaving Commander Rivek's office, Brenat was shameful and confused. He entered the chapel for discipline to flog himself for his failure. The commander watched the first self-flogging Brenat had ever done since he had become an Elite.

Rivek sent spies to the castle to see if his information was wrong, assuring himself that Brenat would lead a group of Elite for the next full moon, to bring an end to this contract.

A few days later, Brenat was summoned to a meeting between Rivek and Asslam about the last moon failure.

Brenat coldly stated, *"The next full moon is a new chance. This time if she leaves the valley, she will not get past five Elites, and your bloody proof will await you."*

Asslam nodded dismissively at Brenat before turning on Rivek. *"If you fail me, the red cloaks will have a war on their hands until you and your like are dead or removed from all my lands."*

Rivek calmly spoke, *"You have used us many times to remove obstacles in your path, we have never failed and will not do so now."*

Brenat walked away so as to hear nothing else. His cold demeanor belittled his internal turmoil between the death dealer he was, the farmer and father he wants to be, and the lover he could be. Brenat set his mind *"That this would be his last kill, then he would say good bye to his parents, go in search of his tigress, and become a farmer; no longer killing for gold. He would be on the ran from the Elites until they thought he was dead. The extra gold would hold him for a year or two, depending on the cost of the farm and how long it took to find his tigress. There would be no more killing for gold ever again."*

The Attack

With the next moon nearing, Brenat left camp with four other Elites and they all took up positions along the forest path from the castle to the cave. Brenat took the cave filled with supplies after spreading his team out along the route, where they could watch the path while they waited for the moon to rise.

Teera came through the barrier as her majestic tigress and headed to the delivery cave. Brenat watched as the great cat appeared as if out of thin air. Their minds touched through their bond as she neared and shifted back to the princess, shocked happiness at being together filled them. Suddenly Brenat realized that he and his men had been sent to kill his own mate.

The twang of the bows being released could be heard as Brenat leapt from his cover, his body pushing Teera into the bushes. The silver arrows having pierced his side deeply with a double thud as they scraped past the bone, stopping the wounds from healing as the blood drained from his side past the silver arrows. With sword drawn he turned upon two of his comrades who were stunned as he swiped with his sword, one head rolled to the base of a tree. The other realized Brenat was a traitor and drew his sword a second too late.

Brenat leapt a fallen tree, his pants catching on a branch, twisting him off balance. Brenat spun with the snag, his katana coming around in a back handed downward swing piercing through the red cloak's chest and heart, ending his existence. Brenat, while freeing himself from the snag, threw two daggers from his belt in rapid succession with his left hand, severing both bow strings of the last two Elites. The daggers narrowly missed the throats of his targets as the daggers sailed into the forest behind them. Brenat advanced on the last two, his katana dancing in figure eights as it proceeds him.

Teera recovered from the push and shifted back to her great cat. She peered through the bushes and saw her mate in a dance of death with his katana flashing in the moonlight. With a low growl and stealth, she moved cautiously into the fray, watching for other unseen threats.

Brenat drew his last dagger while slashing silver swords glinting in the moon light collided with a shower of sparks. The dagger deflected the sword of the other from his heart with a ringing of metal on metal in a flurry of give and takes. Brenat blocked with his sword and returned with a slash. The Elite stepped back just in time as Brenat's sword just nicked the bridge of his nose. Brenat blocked with his dagger again. The second Elite's katana was deflected and it hit the arrows embedded in Brenat's side. He flinched as the arrows cut and moved deeper. Slowed from blood loss, allowed the first Elite's sword to strike a bloody cut on Brenat's forearm.

Teera fearing for her mate's life as she noticed the successful strike and the blood draining from the arrows in his side. Decided to forgo stealth and rushed to close the distance to help her mate in battle.

The two Elites pressed the traitor a little harder, swords and daggers flashing even faster. The two Elites separated trying to keep Brenat between them while his deadly dance blocked the others weapon, always moving to keep both his opponents from getting behind him.

The tigress leapt upon the back of one, her claws shredding armor, flesh, and bone, exposing a still beating heart that she bit, taking it as her midnight snack.

The other Elite's eyes widened as he saw the tigress aiding Brenat, turned to flee only to have Brenat's katana pop through his chest from the back, his heart skewered on the sword.

With the tigress safe, Brenat sheathed his dagger and turned, suddenly dropping his sword. He fell unconscious his energy gone, dying blood pooling at his side as the arrows have worked deeper into his flesh from all the exertion.

Teera, using her claws, dug the arrows from her mate's flesh. Then holding the flesh together, to help the wounds heal. The taste of Brenat's blood wonderfully familiar as she licked to clean and help the wounds stop bleeding. She bit her wrist, pressing the bleeding wound to his lips to give him some of her rich rare blood to stave off death. The powerful white tigress then dragged her handsome, unconscious mate to her hidden valley under the spells protection.

The Reunion

Teera managed to lay Brenat on one of the loungers and shifted to check his wounds, inhaling his musky scent. Seeing that he was again bleeding, she again bit her wrist to feed him more of her blood. She once more licked his wounds, encouraging the healing of the exterior wounds as her blood helped to heal the wounds on the inside.

She sat watching and wondering about him as she sipped a cool drink. Her fingers stoked his cheek before moving to brush a lock of black hair away from his face. Teera removed his shirt to look for more wounds, watching his strong chest as his breathing became slow and steady. Her eyes came to rest on the bonding mark as she traced it with her fingers.

Deciding to clean up before her mate awoke, she went to the heated bathing pools after grabbing a clean robe and towels. The gem encrusted walls sparkled in the flickering candlelight. The warm water fell like a shower that drained into yet another pool.

Brenat awoke, his eyes following every graceful movement and never straying from the beauty before him. He watched through half closed eyes as Teera slid out of her gown, her platinum blonde hair falling past her shoulders. He admired the curve of her neck and the lines of her back that led to her heart shaped hips, that turned into muscular thighs, and shapely calves. She hung her clean towel and gown on the nearby hooks and stepped down the natural stone steps, the water concealing all but the curve of her shoulders. Teera washed her hair, his mark coming into view upon her neck and shoulder.

Brenat stared at the mark and sat up, removing his empty scabbard which fell to the floor with a clank. Teera turned, startled, her bust gently bobbing in the water. He dropped his pants, his arousal springing alive in full view. He stepped into the pool and sank down, sighing as the heated water started soaking into his muscles. He looked towards the princess, his tigress, admiring his beautiful mate.

Teera heard Brenat's thoughts, *"You're so beautiful."*

Teera blushed and thought, " *I love you, my handsome mate."* With an exciting shiver they realized they could hear each other's thoughts.

Teera started bathing Brenat, using the bathing sponge and scented soaps to clean the blood and sweat from his body, cautious of the tender and still healing wounds. He caresses her face, stroking one hand down her cheek and pulled her onto his lap. He claims her sweet lips, kissing her gently, cupping her breast, his thumb caresses her tightening nipple. She wrapped her fingers around his thickening length and straddled his thighs, her rounded belly touching his stomach. His hands grabbed her hips as he slid into her waiting warmth with such longing, belonging, and love. Their lips reclaimed each other.

Their passion built, their hips meeting hard and fast, growled of pleasure reverberated off of the walls. The pool's waves were flowing back on each other, matching the waves of pleasure flowing through them. After what seemed to be an eternity of building, his throbbing pulsating release pushed Teera to her own gushing release.

He bit her shoulder, feeling her coppery blood coat his tongue, then licking the wound closed. Teera, in turned bit his, renewing their bonding marks. With passions spent they licked each other's bonding marks, tracing them with their tongues. Pressing close in a tender embrace, they rested and held each other, letting the warm water sooth their calming hearts.

Teera rested her head on his shoulder, clinging to him with her legs around him. Brenat carried her from the pool to the bed chamber, water dripping off them. The air seemed cool on their glistening body's. Their bodies and minds were almost completely healed. Teera traced her fingers over her mark upon his chest as they realized he was her ghost and she was his.

With slow passion they kissed, their movement matching their heartbeats, slow and rhythmic. His hands caressed her body, while his lips teased at her neck. Her body squeezed him, refusing to let him go. Their need and want responding to each other as their minds melded together just as their bodies did. They were so wrapped in their love they lost where they each started and the other ended. With their release, they finally separated still holding each other as their breathing calmed once more.

Surprise Revelation

Brenat laid beside Teera, tenderly touching her rounded belly. He huskily whispered, *"I love you and your baby, I will raise him as my own."*

Teera's fingers stilled at his words. She looked at him and replied, *"He is your son. You're his father, no one else, it happened on the blood moon."*

Teera felt his confusion and doubt as his mind was in turmoil over the fact that he had been told he had been sterilized as a child. Then there was hope and elation as the reality of the miracle set in. A single tear fell and he kissed it away from where it fell on her belly. They fell asleep, holding each other, Brenat's hand resting protectively on the gentle curve beneath where his child rested.

Brenat awoke watching Teera's ample bosom rise and fell in peaceful slumber until hunger beckoned. Strapping on his empty scabbard, hunger forgotten, he remembered where he had last seen his sword. Following his own bloody drag marks, with all urgency, he shifted, rushing to get his sword.

He found the exit and cautiously he looked for dangers. Brenat bolted from cover to cover circling the area. Secure in the fact he was the only one there, he retrieved his sword. Looking to the old cave, he remembered seeing supplies in the cart, and noticed sunrise was but moments away. He raced the rising light, bewildered at seeing the path so easily marked.

Brenat rushed the cart into the mouth of the mountain entrance. He was pulled off of his feet, his forward momentum abruptly stopped. With a roll and a spin, sword in hand, he faced a solid wall of stone holding fast the back half of the cart and supplies. Brenat sheathed his sword with a huge sigh of relief, half a second later he would have been part of the wall.

His stomach reminded him he still needed to eat, he left the cart to go in search of food. Bernat passed a stretched deer hide and a baby blanket on a loom, a shining light drew his attention. He stopped to admire an impressively stocked armory, before continuing to the entrance and the view of the valley below. A mountain goat on the cliffs above him drew his attention back to his stomach. He shifted with great stealth and ease to fetch their breakfast, before long he carried the cleaned and butchered goat wrapped in its own hide back to the kitchen. Teera awoke thinking of Brenat's location, his thoughts came back to her, *"I'm in the kitchen, my love."*

"Oh, I'm sorry, I'll fix you something to eat," she replied while getting dressed and hurried to the kitchen, grabbing golden goblets of chilled juice and plates, setting them upon the table. Brenat seared the unseasoned goat. Teera with a wrinkled nose and a smirk, grabbed some spices and took over the cooking.

With his body healed of his deadly wounds, after a mere night in her presence his soul felt alive once more. Brenat watched Teera as she cooked, his aura reaching out wrapping her in a ghostly hug, realizing that his body had found the mate his soul had already found at last. Teera heard his thoughts, smiled, and replied, *"You're my ghost, my mate, my love, and the father of our child."*

While sharing the meal Brenat asked, *"While I was bringing in the cart I noticed your route is so clearly marked, yet I could not find the road from that old cave to the entrance before today."*

Teera looked at him strangely, *"This place is enchanted to be sealed against all others. It's my prison for not bearing Asslam any children. I was banished here and I can only leave during the full and new moons, but I must be back in by sunrise."*

Smiling, Brenat stated, *"Well I know why by sunrise. I made it back in by sunrise with the cart of supplies, mostly anyway."*

Teera asked, *"How did you get the cart and our supplies? You should not have been able to get back in once you left the valley, only I can bring others in. What do you mean mostly?"*

Brenat replied, *"There was a problem in my timing on getting back in, but I'll show you what I mean after we are done."*

After finishing the meal and the dishes, they walked to the cart holding hands. Teera s stood, staring from Brenat to the cart.

Her happiness of having Brenat, her mate, there with her almost washed over the fact he had left and got back in without her guidance. He could leave and enter as she could. Then she realized, *"He is imprisoned with her. What had she done? He could not leave even if he wanted to."* Her tears started to flow.

With Teera's thoughts in his mind, Brenat reached and wrapped his arms around her. *"With you in my arms there is no prison."* Brenat pulled her close against him to whisper in her ear, *"Where ever you and our baby are is my home, nowhere else matters. The only thing I miss is not saying good-bye to my parents."* Brenat smiled caressing his mark. *"We share blood now, maybe that is the key to the valley's secret, only those with your blood and mark may enter."*

Teera smiled up at Brenat, *"Would you like to look at our home?"* She pressed close and nipped playfully at his ear lobe. *"It is so nice to have you here. I was so lonely in my small cave."*

Brenat playfully swatted Teera's backside and replied, *"I would love to see more and you're not alone anymore."*

Teera led Brenat through the cave, showing him the armory and the well-stocked pantry. She opened a door across from the main bed chamber into a jewel encrusted room that would be the nursery. She then led him down the hall past the bathing pools and master bedroom, passing eight other closed rooms not in use.

Brenat was awed by the size of the home that Teera considered small thought, *"I could fit my entire town in here easily with room to spare and still not use the spare rooms. Even the corridors were so big that four men could walk abreast and not touch a wall. The kitchen was large enough for a communal feast."*

They continued up the subtly inclined corridor to another door leading to a veranda. They stepped out onto intricately carved marble tiles, and sat on a marble bench. They looked out over the massive valley floor which was longer than it was wide, with a lake to one side. Grasslands were cut down the middle by a creek surrounded by forest that climbed from the valley floor up the mountainous slopes. Barren rock and lichen took over the steep slopes to the snow topped mountain peaks that completely encircled the valley, finishing the view.

Teera pointed out the porch, down and to the right. He saw the cave's stone entry way with its butcher block table, hide stretchers, and small stack of wood with its own chopping block.

He turned and looked at Teera. *"WOW, I have traveled far and experienced much but nothing like this. How is this all possible?"*

Teera, sat watching him, replied, *"It had always been here, my parents just added to it and had it enchanted when I was banished here."*

They walked back inside hand in hand down to the entrance, from the porch through the trees and to the grassland below. They walked along the creek to the mountain glacier fed waterfall and lake at the southern end of the valley.

As they walked, Teera absently remarked, *"When Asslam*

finds out you're the father of the baby, he will kill you. What will your people do when they find out you killed those others?"

With somber truth he replied, *"When Asslam hired me to kill you and our baby. Had I known who you were then, I would have slit his throat and removed his heart right on the spot. Yes, I would have forfeited my life immediately thereafter. I would consider myself lucky to receive a quick death when my people find me. The Elites will not stop until the contract is fulfilled or Asslam is dead. I must kill Asslam or die trying. I will not allow any harm to come to you or our baby."* Brenat stopped and turned to Teera in stunned surprise, *"I still have trouble believing how I could be the father, I was told that I had been sterilized shortly after birth by my sister."*

Teera answered in hurt and anger, *"You don't believe me? I got pregnant the night your wolf mated with my tigress,"* her eyes started to flame in anger.

Brenat held her in his arms, *"I believe you. It has to be a miracle, for I have always been told I would never be able to have children of my own."* He laughed a deep laugh that startled himself as if he had never heard himself laugh before. *"Thanks to Asslam bringing us together after so many years apart, we are to have our miracle baby. After being on assignment for so long after the blood moon I thought I had lost my tigress and maybe my ghostly friend. Because of him I have my mate and we are going to have our baby and be a family."*

Teera asked, *"What about your parents and siblings? How did you grow up?"*

Brenat looked at her, *"In the short version, I was raised a killer by the militia, I would rather be a farmer with my family and help with the apothecary."*

"No," Teera exclaimed, *"Tell me about you, your family and growing up."*

Brenat nodded, taking a moment to think before answering a question he had never had to answer before. *"Elsie and Sid bought me and my older sister, Rose, from slavers when I was a* baby. *My parents own a farm, but really dabble in the mystic arts like spells and potions, with many books on legends and lore. They keep the knowledge of days gone past. Rose married and moved away when I started my warrior training. I think they keep the farm for me because that was my only place I could find peace besides you on the full moon. Now my existence is with you. We'll live here and raise our family in peace."*

"*How do you think we have our baby? You were sterilized and I never gifted my husband with an heir even after five years,*" inquired Teera.

Brenat shrugged, "*I have no idea, but if we ever get the chance we could inquire at Blessed Miracles, that is the name of my parent's apothecary shop, they'll know.*" He pulled Teera in for passionate kiss then together they continued to the lake.

Passion in Paradise

Teera stood, leaning her back against a tree as they looked out over the lake. Bernat leaned into Teera, his arms lifting hers and pinning them above her head against the tree. He claimed her lips, his tongue moving in to taste her. Pressing his body against hers, his excitement easily felt against her belly through his pants. Teera panted softly at his dominating stance as she returned his kiss with passion, and longing. Her tongue danced with his as they kissed their bodies molding together in heated passion.

He slid a hand down under her dress so he could feel her hot moist readiness. Her hips moved into the touch of his fingers. Letting go of her hands, he freed himself, reaching around and lifting her. Her legs wrapped around his hips and her arms wrapped around his shoulders, their kiss deepening. Her warmth enveloped his throbbing length.

Teera's back pressed into the rough coolness of the tree, their smooth heat followed the beat of their hearts in a rhythmic dance. An eternity in bliss turned into hip bruising, frenzy need, and want, ending in a passionate release. They laid back in the grass, still entwined together, while they rested.

Kissing Teera, Brenat smiled, *"Let's get some food before I take you again,"* his arousal was already stirring near Teera's thigh. With a growling stomach, Brenat grabbed a knife from his discarded pants before running to the lake. He called back over his shoulder, *"Grab some kindling,"* as he dove into the water with hardly a splash. Resurfacing to catch his breath that had been stolen by the cold waters, he heard Teera laughing at his shock. He dove back down while thinking of his retaliation and smiled. His eyes focused on a large silvery fish swimming lazily beneath the surface. He brought it back on his blade. As he came out the water, the thought from earlier on his mind.

Teera laughed, *"You can just shake off that cold water right there, also you need to learn to guard your thoughts better."* She had started the fire while he had been fishing and added another piece of wood to it as she said, *"Brenat, you might as well clean the fish while you are beside the water."*

Smiling Brenat shook off the cold water, letting the noon day sun warm and dry his nakedness, as he cleaned the fish.

The fish sizzled over the fire as the warm sun shone on their naked bodies, while they sat, enjoying each other's company.

Brenat inquired, *"What happened to you for those five years we were apart? We went from almost nightly visits to nothing. When did you arrive here in the valley? I could only find you on full moons as the pull was stronger. The blood moons were always hard to remember and vague, however, the last blood moon I will clearly remember forever."* Brenat divided the fish. *"If you need more, Love, I will get another,"* he said before he pulled off a chunk and savored the hot white meat. Brenat stood up and with a playful bow asked, *"What was life like for you growing up, your highness?"*

Teera told him. *"From the time I was born I was betrothed to Asslam, to end the war between our two kingdoms. He never really wanted me except to get an heir. When I came of age we were married and he took me to his castle. He had powerful magic and several witches. For five years he tried to get me pregnant and couldn't no matter what he or his witches did to me. He hated me before, but his hatred is worse now that I am pregnant and he knows the baby is not his."*

Snuggling closer to Brenat, Teera continued, *"My parents are great and loving. They do all they can to help me. My parents also know Asslam is not the father. My parents had this place built for me as a refuge from the empathy I have. All my life I have felt the pain and emotions of others except when you "my ghost" were near, then only your emotions could I feel. What was it like for you as my ghostly friend?"*

Pulling her closer, Brenat nuzzles her before speaking, *"Well as a ghost you were real; the trees were real. Walls were visually there, but immaterial. Other people were there, but had the same effect as closing your eyes and sensing the things around us. I never knew you were a princess or even which castle you lived in. My nights away from you, I was always cold, dead, and in my own little mental prison."*

They sunned themselves beside the lake while they talked, Brenat's fingers drawing circles on Teera's belly. Teera yelped in surprise and placed her hands over top of Brenat's on her belly. They smiled at each other, feeling their child kick and move, truly realizing that their baby was real. They were soon to be parents of their own little miracle. Brenat smiled, *"I guess he will be a fighter with the way he is punching at my fingers."*

As the sun started to set over the western end of the valley, they got dressed and headed back to the cave. They sat together on the veranda and watched the sunset and the stars that came out to play with the waning moon. When the chilled air from the snow topped mountain brushed down their backs, Brenat picked up his love and carried her to their warm bed.

In the morning Teera stretched and reached for Brenat. Feeling his absence, she reached for him with her mind and found him sitting on the porch, drinking wild mint rose tea. At her inquiry, he smiled and mentally replied, *"Pour yourself a cup and join me my love."*

Joining him on the porch, the tea's subtle scent pleasantly drifted in the air. She leaned forward and kissed Brenat before she sitting beside him asking, *"What were you doing up so early?"*

He smiled and replied, *"I got up and put the crib together."*

She smiled as she heard Brenat's thoughts and plans for their future. *"I will need to grab a diamond willow branch to attach to the crib so I can hang the mobile. The wood pile is low and I need to cut a few cords before winter. On our side of the lake I can teach him to farm and hunt. There is plenty of deer, elk, mountain goat as well as fishing and wild berries for lazy days. The only predators I have been able to find is us and a family of black bears, who guided me to the bee hive, I can make mead."*

After taking a sip of her tea, she laughed, *"Do you think you will be able to make time in your busy schedule to hold and kiss me?"*

"Always my love." Brenat grabbed and kissed Teera deeply, holding her close. He smiled, *"But right now we have a nursery to finish for our baby. Let's go get the willow branch I need for the mobile."* He took Teera's hand as they headed towards a stand of willows that Brenat had noticed earlier. With an axe he took one branch with a long soft bend and a dozen others. They both carried up the branches. They peeled the bark, leaving the bone white wood, weaving it vertically through the crib rails so they bent and came out over the crib then secured them with rawhide straps. The mobile was then hung and tested, as it spun its carved jeweled figures glittered from the candlelight that played over it and the jeweled ceiling.

Leaving the nursery, they went out onto the porch with the other branches. Where Brenat took the other branches and wove them together, a high back loveseat slowly took form, also secured with rawhide straps. Then, with a hide pulled from the stretcher, he covered the chair he made, pulling Teera onto the seat with him. The flimsy looking wood held both with ease as he kissed her lips while holding her in the soft chair he had made for them to relax in.

Teera looked at the beautiful chair, *"Brenat, where did you learn to make furniture?"*

"When you train to kill vampires, lycans, and other creatures, the natural properties of things one could find around you could come in handy. When not on assignment, my mother's books have given me a lot of information. The essence of wood and plants just flows to me, just like your empathy lets you attune better with the animals and people you live around."

Sweaty and covered in sap after the day's work with the sun late in the sky Brenat headed for the bathing pools. Removing his shirt, Teera watched his muscular back and stared at all the scars that ran like whip marks across it.

Teera walked to the pools, slipping out of her gown and into the warm water. She started washing his back, tracing the scars with her fingertips. *"Brenat, those marks on your back, they look like whip marks. What happened? Why were you beaten and by whom?"*

Brenat replied casually, *"Most are the marks of my training and my rank of the Elite. Some are for failures from long ago. The most recent were from failing to kill you the first time. The Elites have a strict rule for failure, better to die trying then report a failure."*

Her fingers caressed his body, smiling as she started kissing his neck and nipping playfully.

Wrapping her in his arms, he pulled her close in a loving embrace. His want evident as it pressed against her belly. Tenderly he took her, filling her with his want, need, and passion. She clinged to him, her body craving his as much as he craved her. Their passion built to a powerfully tender release, culminating in whispered words of love. Holding each other as their hearts settled back to a normal beat, their bodies entwined, resting. They separated only when the baby declared it was hungry with some repeated kicks that made the water ripple.

Teera headed to the kitchen to cook up some rabbit stew. Breaking the wax seal on the pottery, she poured the stew into a cauldron, adding a few fresh herbs and some fat rendered from her last hunt.

Cleaned and ready, Brenat joined Teera and after a modest feast, they retired to bed wrapped in each other's arms, as they slept.

Teera awoke to the rhythmic sound of wood being cut, and the scent of left over stew warming in the cauldron then all went quiet. Getting up, Teera went to investigate and found Brenat marking off a place for a garden as well as an area for the cow. Smiling, Teera felt his happiness at being able to relax and farm. She sent him her love and reminded him that fresh eggs would be nice with their breakfast.

Brenat, while hunting in the tall grass for some eggs from the chickens that Teera's parents had set loose in the valley, heard the unmistakable shake of a Rattler and thought snake for supper might be a tasty idea. Hunting the snake was easy part, but he also had to kill it. As he circled it, Brenat's foot caught in a gopher hole and he started to fall. The snake struck, its venom dripping fangs heading straight for Brenat's face. Brenat caught the snake's head just before it could sink its fangs into his face, then drew his knife cutting off its head. He sent a thought to Teera how about snake for dinner before struggling to coil an eight-foot snake. Walking back to the cave, Brenat held up the rattle and gave it a shake, thanking brother snake for the nourishment and toy for his boy.

With warm days, Brenat explored the valley with Teera. They gathered eggs and caught birds or fish for their daily meals. They spent cool nights wrapped in each other's arms and passion. Brenat explored Teera's valleys, hills and curves at every opportunity, and Teera explored Brenat's body with equal enthusiasm. The child already played with the rattle by bumping it while it was on Teera's belly.

New Surprises

They were relaxing one morning when Teera told him, *"I should show you the lookout my mother had built, so I could always see the castle. It is a long trek and we can take supplies* up like wood, we can bring down some of the meat I stored and froze up there."

Brenat, intrigued, asked, *"Shall we head out tomorrow then? We could make a pack to carry up with us."*

The next morning from the veranda, Teera led Brenat up rarely used stairs. Many hours later they came to a hollow between two peaks that formed a snow covered plateau that had a small wooden cabin. It had a large spy glass that let her see her home clearly and protected her from the elements.

In the cabin Teera started a fire to take the chill out of the air and added mutton soup from the cold storage to the cauldron over the fire. All the while Brenat, used the spy glass, until the air is warmed by the hearth fire. The smell of soup drew him to the small table, the love in Teera's eyes warmed his soul. After the meal, Brenat took the hot cauldron outside, it hissed as he filled it and the used bowls with snow. He carried all back in, set the cauldron on its hook near the fire.

Grabbing Teera, his love filled his eyes and mind. His lips took her lips and slowly he undressed her. His lips kissed each newly exposed flesh her neck, shoulders, breasts, belly.

Teera guides him to a bear rug in front of the fire before she straddled him, guiding him into her warmth. Brenat's hands were on Teera breasts and his lips suckled her hard swollen nipples, their passion building with the speed of their hearts to an explosive conclusion. Sweaty they kissed, tasting each other's tongues. Their passions were spent. Exhausted, Teera rested her head upon his chest, his arms holding her close, they slept as the hearth fire cackled and burned.

They woke to a dying fire and a chill in the air, their shared warmth just barely kept it at bay. Brenat stepped out to grab more wood, the cold air raising goosebumps on his naked chest. As he noticed the bright stars, he briefly wondered how his parents were doing, before he returned inside and restocked the fire.

Teera called to Brenat, *"Come lay back down until morning."*

Brenat's eyes were alight with passion as his arousal swelled as he watched Teera sleepily reach for him in the glow of the fire light. Brenat's voice was husky with passion, *"I've got a better idea before we sleep until morning."*

Teera smiled and moaned as he joined her back in the bear skin, his lips claiming her once again. With the morning light they packed up, taking one last look at Castle Black before they headed back down the mountain side.

Later, back on the veranda, Brenat asked her about any other secrets she had not told him yet about their home. Teera looked towards Brenat. *"Yes,"* she replied, *"There is a heavy double barred door on the south-west side of valley that goes through the mountain and comes out with an ocean view. My father added it as a secret passage in case the enchantment ever failed and I needed to escape to safety."*

With the new moon coming they decided on a night time adventure to check out the escape tunnel. After a day's travel of running with each other, they came to the tunnel. By dusk they had the debris cleared away for the entrance and opened the door, they noticed it could be barred from the inside. As it was a tight fit for even one person, Brenat decided to check it out alone while Teera stayed outside because her belly made it awkward for her to travel in tight places. Brenat shifted into his wolf form and headed into the darkness of the passage.

Brenat, several times had his face full of spider webs, and the feeling of things crawling in his fur. He also felt several squishy and crunchy things leaving something gooey on his paws as he traveled. Even with his enhanced sight, there is no light and no way to turn around. So as not to feel alone, Teera sat at the entrance mentally telling him how bright the stars were in the moonless sky. As the night went on, she fell asleep as she waited for Brenat to return.

On and on Brenat traveled, he smiled as he felt Teera drift asleep. Before long, the smell of the sea came to him, it revitalized his hope when he came to a door where the fresh air seeped past fine cracks.

Brenat opened the door inward which took a little effort as years of disuse had made it stiff. He went out into a heavily forested area where he saw the sun as it glinted off the ocean below through the trees. Teera awoke with a start the morning sun bright on her face. She called to Brenat her mind, unable to reach him through the barrier as he stood outside.

With Teera's mind absent from his, they both feared the worse. He entered and barricaded the door once more, heading back to Teera. Somewhere along the darkened path through the mountain their minds touched once more to their relief.

Brenat made his way back to Teera, by late afternoon he came out into the sunlight, covered in things he prefers not to think about.

Teera asked, *"How was it? Is it clear? Could we easily get through it?"*

Brenat replied, *"It is tight, oppressive, and a little claustrophobic with enough little creepy crawlers that only the heartiest of souls would follow your escape. There were moments I felt I may get stuck and remembered a mountain of rock was just sitting there above me ready to crush me at any time it chose to. As a matter of fact, if you were not in my mind I would not have come back. So unless you were running for your life you should never use that route."*

Teera reached over and pulled a stubborn spider from Brenat's hair, dropping it to the ground where it scurried back into the tunnel before Brenat closed the door. He washed away the crawlies in the nearby creek while Teera made him something to eat.

The Legend and The Tiger

Teera inquired, *"Brenat do you remember anything about your natural parents or where you lived? You were born a Royal, just like me, only you were born a wolf. I suspect you're one of the lost wolf royals thought to be killed long ago. Do you know anything about the legend of the royals?"*

Brenat said, *"No, only what I was told, which was that my sister and I were sold after our village was destroyed. All my other family are dead as far as I know, I only have my adopted family. The only thing I know about royals was in my training on how to kill them. I never really needed any extra knowledge other than that royals are often multishifters, usually wolf and something else. Some have abilities with the elements, some even have the ability to shift a single body part, hand to paw, for example."*

Teera's voice took on the royal instructor's tone. *"So you were never told the legend? I will tell you the legend as it was taught to me..."*

"In the early days, Lucifer was the first archangel, God's first creation. He loved his father unconditionally and followed his every order."

"The human race was created and he was ordered to love these flawed and hateful creations more than his father. He could not do it

and it caused a civil war in heaven. This war raged for a thousand years. Lucifer and the other angels that sided with him lost and so were cast down from heaven."

"In revenge Lucifer created immortal beings he called Vampires. God watched from the heavens as these immortals took the lives of the innocent humans. God created beings of his own to restore balance, he created lycan wolves to destroy the vampires. He also secretly created several beings with royal bloodlines to push the balance more to his side. The Royals consisted of tigers, bears, wolves, jaguars, panthers, dragons and lions. They were stronger, bigger and more powerful then the regular lycans.

"Once Lucifer discovered this, he set out to destroy all the royal blood lines, he made many attempts to kill them with vampires, demons, and witches. They were thwarted until one lowly witch helped her master with the task by corrupting a royal to help destroy the royals. The witch found a young royal hungry for power and gave him a feast of his own father thus, corrupting the royal. His hunger to eat all life grew. Hate and malice made him powerful yet. Love and hope were painful and weakened him. He began the journey of corrupting the innocent until all the royals were hunted to extinction, and all life would follow. As a reward she became Lucifer's mistress and was given powerful magic to help her do his bidding"

"A few escaped and lived as humans to remain undetected soon these remaining royals passed into legend. The legend also told of a princess with this royal blood that would set the righteous path in motion, her child would restore the balance of good and evil."

"Lucifer created an Elite group, filled with hate, sin, and war to find and kill this princess, thus insuring the destruction of her child. Not knowing that God had created from one of Lucifer's own group of special assassins, the other half of his plan to restore the balance."

Teera's voice became husky and passion filled, *"Brenat, you and I are royals. You are a wolf and I am a tiger, but I can turn into wolf too. I was, for the longest, the only one of my kind. Brenat, you should know that you are like me now, you are now a tiger too. I want to see my mate's tiger and coloring."*

Teera smiled, her eyes changed from blue to green, then to a deep golden amber. Her hair and skin rippled and grew striped as she arched and fell forward. Her smooth form gracefully shifted into that of a massive white snow tiger the size of a pony. She worked her jaws and her large canines elongated. Her saucer like paws, when she flexed, showed off her dagger like claws. Purring, she rubbed her long and sleek body against Brenat.

Teera nudged Brenat through their mental bond and he felt his wolf merge with his tiger. Reaching to touch her beautiful coat brought about his shift. His course, jet black coat became sleek with gray stripes. Flexing his paws, he reveling in his new retractable sword like claws.

Teera watched as Brenat shifted. Purring, she rubbed along Brenat, reaching up to licked his muzzle. Her feral need and scent hit his senses, as she turned and raises her hind quarters. Brenat mounted her with a growl, with every thrust Teera met his with her own hard fast feral passion. They pounded against each other until they released with roars. They laid with each other resting on the barren rocks of the mountain side sunning themselves. Ears suddenly twitched as they heard a bull elk bugle to his herd, as it called the others away from the two predators. Stomachs rumbled at the thought of the hunt and fresh meat.

They ran down the mountain side past trees and boulders onto the plains with tall grass. They sat, tails twitched, as they sniffed the air and watched the deer and elk graze.

Brenat looked at Teera, *"Any preference love?"*

Teera thought back, *"Elk, our son is starving, as is his momma."*

The two cats slinked through the tall grass like shadows moving at dusk, they closed in on their prey. Teera crouched, ready to pounce, awaiting the signal.

Brenat left Teera to continue to slink downwind before sprung high into the air with a roar, joyous in the chase. The elk, fearful and reckless, bolted for freedom and safety.

Brenat cut the herd in half, to chase many to where Teera hid and waited. With a burst of speed he cut another from the herd, the others bolted to the safety of the rest of the herd across the creek.

He chased a dozen elk Teera's way, before they split again with four young bucks wide eyed, fleeing in terror, as the predator wanted to ran them to exhaustion. Two elk peeled off to the right, to cross the creek and join the others. Two continued to run through the tall grass, headed straight to where Teera hid and waited.

Teera smelled the sweat and fear of the prey and felt the pounding on the earth as the elk grew near.

Brenat's excitement broke through it all in a single thought, "*NOW!*"

Teera leapt, claws out, and with a single swipe severed the spine of her prey, using the crumpling prey as a spring board, she leapt towards the other. One hind claw snagged on a rib before it's release, causing a split second delay as the second prey veered and kicks out, the hoof tore open Teera's shoulder.

Brenat felt Teera's pain and watched the kick as it brought Teera down. The elk turned away from the two predators to rejoin its herd.

Brenat, the chase forgotten, was beside Teera in two strides, he licked her bleeding shoulder and nuzzled her to reassure himself she lived. He checked her for broken bones, and found only a gash and bruised flesh, with one elk bled out, almost completely forgotten.

Brenat focused his fierce stare on her with a concerned

growl *"You and the child could have been killed."* His paw held her down as he checked again for any wounds.

Teera chuffs at his scolding, *"I only wanted to help. It only got me as I misjudged my leap."* She tried to hold in a whimper as she started to get up to feed and finish the kill. Brenat growled as he continued to hold her down while he checked her over one last time.

Once able to get up, Teera started to limp to the lake for drink with Brenat's help. As she drank, Brenat went and brought the elk for them to eat. After they ate, she fell into asleep to heal, during which she shifted back to her human form.

He stood, watching her rest, his mind shifted from pride at such an efficient kill to the concerns and potential deadly scenarios. *"The hoof could have sliced open her belly, she could have busted a rib and punctured her heart or the baby, or an unlucky hoof strike could have crushed a skull."* His mind slowly calmed with the realization that Teera and the baby were both okay.

Brenat shifted back, hands were better than paws to care for his mate.

Teera whimpered in her sleep, she wanted and needed her mate close. Brenat picked her up and carried her back to their cave house, he laid her gently in bed.

Going back for the elk, Brenat looked up at the sky and thanked anything that might listen for Teera. He slung the remains of the elk on his back. He returned to the cave to skin and butcher what was left. Teera rolled in her sleep and cried out for Brenat to hold her. Brenat heard the call and went to hold her, he observed the bruise, until she regained peaceful sleep.

Then Brenat grabbed a pack, and bounded up the stairs to the veranda. Up the mountain side with all the speed and agility he could muster. He traveled to the edge of the snow pack, still hours from the look out. He filled the pack with snow and ice and then headed back down with reckless abandonment.

Brenat took the snow from the pack and wrapped it in a soft cloth, placing it on her shoulder. He placed the snow and ice that remained in the pack into some pottery and stuffed it in the cold spring storage room, then tossed hides over it to keep it as cold as he could. Before going to lay with his wife, cautious of her wounds as they healed.

Teera awoke as their baby kicked as Brenat snored in his sleep. She snuggled close to Brenat, Teera and the baby settled to drift back asleep.

Later when Teera awoke again, she slid out of bed silently as to allow Brenat more rest. She saw the stretched hides as she went to the kitchen to fix breakfast.

Brenat, felt Teera move, and watched her graceful, naked form, then remembered to guard his thoughts. He noticed her strong calves flex with every stride. He looked up past the legs that made an ass of themselves as they swayed to her movements. Her hair moved across the small of her back in time with her hips. When she brushed a wayward hair behind her ear. He smiled to himself, *"Yes, that would be the first place he planned to kiss."*

Teera sliced the readied meat over the fire to sizzle, before she squeezed some fresh juice. Then she turned to wake Brenat, she noticed he was already awake. She noticed how his eyes were alight with passion as he followed her hips up her body, stopped at her full breasts, before he continued to the curve on her neck up to her luscious kissable full lips.

Teera smiled, *"Good morning, Love, your breakfast is ready. You were up late last night."*

Brenat, with a sly smile, replied, *"Yes, I suppose I could eat first then have you for dessert. I did not want the hides to go to waste, they would make a great blanket for our child."* He noticed how Teera's belly moved to his voice.

Teera laid her hands on her belly as the baby moved, smiled, *"I think he will love it."*

They finished their meal, Brenat kissed a wayward drop of juice from Teera's lips, before he headed to the bathing pools. Teera followed Brenat to the pool, after she fetched fresh clothes and towels. *"Honey, is there anything else you'd like?"* she asked.

With a smile Brenat answered, *"YOU."*

She smiled, and slipped into the pool. Started bathing Brenat with the scented soap to scrub away the sweat from yesterday's exertions. She sponged and soothed the roughened flesh, she noticed his lean firm muscles and the pale scars on his back from the obviously many deep whip marks long since sealed into his flesh. She traced a few with her fingers and her smile returned as she remembered her bath training. Worked her way around to his chest, she sponged, and traced her mark. Dropped the sponge, she gripped him gently, felt him swell in her hands.

Teera, took a deep breath, slipped beneath the water and took his length in her mouth. Her tongue circled his shaft's mushroomed head. Her hands caressed his thighs and jewels. He tensed and moaned in pleasure as he swelled and throbbed in her in the mouth. Encouraged she took him deeper as he tickled the back of her throat, she swallowed to accommodate more of him. She sucked harder, her head bobbed up and down while she rubbed and squeezed his jewels until forced to come up for air. She looked at him, their eyes blazed with passion.

He caressed her face, stroked one hand down her cheek and pulled her onto his lap. He claimed her sweet lips with his. The kiss deepened as he reached to cup one of her ample breasts, his thumb caressed her tight nipple. Brenat's arousal throbbed against her thigh, when she moaned in pleasure. His other hand slid down and tested her readiness. She opened her thighs to his touch, his fingers sent a shiver of pleasure through her. Another soft moan escaped her lips as their tongues tasted each other. She turned and rested her hands on the edge of pool looked back and beckoned. He grabbed her hips, his arousal pressed at her entrance. She pushed back onto him and moaned with pleasure. His growl of pleasure reverberated off the walls.

As she pressed against his hips, his arms encircled her and his hands gripped her ample bosom. They started to move in wild abandon hard and fast, water splashed over the edge as her ass slapped his hips every time she impaled herself upon him. Their passions rose, his balls tightened as her body gripped him. She screamed his name, the rough stone edge cut into her hand as they peaked together, her body milked him of his seed.

They sat back in the water, he lifted her hand to his lips, and licked the minor cuts closed. They watched as the water settled back to gentle waves, their heartbeats matched. Their passions sated for the moment they embraced and rested.

Leaving Paradise

Teera checked then stretched and scraped the hides, worked them to make them soft for the baby's blanket.

The wood was low, Brenat grabbed an axe and in minutes the rhythmic whack and crack of wood being split was heard. His mind wandered to the beauty of the miracle, then worry hit. "*What if there is a problem? I know nothing about babies. What if the baby gets sick or hurt and cannot wait for the moon?*" His mind raced, sought solutions and found more worries. His mind pushed in urgent need to save his mate and child. His guarded thoughts slipped and Teera heard "*On the next moon I have to get out and talk to my parents about the magic of the valley, so I can bring Teera out in case of problems.*"

Teera reached with her mind, "*It is okay. We will be fine, just us. Supper is almost ready, get cleaned up. By the way, Love, I think that is enough wood.*" She laughed.

Startled, he spun on instinct; the axe at the ready for no one had ever snuck up on him before. He calmed as he realized it was Teera. He looked around, and he realized he would carry wood for the next two days.

Brenat stacked wood, cleaned up and between bites said, "*Teera, my heart, with all the dangers that could happen to you and the baby. You should be at the castle where others could help you. The full moon is less than a week away. I will go get our families to help so you can have the baby in the castle, I'll go alone because the Elites will be outside waiting to for you to leave here."*

"Brenat I cannot, for I have to be in the valley before sunrise or I will die." Teera reminded him.

"OK, then I must get my parents first, for if there is a way to get around that part of the spell they would find it." Brenat placed his plate in the wash water.

"Brenat, you cannot leave either the sun would kill you outside the valley just as it would me." Tears slipped silently from Teera's eyes.

"No it won't, Teera, for when I used your escape tunnel I went in and out when the sun was up. Would it not be better to be able to come and go from the valley as needed to ensure our child's well-being? Teera, I will survive and get my parents, they will find a way to circumvent the mystical barrier. Then Sid, Elsie and I will go see your parents to help enlist their help to secure your path from the Elites and get you safely within the castle walls, away from the Elites' deadly intentions and protect you from others that wish you or our child harm. The moon is a little over a week away. Let's go sit on the veranda and watch the stars. You can tell me of your life and family at the castle along with what you know of Asslam. In order to stop the assassinations and ensure your safety, I will kill Asslam and all others that wish to do you harm," Brenat kissed Teera's tears away.

Later, as they snuggled together on a lounger, she told him of how she grew up and snuck out of the castle through the secret passage none knew of but the royal family. She told him about how she was taught to avoid the pit falls and spear traps in the secret passage.

A plan formed in Brenat's mind and he asked *"Teera, when I get into your father's office, what could I say to him that only you and he would know?"*

Teera thought and then replied, *"My father gave me my first drink of his special aged whiskey. It was from the secret bottle he keeps hidden in his bottom desk drawer under a false bottom that he does not share, even with other royal guests. It was the day before my marriage and he told me not to tell Momma. My mother does not like father to drink."*

Brenat told Teera the plan. *"We shall wait at the entrance until just before moon set. Once the barrier locks you away, I will leave. I will go to my parents and we will make our way to the castle. I will build a signal fire when I arrive at the castle and we will see each other at the following moon rise."*

They spent their remaining days until they must be separated hunting, watching sunrises and sunsets, and making love as much as possible before they had to say goodbye for a time.

His weapons and armor were cleaned and his silver katana sheathed. His bow was slung and the quiver was filled with silver tipped, holy oak arrows. He was geared for battle if stealth failed. They stood just inside the mystic barrier and held each other, while they watched the shadowy figures that laid in wait just outside the entrance. Moments before sunrise, with a final kiss, Brenat stepped out, still hidden by the foliage. He turned to watch Teera as the sunlight hit the entrance and the stone locked her away until the next cycle.

Teera watched as the wall resealed, and locked her back in her prison. Their bond broken, she could not hear him, she was alone once again. With tears in her eyes, she headed to the lookout where she hoped to see him below.

❂ ❂ ❂ ❂ ❂ ❂ ❂ ❂ ❂ ❂ ❂

Brenat observed the shadows, an Elite walked within a hands breadth of where Brenat was hidden, he stopped to look around before he moved on. Brenat, with his hand on his dagger, ready to attack if the Elite had turned to look at him. Brenat relaxed as he realized he was still just inside of the mystical protection. Still as a rock and silently as a shadow, he watched until the sun hit its peak and the Elites moved on to report another failure.

Brenat followed the Elites for three days and nights back to their camp. They disappeared behind their walls before he continued to travel for another two days and nights. He never stopped to rest until he got to his parent's store.

Planning Teera's Escape

Watchful and cautious he snuck into his parents shop through the back door. Noticed a ham on the counter, he stuffed his mouth full and grabbed another chunk to carry with him.

He continued to the front of the apothecary shop where his mother and father worked. With stealth he watched through the bottles and jars as his parents worked. His thoughts drifted back to when he was a child. *He use to watch his parents from that very spot, concealed by the many jars filled with liquid and creature parts too numerous to name.*

After their last customer left for the night, Sid secured the shop and closed the curtains. Elsie put away the cash box and called out, *"Brenat, it's safe to come out now."* Pulling him from his reminisce, the boy once again became the man. He was not surprised that they knew he was there, they had always been the only people he had never been able to sneak up on. Brenat started to speak but Elsie shushed him *"Go help your father load the wagon."*

They loaded mystical books, potions, and strange smelling packs. *"We knew you were coming and in need. The wagon is ready; we will talk after you get some rest."*

Brenat hid in the back of the wagon and told them to head south on the Obsidian Mountain Road to Castle Black. Brenat fell asleep, the wrapped warm ham clutched to his chest.

Sid looked at Elsie with a smile, *"You think I could get some of the ham now or do you think he would bite me if I reach for it?"*

Elsie laughed softly, *"Not if you're quick he won't. I'd like some too, we have a long trip ahead of us."*

Sid and Elsie snacked, as well as chatted through the night about the wonderful scenery and how they had not been that way in years. Brenat stirred the next day with the setting sun. Grabbed a mouthful of cold ham that was beside him, he scanned for subtle signs of shadowy danger.

Sid answered, *"We are clear for the moment. We were followed for a while, but they moved on."* As darkness fell Elsie's and Sid's eyes seemed to glow with intensity, as they waited for Brenat to speak.

Brenat started, *"I found my mate on the Blood Moon before leaving on that three-month assignment. I was also hired to kill the princess and bring back the dead unborn fetus as proof to Asslam. I had to kill the other Elites when I realized who it was I was sent to kill. Then Teera saved me by giving me her blood when I was mortally wounded and she carried me into her valley, which is her prison."*

He saw the question in Elsie's eyes, Brenat said, *"Yes, the child is mine. Yes, Teera bears my bonding mark and I bear hers."* Showed them his bonding mark, he continued, *"I left the valley to get you to help me find the secret to help Teera and the baby escape the valley. I need to tell King James and Queen Rizalle to set up a signal fire. There's a secret passage into the King's office I will use to get in. Teera told me a secret that only she and her father knew involving the aged whiskey that the king hides from the queen. Also, I have to kill Asslam to remove the threat of assassination from my family. I am safe from the Elites as long as they believe me dead."*

Brenat, Sid, and Elsie took turns sleeping, searching through the books, looking for obscure mentions of the valley's magic, and driving the cart. They stopped only long enough to feed and water the horses.

As the castle came into view, many days later, Brenat slid from the back of the wagon, like a clouds shadow he passed through the night, and headed for the secret passage. Brenat was inside long before Sid and Elsie reached the castle gates. The wagon was given a search, complete with spears that poked at the piles of blankets and clothing, before being let through the gates.

Before long, Brenat was through the secret passage, moved past the silver dart traps, the holly oak spears and the pit traps that would kill lycan, vampires and mortals alike. He waited in the secret passage behind the book case and listened to the meeting about Asslam's upcoming visit. Brenat heard the leather chair creak as King James sat back and relaxed. Before long he heard the king began to snore and Brenat smiled.

Brenat moved from the passage with the speed of a cobra strike. The silver dagger burned as it touched the king's throat, waking king James. Brenat whispered in James's ear, *"I'm Brenat, an Elite. I'm here to give you a message from your daughter."* He sheaths the blade and moved to sit down in front of the king waited while the king regained his composure.

Brenat pointed to the book case, *"I came through the secret passage and I'd like a glass of your special aged whiskey that you and Teera shared the day before she married to Asslam. Do you need me to tell you where it is or do you already believe me?"*

James went to the liquor cabinet and reached to the back to pull out a bottle of aged whiskey and two glasses. Brenat smiled, *"No sir, the bottle in your bottom right hand drawer of your desk under the false panel."*

James looked at him, then put the other bottle back in the cabinet. He sat at his desk reached in and pulled out the special bottle. James was back to his regal self as he felt the burn mark fade on his throat.

He looked Brenat over as he poured them both a drink, *"Well, Brenat, you sure know how to make an impression, what is the message?"*

"Teera is waiting for a signal fire from your northwest archery tower so she will know I am here," Brenat stated.

Queen Rizalle came in to tell her husband supper was ready in their private room noticed the stranger, that she stared at with distrust.

James looked at Rizalle, *"He is here with an important message from Teera and has proven himself adept at by passing our security."*

Rizalle shut the door and sat beside James who nodded to Brenat to continue with his tale.

Brenat took a deep breath, *" I'm the father of Teera's child. Asslam plans to kill your daughter and our child when she steps out of the valley. The Elites have already tried three times. I know this because I was the first one hired by Asslam. For the baby's sake, and hers, we need to get them here to the castle. The only way to stop the Elites is to kill the contractor, Asslam. I plan to kill Asslam, personally, to save her and our child before the red cloaks realize I am still alive."*

Taking another deep breath, he continued, *"You could call your guards and kill me now, but the Elites would get your daughter, or you could help me save your daughter and kill Asslam. My parents will help find a way for her to leave that valley prison for more than a moon rise. Just so you know I speak the truth."* Brenat bared his chest and showed Teera's bonding mark, then took a sip of the whiskey while he awaited their decision.

James looked at his wife. Brenat watched as Rizalle's eyes turned from glowing amber to flickering flames as she took in the information.

Growling, Rizalle went to the door and told a guard to summon the betas for a war meeting. Turning to Brenat, Rizalle coldly said, *"When this is over, young man, you have more explaining to do."*

Brenat smiled and said, *"May I interrupt your wrath for a moment? Before you summon all into a meeting, you should know that you may have spies in your midst. The Elites are good at what they do and placing spies is one of the things they use to do their job."*

Teera's parents gasped and glared at Brenat in disbelief, *"You have a lot to answer for,"* they both growled, *"First can you identify the spies before we go into the counsel room? They'll enjoy our dungeon for the remainder of their short lives."*

Brenat replied, *"Yes I can, each Elite bares six horizontal marking scars running on each side of their backs to let others know they are Elites. Bring in your most trusted people one at a time, check their backs, if they refuse kill them out right. Do that until you get four you could trust. Once you do that, drag me to your throne room with my back bared and in cuffs, it would be obvious you have caught one of the Elites and get that signal fire lit for Teera. The spies would see me being dragged into the room, the report would go out and they will flee or die. Bring the scouts in first to assist in checking the warriors. Send four man teams to do room by room searches until the castle is cleared and all of castle staff had been checked. Record the names of anyone missing."*

To James and Rizalle's shock, Brenat shifted his left hand into claws and then watched as he reached across his face, ran his claws deep into his flesh from forehead to chin, scratching the bone. With blood blinding his right eye Brenat tore off his armor and unbuckled his weapons. He then ran his claws from his shoulder across his chest and down to his waist. His silver dagger followed each claw marks to slow the healing from minutes to hours. Finally, with silver spiked cuffs, he shackled his hands and legs. Blood dripped from the wounds as well as his wrists and ankles. He fell over unconscious, his healing halted because of the silver's poison.

Rizalle brought in her first guard who noticed the bloody body lying on the floor. James aimed the crossbow at the guard's heart, then ordered him to turn around and remove his shirt so they could see his back. Soon, each of Rizalle's and James's personal guards were cleared individually.

One of the guards was ordered to start the signal fire, then to go to the throne room. James and Rizalle, along with their seven remaining guards who dragged Brenat between them to the throne room. Brenat was tossed at the foot of the thrones for all who entered to see. With swords at the ready and crossbows cocked, the scouts got checked next.

The warriors then filed in one by one, every time four were cleared, they were sent out to search the castle, long into the night, until the last of the castle staff were cleared.

Meanwhile, the guests Sid and Elsie, were called into the throne room, where they saw their son, stripped, bleeding, shackled, and laying on the floor. Their faces briefly betrayed their knowledge of him. They were asked to show their naked backs, which they both quickly did. Once cleared, Sid and Elsie were taken to James' office and asked why they had came to the castle.

Sid said, *"We are here to aid the princess and the child."*

James and Rizalle stared at Sid in shock. Rizalle ordered breakfast and Brenat brought to their office. Soon breakfast arrived, followed by Kenny and the personal guards who dropped Brenat unceremoniously to the floor. Rizalle ordered the guards back to their posts and had Kenny remove Brenat's shackles. With the shackles gone, the healing was allowed to begin.

After Brenat regained consciousness, he reached for some of the breakfast on the table without asking, again surprising the royal couple and parents. Kenny growled a low warning, Brenat smiled at the growl and introduced his parents to James and Rizalle. Elsie sighed in relief then scolded, *"Brenat, don't forget your manners. What has gotten into you?"*

Brenat looked up from the food, *"But Mom, I'm hungry and we're all family now."* He then apologized to his parents for the necessity of the ruse. Kenny looks from the strangers to James in stunned silence at Brenat's words.

Sid, a bear of a man, said with a chuckle, *"If you were not so big Brenat, I would put you over my knee for a whipping you would not soon forget."*

Elsie started nursing Brenat's wounds with none to gentle care. She applied a healing poultice saying, *"This will sting, a lot."*

Brenat hollered, *"OW MOM, I said I was sorry, really I'm sorry for scaring you, but we had to make it look real. MOM, OW! I said I'm sorry."*

James and Rizalle started laughing at their new son-in-law whom they had seen take so much pain, suddenly hollering and struggling to escape his small, sleek mother as she treated his wounds. Kenny fought to hide his laugh but failed and soon joined James and Rizalle.

Brenat, once treated, asked the question on his mind, *"If a problem arises during child birth I cannot help her. I can bring her to the castle on the next moon, while you sweep the path clear of Elites, but how do we keep her safe when the moon sets?"*

Elsie interjected, *"That would not be a problem, for your bonding and blood sharing took care of that. Teera's blood allows you into the valley and yours lets you live outside the valley. Your blood allows Teera the same ability as you. you both now share the same abilities, son. Magic works in mysterious ways, but let me check my books to see if a counter spell is needed. If it should be needed I will start on that as well."*

With wood added to the signal fire every hour, the fire was kept burning day and night. Some cedar greenery was added to scent the smoke.

The castle was alive with everyone being searched from the rampart to dungeon, as well as everywhere and everyone in between. James waited for the reports on any Elites that had been found and killed, as well as any reports on those people who were missing. With the sun high in the sky and the castle was still in full search James, Brenat and Kenny sipped on whiskey coffee until the last report was delivered. The report showed one cook, a warrior beheaded, a stable hand, and two gate guards unaccounted for.

James wrote a letter to Asslam with barely restrained rage, putting a plan into motion. The fastest scout, Walt, was sent on the fastest of horses. That were equipped with mythical shoes that turned miles to minutes, and also allowed the horse to ran for days without need of food or rest. The message had James' seal and was to be delivered to Asslam personally. Walt was to return with Asslam's reply. James hoped the leach Asslam took the bait.

Walt arrived at Asslam's castle before the week was out. Even with the mythical shoes the horse seemed a little winded. With the sealed letter in hand he was escorted in to see Asslam. Asslam broke the seal and read the message:

"Asslam, King of the Vampires. My people have captured an Elite, my best medical personnel, even at this moment, are just managing to keep him alive. My people got a little overzealous when they caught him trying to kill their princess (your queen). I request the use of your high inquisitor, renowned for getting answers others could not, to gather information about who is trying to re-ignite our war by killing our allies and my daughter as well as your unborn son."

Asslam took a moment to think, *"If I took the child, its power would be mine and I would be able to control the world as the legend foretold. With the child, Teera would no longer be needed and she could mysteriously die in childbirth."* His mirth was alight in his eyes, for his original plan had worked out even better than just killing them both outright. He called his witches to activate a spell that would allow the valley's daylight death to be canceled. Then called upon his scribe to bring him his seal as he quickly wrote his reply.

"King James, King of the Lycans, your request is prudent, I shall come immediately with my inquisitor and troops to escort my queen and son home. The daylight death spell is being countered as I write this letter. Together, our two kingdoms would bring about a new millennium of prosperity. Your grandson, my son, would ensure our most prosperous peace."

With the reply sealed, it was handed back to Walt, who was sent immediately to return to Castle Black.

Asslam conspired with his chief interrogator. The chief interrogator said, *"A good showing of a concerned husband was needed until the bitch gave birth. With some proper interrogation of the red cloak another wedge between the dogs and their allies would be set."* Asslam expanded his entourage for this trip so he could properly protect his queen and son for their return to his castle.

While Keres had her witches working upon the cancellation spell, she communed with her real master. The smell of sulfur permeated Keres's alter as her master appeared.

Lucifer looked down at Keres, *"I have new instructions for you, Witch, you will soon be helping a new king of this castle, one just as ambitious, but more conductive to my plans. You will need to aid in Asslam's demise upon the upcoming trip to open the way for his successor and my newest servant. You will both be instrumental in the destruction of my enemies."*

Birth and Death

When Teera lost contact with Brenat when the portal closed, to keep the sadness at bay she carried up some supplies and extra wood to the look out. Where she sang and talked to the baby and made him some cloths while she watched for the signal fire.

As the days turned into weeks and the absence grew ever longer, the wood supply ran low and Teera decided to head back down from the lookout in the morning. With one last tearful look for a signal fire, her heart leapt at the sudden appearance of a bright beckoning light coming from the archer tower. She now knew Brenat was there and would soon return, with a touch of panic she thought *"If mother didn't kill him first."* She giggled as the baby playfully punches her bladder and Teera stopped contemplating the fire, to go pass water. That night the sight of the fire made her sleep, full of pleasant dreams.

The following morning, she saw the castle come alive, the people were like a swarm of ants protecting their home. The unified howl reached her ears, bringing tears to her eyes as even from the distance the howl was calling her home. She felt the challenge to any that would do harm. Even the baby kicked as if answering the call from home.

Smiling, she headed back down to the cave. Following the long walk, she went to rest in the pools. The baby had grown to the point that it was difficult to do much.

She sat and thought about the activity at the castle, and wondered what had happened to cause all that was going on. The baby moved more often and seemed unable to settle after the excitement of the howl. She wondered who would arrive first, Brenat or the baby.

Not knowing if Brenat would return with help, Teera prepared for the baby and birth. She guessed at what would be needed as she had never been to a birthing nor been around babies.

Days later, while cleaning, Teera felt the baby's pressure to join the outside world, she barely made it to the bed and await his arrival through the bouts of pain. Teera cried out as the pains had became worse, at times so bad that she felt as if she was being torn apart. Suddenly she felt pressure then a gush of fluid as her water broke, which was followed by a sharp stabbing pain. In her pain, she felt a problem and tried to reach Brenat, wishing he was there. As hours turned into days of painful labor, with a final scream, Teera brought the baby into the world. He howled his arrival, while Teera laid weak and bleeding from the difficult birth.

She pulled the baby close, wrapping them both in the clean top bedding, as she used the last of her strength and used the bottom bedding and tried to stop the bleeding that poured from her. They laid there, the baby fed from his weakened mother. Teera was unable to shift to heal herself as her body cleaned itself of the last of the pregnancy. She pushed the soiled bedding away from them and again tried to stop the bleeding with last of the clean bedding. She just hoped Brenat would arrive in time to save them both or at least their son was her last conscious thought before she passed out.

❁ ❁ ❁ ❁ ❁ ❁ ❁ ❁ ❁ ❁

James called his three most trusted betas, and half-brothers, Silfer, Kenny, and Dukut. Silfer and Dukut were his half-brothers by his mother's second marriage after his father's death in battle. None knew that Kenny was in fact not just his most trusted royal guard but was in fact James's brother by his father and his father's mistress. Only Rizalle knew how close Kenny and James were and that they were brothers. After Silfer and Dukut arrived James introduced them to Brenat and told them of Asslam's plans to kill Teera and the child. The death of Asslam was soon agreed to being the only way to secure Teera's safety, James gave each an assigned task.

Kenny was ordered to take a quarter of the troops and scourer the forest for enemy, then he was to guard a hundred yards on either side of the path to bring Teera home. Silfer and Dukut were each ordered to take troops to guard the two southern roads and to ambush Asslam. James told them that whoever brought back Asslam's head would become regent of Asslam's castle. As Dukut and Silfer left, they vowed to each other that whoever won the honor, the other would became the winner's second in command.

Brenat went with Kenny to escort Teera from the valley as he was the only one able to get in. James, Rizalle, Elsie, and Sid sat drinking James's best aged whiskey when not pacing in a mixture of worry and impatience. Waiting was something none of them had ever enjoyed and the four quickly became friends.

❊ ❊ ❊ ❊ ❊ ❊ ❊ ❊ ❊ ❊

Silfer left with a sly smile after he called upon some witches that owed him favors. The witches were ordered to assure that Asslam took Silfer's road, they mystically secured the area to deaden Asslam's magic where Silfer had set up his ambush.

Dukut, confident in his power, set off on his route while his troops all sang boisterously, as always, to the praise of his conquests. The troops set the drum beat with swords upon shields in time with the pounding of horses' hoofs. The troops raised their voices in a war cry *"DUUKUUT"* then the song continued:

"Dukut is known for his ferocity in war and the enemy tremble at his visage. DUUKUUT

Dukut's helm is a demon skull that he killed and scraped the brain from. DUUKUUT

Dukut's giant war axe he made from the hip bone of a silver dragon he slayed. DUUKUUT

Dukut's horse is a nightmare that he lassoed one night as a pup and pulled into the land of the waking. DUUKUUT

Dukut could punch through a warrior, armor and all to get to his enemy on the other side. DUUKUUT

The glory he shares with all who ride by his side. DUUKUUT"

The song continued as they rode out of ear shot.

Kenny and his troops howled their rage filled challenges as they fanned out through the forest. One hundred yards on either side of the path, all creatures, large, small, and ghostly fled the onslaught of the lycan army whose single purpose was to bring the Princess home safe no matter the cost.

The path was soon cleared, the troops stood guard, once more they let loose a roar that reverberated through the trees and off of the mountains, challenged any to break their barricade of tooth, claw, and sword. Vigilant, the troops stood and waited for moon rise for the princess's return.

News reached Asslam that one of the roads to Castle Black was washed out by a flash flood. Asslam set off with his entourage. Keres stayed back at the castle to ensure the releasing of the spell that would free Teera from her prison. Asslam headed happily north, he smirked to himself and said, *"James is handing over his daughter to her executioner like the beguiled ignorant dog he is. I suppose I should toss him a bone and say good doggy."* Asslam laughed at his own joke.

With his magic, Asslam surrounded his whole entourage in a mystic bubble, though everyone was only moving briskly, the miles passed by faster than flying on the back of a dragon. On cue, his bubble dissipated. The trees that were blurred by speed only moments before, could be seen as individuals as the entourage slowed as if moving through mud.

Silfer sat ready to spring his trap. Under the light of the full moon Asslam's magic was sapped as he came into view. Silfer's troops charged, the archers let fly their arrows, and the sky brightened as the blazing holy oak arrows peppered the enemy troops.

With many vampires going down under the first volley, they took cover and drew their swords. After the second volley was let loose, several horses lay dead and many vampires had gone up in flames, the melee grew worse. Silfer's charge fell upon the surviving vampires who tried to muster a defense of two wounded vampires to four lycans. Over whelmed, outnumbered, and wounded, the vampires fell in minutes under sword, tooth, and claws. Any vampire that turned to flee were cut down in their tracks by the archers, then torn apart and lit on fire.

Asslam, with a wave of his hand and a spell on his lips, easily deflected the first volley of arrows around him. His personal guard, Kaplar, drew his sword and covered his master's body with his own, took another volley of flaming arrows onto himself until the fire melted the flesh from his face and his heart was pierced by one lone arrow out of the score imbedded and burning in his body. Asslam threw the burning corpse high into the air where it finally burst into a ball of fire. Kaplar's last deed was taking out another dozen arrows that were on their way to his master. Asslam, although spouting holy oak arrows like a flaming porcupine from yet another volley, drew his katana, slicing through spears, bone, and armor, killing a dozen lycans. The clash of metal on metal rang out along with the crushing of bone from severed limbs.

Silfer came to face Asslam with his battle axe. In a flurry of blows, the ringing of metal upon metal could be heard and sparks flew as the two skilled warriors battled. Silfer fell back under Asslam's powerful assault.

Asslam's strength suddenly left him and he shivered as an unseen presence howled its arrival into the world and in that moment, Silfer's axe separated Asslam's head from his shoulders. It rolled to a stop with dead eyes staring at a rare single black rose that seemed to have appeared, as if by magic, among the bloody and burning corpses.

Silfer picked up Asslam's head, stuffed it in a bag, ignored and stepped on the flower. His troops headed back to the castle with his prize in his hand. With a sly smile, Silfer knew that Dukut would be doing his bidding from that day forth.

As the moon rose, the portal to the valley opened and Brenat rushed to find Teera. He heard a tiny cry directing him to Teera and his newborn son. Seeing her pale and dying, he fed Teera some of his blood to give her strength until they get to the castle then fed his son from the same gash. He wrapped them both in a deer hide blanket and carried them to the dilapidated cart before he pulled them through the barrier.

Teera looked up, smiled weakly at her beloved mate. *"Brenat had saved them,"* she thought just as she fell asleep. The soldier's close ranks around the cart to protect the precious cargo. Kenny sent his fastest scout to the castle with a message to James that said *"Baby born. Teera Hurt. Have doctors ready."*

When the cart arrived through the castle gates Elsie, Sid, James, and Rizalle were there. They checked on their daughter and grandson before the cart even stopped moving. A wave of noise was taken up by all, as the troops entered the castle courtyard.

The cart is moved to Teera's secured garden until she could be moved to her room. Brenat picked up the baby, held his son as Elsie examined first Teera and then the baby. He stares in wonder at the miracle that lay in his arms while running his fingers along Teera's cheek steadily, he talked to her and begged her not to die.

Elise smiled at her new daughter-in-law and grandson, *"Teera will be okay but she will need a lot of rest and must remain in bed to heal fully. Luckily she was rescued in time. As for the baby, he is amazingly healthy."* Teera nuzzled Brenat as he held her in his arms, watched as their son nursed with ravenous hunger as she drifted asleep to fully heal.

Rules Change

Everyone rushed to see what the ruckus in the courtyard is just in time to see Silfer arrived, with his gory prize. Dukut accepted his role of being Silfer's second. James and Rizalle publicly announced Silfer's regency of Asslam's former lands.

Before the day was out Silfer, Dukut, and Kenny, along with Kenny's aide Arris, headed out with half the warriors as well as the junior warriors, to Asslam's former castle to cull any resistance. The speed of the takeover turned years of battles into months, and stopped any resistance before Asslam's nobles realized there was a new lord in control.

Upon his arrival at the castle, Silfer grabbed Keres, squeezed her breast through her gown and whispered in her ear, *"Your spells to counter Asslam's magic worked perfectly."* Silfer nipped her neck and Keres moaned in pleasure, she arched her neck to give him better access while they watch her witches' coven continue to move their supplies into the extensive library. The scribes stood against the opposite wall, watched under guard as the witches took over their library.

A guard turned to Silfer, *"Sir, what do you want us to do with the scribes that we have rounded up?"*

Silfer replied, *"Take them to the dungeon. They can help build my new arena. They can earn their freedom like all the other prisoners by fighting for their freedom once it's built."*

Kenny stopped the guards as they were headed to the quickly crowding dungeon cells, " *What are you doing with the scribes?"*

The guard replied, *"Silfer has ordered them to be taken to the dungeon to await their turn in the arena after it's built."*

Kenny hid his anger and nodded before he replied, *"Make sure they are properly fed immediately upon imprisonment and they do not need to be tortured or questioned by the inquisitor. Is that understood?"*

The guards saluted, *"Yes Sir,"* as they led the newest prisoners away. Kenny's eyes briefly shifted to red in his anger before he regained control of his emotions and they returned to their normal blue.

With a ready supply of humans, vampires, and lycans from his cramped dungeons, Silfer's arena was built in a several months. Kenny oversaw the prisoners, guards, and construction. Everybody who worked well were fed well and the use of whips were minimized so the prisoners worked better.

When Asslam, the king of vampires, died, the vampires that were left found themselves with three choices, either ally themselves with Silfer, end up as arena fodder or flee to red cloak controlled areas.

Kenny was also placed in charge of the city policing and the castle guards. His strict, honorable, fair treatment of all earned him respect among warriors, guards, and populace alike. When Kenny found the occasional child locked in the arena pens, he had them released into his care where he placed them in the orphanage he had started to save them from the arena.

There was more than one guard that was stripped of their duties to be placed in the arena pens when caught taking bribes or unwanted liberties with the female populace and prisoners.

When families visited the prisoners, they were never accosted by the guards or forced to pay or service their way to have visiting privileges. Kenny became respected by the prisoners as well.

Dukut was sent out to hunt vampires, bandits, and other criminals, regardless of race, from the surrounding countryside and towns to have enough participants put on a one-day show once a month. Dukut culled villages and enemy camps, soon developed a reputation as a fierce war general. He always brought back some survivors. When vampires became hard to find, humans and others took their place.

It was said that if Dukut was coming for you, it was best to just line up to be taken prisoner than to be staked and roasted like a pig while he hunted for your family and friends. Many towns, upon hearing that Dukut was in their area, started lining up all of their people. Dukut handpicked through them until he found the criminals that were to work off their crimes in the arena.

Silfer, with the aid of Keres and Dukut, rapidly gained control of arena city and the surrounding area. He also became more feared then Asslam ever was. There had been a few nobles and their entourage that had been ambushed by bandits upon leaving the city after insulting Silfer.

Silfer pretended to discover them while he checked the slave pens, they were welcome to buy their freedom. The witch Keres was in charge of finalization of the deals. Soon they signed into a bloody contract that had many wishing they had took their chances in the arena instead.

When Silfer found a worthy worker, he pulled him from the work crew and offered the worker an opportunity to earn his freedom, all he had to do was survive a year in the arena. Everyone accepted the new placement graciously or they were publicly whipped until they accepted and was sent to training.

James got regular reports that the city is now under control. Silfer and Dukut were expanding the territory while culling any resistance in the country side from vampires and their allies. The arena was in various stages of construction.

James and his family were invited to opening day of the arena games, but with the ceremonies approaching fast at Castle Black, they decline the invitation. James congratulated Silfer on his running of his new area and of all the respect and honor he had earned from the populace.

The opening day event was scheduled, the spectacle was to be extravagant. Many of the populace were encouraged to attend to watch friends, neighbors, and family participate in the arena games under threat of joining them. Many aristocrats and nobles from all over were invited to come bet and watch the three-day event, that was to be filled with brutal carnage.

Silfer, with a growl, set aside the message in anger as his plans to take the royal family at the opening of the arena were no longer an option.

With the arrival of the letter from King James about the upcoming naming and public wedding ceremony, Silfer wondered what would happen to his castle and his newly acquired power. He had called Keres to him to see what would become of him after the ceremony.

Keres told him of the legend and that if he married the princess and got an heir from her, he could rule all of James's realm and then the world. First he had to stop the wedding and kill Teera's son or gain control over him. Power hungry, Silfer formed a plan that would allow him to succeed where Asslam had failed. With Keres's help and a promise to Dukut that he would rule Castle Black. The three soon planned to celebrate at the ceremony and enhance their power.

Silfer, Keres, Dukut and a selected group of nobles loyal to Silfer arranged to attend the wedding ceremony.

Many scribes, grown strong from building their muscles while forced to build the arena, were later forced into hand to hand combat to fight and kill each other unless a family member paid for a single day's reprieve from the arena. Only the gladiators that fought well and received a sponsor were spared having multiple battles in a day, as they earned special treatment that their sponsors paid for.

Vampires battled to the death at night under the glow of torchlight. The humans fought in the afternoon while various other races battled in the morning. The winners from the first and second day had to fight each other on the third day. The overcrowded dungeon soon thinned out, which resulted in a great weekend of prosperity for Silfer.

Back at the Castle

Teera awoke to hear a heated discussion between all four of the grandparents about their grandson's naming ceremony and their children's upcoming wedding ceremonies both the private one and the more formal one that everyone would be invited to attend.

She glanced around for her son and Brenat, *"Brenat"* she called out only to be interrupted as a large blue-black raven suddenly flew to the baby's crib and dropped a rabbit into it. All six of the adults watched in stunned silence as the baby started to gnaw on the rabbit's ear, as the bird flew back out through the open veranda doors and disappeared into the garden. Brenat looked at Teera with a shocked smile. *"I think he's hungry,"* Brenat said as he picked him up and carried him to Teera so he could nurse.

Looking up at the grandparents as they continued to argue over what the baby was to be named, Teera announced, *"His name is Joel, we chose his name when we were in the valley."*

Their parent's continued to prepare for Teera's and Brenat's official formal wedding along with Joel's formal coronation and naming ceremony as the months went by. A small private affair had been seld once Teera had recovered from Joel's birth.

Everyone watched as Joel appeared to grow very rapidly

over the next few months; even faster than other lycan children. His appetite and special gifts were also more astounding and larger than expected in one so young. Both his parents and grandparents were soon not the only ones that watched as well as wondered just how powerful the young prince would become.

Meanwhile, Joel was unaware of the interest he was causing as he was finding many great adventures in the castle. Shortly after learning to crawl, he repeatedly slipped away from his nanny, causing mass searches throughout the castle and grounds, only to be found hours later at the top of the archer towers sharing a rabbit with a horned owl. Another time he was found raiding cookies in the kitchen with a raccoon. Most often he was found curled up and asleep in James' large, comfortable office chair. It had caused more than one frantic nanny to comment about how he could disappear faster than the best scout.

Still, between the regular search parties for Joel and all the ceremony preparations, Teera, Brenat and their adventurous son found time to spend together as a family.

One day the castle was roused to a ruckus of pots dropping and the kitchen staff screaming in fear as they came running out of the kitchen. When asked by the guards what was wrong, the kitchen staff stated that there were two hell hounds loose in the kitchen, just as the hell hound keeper announced the pair of alpha hell hounds were missing from their kennel in the dungeon. The warriors and the hell hound keeper, all fully armored, went to the kitchen to investigate, but no sign of the hounds could be found.

The search and ruckus brought an all-out panic when the searchers were alerted that Joel also could not be found by his nanny. Fearing the worst, the castle went on full alert, searching for the two hell hounds and Joel. All of the children and noncombatants were ordered to stay locked in their rooms until the hell hounds were found and recaptured.

James headed to his office, checking to see if Joel was hopefully asleep in his chair. Opening the door, he stopped and exclaims, *"Holy Crap!"* There was Joel sharing a hunch of meat with the two alpha hell hounds who were acting like well-trained pups playing and eating with Joel.

The guards reacted to James's astonishment, drew their weapons and moved to protect James. The two huge hell hounds, when they saw the armed intruders, moved to protect and guard Joel with hackles raised, teeth bared, flames licking at their lips, and a growl that would scare the dead back to their graves. As they prepared to attack Joel rested his hands upon the hounds, causing them to calm and sit at his silent command. Joel walked over and gave his GAPA James a hug and announced with pride, *"See my new puppies. Their names are Howy and Kwap, momma is gonna wuv 'em. Thank you GAPA for naming them."*

The guards stared wide-eyed, struggled unsuccessfully to restrain their laughter.

James, with the wits of a true leader, ordered the guards to see that an area in Teera's garden was secured, so Joel and his two pets could have a place to play where the populace would not accidentally come across them.

James also ordered better security in the dungeons to ensure that Joel did not acquire any new and even more dangerous pets, the guards quickly left to follow his orders.

Brenat and Sid entered only to both stop short at the sight in James's office. Joel launched himself at his daddy excitedly, *"Daddy wook at my new pets, Gapa James named them Howy and Kwap!"* Sid started laughing.

Brenat looked at James and shook his head, *"I would not want to be you right now."*

James muttered, *"Me neither, Rizalle is going to kill me."*

He looked to the other two men asking, *"How are we going to get out of this without our wives killing us, or worse?"*

Sid and Brenat both replied, *"What do you mean we? You're in this one on your own."*

James responded, *"Want to bet?"*

Joel, unaware of the trouble he had started for his father and grandfathers, returned to playing with his two massive pets, Howy and Kwap.

Within minutes, the alarm was canceled and Teera felt the castle go from high alert to high mirth. The mirth was soon passing through the castle faster than the alarm had, she joined her mother and Elsie as they headed towards James's office.

Rizalle, Elsie, and Teera arrived in James's office after passing more than one laughing guard. Opening the door, they observed the three men drinking while watching Joel play with Howy and Kwap. Noticing the ladies, Sid and Brenat looked at James, then got up to leave. Brenat told Joel, *"Come to the garden and bring your new pets with you."* Teera and Elsie eyes flare between mirth and astonished anger, as they watched them leave before following. Through their bonds, the mental interrogations started.

Rizalle shut the door to offer her and James some privacy before long a loud voice came through the thick door, *"YOU NAMED THEM WHAT?"*

With Joel developing faster than a normal child Teera, Elsie, and Rizalle, spent time teaching Joel reading, writing, and arithmetic between preparing for the joint ceremonies and castle duties.

Sid, James, and Brenat took turns teaching Joel swords, hunting, tracking, and archery while trying to stop Holy and

Krap from fetching the arrows out of midair, between their castle duties and after a game of search for Joel. Each night Teera and Brenat relaxed into each other's arms, loving and renewing their bond while Joel and his pets slept.

Brenat woke early one morning and sat drinking his coffee in the garden while he watched as Joel played with Holy and Kwap. He chuckled at their names before he mentally told Teera, *"Thank you for this gift you've given me, I love you and our son so much."*

Life at the castle soon returned to almost normal as everyone became accustomed to Joel chasing the two hell hounds through the throne room and around the castle. While the strangest sight that made everyone stare, was the day, Holy and Kwap came through the castle carrying a leg bone between them, each with an end in their mouths as Joel hung from the middle of it by his teeth.

In a few short months, Joel's head could be seen just above the hell hounds back while he walked with his pets. Most of the castle inhabitants gave Joel and his pets a wide berth due to how protective of Joel the two hell hounds were.

Ultimate Betrayal

Invitations were sent out, to the lords and ladies far and wide.

Upon reading his invitation, Silfer put his plan into play, nourished by Keres's ambition. Dukut was ordered to do his part. Kenny who was treated as nothing more than a lead guard, was ordered to stay at Silfer's castle. Kenny had no trouble with that as both he and Arris had attended the private ceremony earlier while on leave, at which point they had been made god uncles to Teera and Brenat's son, Joel.

The walkway was lined with gardenias, their subtle scent wafting in the air, ceremonial armor and weapons shined as the honor guards guided the guests to their seats. Brenat, in a special dress tunic that felt too restricting, watched Joel to make sure he did not get his special dress clothes dirty as he straightened Holy's and Kwap's collars then combed their fur again. Brenat still was amazed at how well the two large hell hounds behaved for Joel, yet they barely tolerated anyone else.

Silfer, Dukut, and many more royal guests, each with their own personal guards and their armor and weapons shined for the occasion, were seated. Red cloaked monks attended to add their blessing to the royal ceremonies.

With everyone placed, the harpist played a light pleasant tune. Teera, walking down the aisle in her form fitted gown with a modest train and her lace veil fluttered lightly on the breeze as she was escorted by James. Rizalle, Elsie, and Sid were seated in the front pews. Brenat and Joel, along with Holy and Krap, awaited Teera at the altar.

As the wedding ceremony started and Brenat noticed that Joel's eyes turned a crystal blue and he had started growling at the red cloaks. The hell hound's hackles were also raised, their fiery eyes glittered as they too stared at the gathering of monks. The monks' attendance in such a large group had already made Brenat uneasy, he had voiced his concerns to James. The monks had assured both James and Rizalle, earlier that the death warrants on both Brenat and Teera were no longer active. They stated that they had come to bless one of their Elite's marriage and the coronations of both him and his son into the royal family.

Brenat whispered to Joel hoping he and the hounds would settle down and asked, *"What's wrong?"*

Joel told him *"Bad, Daddy they bad, they hurt. Kill them Daddy. Make them go away."*

At that moment Rizalle's eyes widen as just as the royal priest was about to start the ceremonies, the red cloaks leaped up from their seats to start killing and feasting upon those between them and the altar. As James called to his guards to protect everyone, Silfer, Dukut, and their guards started killing the guards of the castle. Suddenly complete mayhem broke out as the noble guests turned on the people of the Castle and begun killing everyone they could.

Brenat tossed Joel to his parents and ordered them to run as he heard Silfer command someone to, *"Grab the boy"*. Five red cloaks separated from the fight to chase Elsie, Sid, and Joel through the castle.

Brenat shifted to join the fray a split second behind Rizalle. James turned half shifted to join the fight and was killed when Silfer's axe cleaved into his chest. Rizalle leapt towards

Silfer, only to be cut down by Dukut.

Teera had started to shift to her royal tigress just as a heavy bolt glanced off the side of her skull, her veil carried away by the wayward bolt. Brenat killed several red cloaks while he tried to reach Teera, before he was swarmed by the Elites. Soon he laid unconscious at their feet not far from where Teera also laid. The hell hounds attacked, leaving a path of torn limbs and bodies that ended where Holy and Krap laid dead killed by many heavy silver bolts, still sharing a red cloak corpse between them.

The Castle's warriors, guards, and inhabitants were caught off guard by the surprise attack. Not sure who is friend or foe, they tried to team up with a partner and mount a defense of their home. They were valiant and ferocious in their defense but were heavily outnumbered by the attackers. The battle raged on, but the people of the castle were overwhelmed and massacred after many hours of bloody vicious fighting.

Elsie and Sid took turns as they carried Joel through the secret passage to the mountain range, then north before the pursuers even found the passage left open in James's office. Two of the pursuers their copses were left to rot upon the traps that had claimed them, while the three remaining were slowed and moved with caution until they exited the passage to resume their chase.

With the Castle inhabitants and the guests that had been allied to King James all dead, the red cloaks feasted upon the dead and then dragged Brenat's bloody chained body away.

Dukut looked up as he noticed a bloody veil floating down on the gentle breeze. It landed upon the mounting pile of corpses, with a shrug he tossed the torch on the pile of dead castle inhabitants and guests. The Flames engulfed the bodies, the smell of burning hair and flesh over powered the aroma of the crushed gardenias. With the Pyre burning, Dukut stood watching the flaming victory.

Silfer approached, slapping him on the back, *"Well now you are the regent of your own castle. Very few can say that in one battle they have took over a castle and destroyed almost all its former allies. You're in charge of hunting bandits, send rebellious heretics and anyone still showing the slightest loyalty to the late King and Queen to me for interrogation. They would spend some time in my arena."* Silfer looked around *"Where have you put Teera?"*

Dukut smiled, the flames glittered in his eyes, *"She seemed to have went missing during the battle. She could not be far; I have people searching for her as we speak."*

Silfer raised an eyebrow, *"Continue the search for Teera. When you have found her, leave her in the dungeon for a little while until I return for her. Make sure there are absolutely no survivors in the castle to tell what really happened here, I am headed back to Arena City. Keep me posted on the progress of your new castle, Dukut."*

Broken Arrows Are Formed

Eve came out of a kitchen door to watch the ceremony and gasp as she saw the attack happen. She watched as Teera was struck down then rushed past the warriors, friends, and foes, to grab Teera and drag her to the dungeons while the fierce battle raged.

Eve put Teera in the furthest cell, then released all of the creatures into the dungeon main area and hallway. Rushing back to where Teera laid, she managed to just slam shut the door as one of them hit the door. Eve checked on Teera, seen that she was still alive but unconscious and bleeding from a gash on her head.

Eve lifted Teera, maneuvered her into the secretive maintenance tunnel. She pulled the lever that flushed each cell with three inches of water from the moat then replaced the block of rock in the wall. She sat Teera up bracing her against the wall so the flood of water that came down the tunnel wouldn't drown or pull Teera under.

Eve watched the water wheel as it picked up the water and dumped it into the trough that flushed the cells clean through the tiny window. Waited until the water filled the trough of the last cell and had started seeping down from the tiny cracks where the troughs touched the walls. She then rushed back into her old room she had shared with her master, pushed the lever that reversed the water before she again rushed back to Teera. She pushed the rock back into place, that concealed their escape.

The moat smell covered the scent of their escape. Eve then pulled Teera down to the grate where the water entered and removed two bars, then proceeded to drag Teera through the three foot gap she had created. The moat level had dropped about three to four feet, they floated in the moat, hidden by the shadows. The noises from the water wheel and the counter weights that redirected the water back into the moat covered any noise they made during their escape, yet did nothing to cover the screams of the dieing, nor the sounds of the battle that raged in the castle.

The moat was soon refilled and concealed the barred tunnel again as Eve maneuvered Teera limp form to the opposing shore. Sounds of the battle could still be heard as Eve managed to get Teera deeper into the forest's dark center to hide.

Eve finally found a place where they could hide under a giant pine, its lower limbs so long and heavy that they touched the ground, it created a dark shaded space around the trunk. Their scents were hidden by the sweet scent of pine from those that searched for anyone that might have escaped the massacre.

As they rested Eve checked Teera's head wound and treated it the best she could by wrapping the wound with part of Teera's already torn wedding dress. Unsure what to do next, she sat and hoped Teera would wake before an enemy found them.

Teera groaned as she woke many hours later, suffering from nausea and sickness because of the head wound. The gash in on her head was almost completely healed but she still had a pounding headache. Eve fed Teera some of her blood, knowing she required blood to survive because of her rare bloodline and thought *She hoped that would be enough for the princess* then blushed at her error, *for Teera was now the queen since her parents had been killed.*

Feeling Eve fretting over her, Teera reassured Eve. Then she asked, *"What happened? Where are we? Where is Brenat, my son, Joel and my family? How did we get here?"*

Eve relayed the story, *"The red cloaks attacked and started killing everyone, Silfer killed King James and Dukut killed Queen Rizalle. Sid and Elsie ran with Joel, five red cloaks followed them. Brenat was overwhelmed."*

Teera asked, *"Eve, how did we escape?"*

Eve told Teera about their escape from the castle to where they now rested several miles away from the castle. *"When the battle started and you were hurt I dragged you to the dungeon and out the escape passage through the maintenance tunnel that my former master built. He was the one that you saved me from, but because I helped my old master so much, my status as omega has never changed over the years."*

Taking a deep breath Eve continued, *"I have been glad to be part of Castle Black. I thank you for sparing my life and helping me get past my time being kept as a pet to that jailer. After the search King James did, I realized he was a red cloak spy. Many times after, he took me with him and I had to wash him and saw the scars."* She rubbed the old brand mark, which looked like a broken arrow, that her former master had used to claim her as his property. Eve cried, *"Thank you for showing your parents that I was not just a pet and letting them see I am a shifter too."*

"You saved me long ago and I was finally able to aid you, my queen." Eve cried, *"I'm sorry I don't know if anyone from the castle survived. It did not look like we would win when I dragged you away."*

They held each other and Teera cried thinking about how her parents and Brenat had been cut down. She cried even harder as she realized she could not feel Joel. She thought *my baby must be dead along with Brenat, Sid, Elsie and my parents.*

Eve, not really having a plan, took a still weak Teera to where she had been born and raised before she had been taken, it was a burnt out old farm house that the wilds had taken over again. They went to the stone fireplace and its four foot clearing where once Eve's family cabin had stood. Wild raspberry bushes eight feet high had taken over every other spot of what used to be Eve's parent's old farm house. They sat down in the clearing, Eve moved a stone to get to a hidden stash of tinder. She smiled, *"When the sun goes down we can have a fire for warmth once I gather some fire wood."*

As the moonless night drew on, Eve and Teera sat and contemplated the betrayal to her family. Teera vowed vengeance on her uncles, Silfer, Dukut, and all of the upper echelon of the red cloaks. The two young women sat sharing tears and laughter of times now long gone until they were surprised by the arrival of two boys from the castle.

Reed and Dru burst through the raspberries and knelt before their queen and blurted out, *"We smelled the smoke and followed it cautiously. When we heard you crying and laughing we rushed to you. What do we do now? How are we gonna fight back? What do you need my queen?"* Teera smiles *"How about telling us your names might be a good start."* The youngest of the two young men blushed then said after bowing to his Queen, *"I'm Dru from the stables and this is Reed, He was apprenticed to the blacksmith."*

With raspberries as their night meal, Teera told them, *"Please calm yourselves. I feel your emotions and it can become hard when all of you are so full of conflicting emotions that are directed at me."*

Teera soon noticed that even with Brenat gone, she had more control on how much she felt from others. She could suppress some of the others' emotions without being overwhelmed. Teera cried, feeling Brenat's absence once more.

The boys apologized and knelt with their heads in the dirt thinking they had caused Teera's distress. They only rose after Teera reassured them that they had not caused her tears.

All of them were emotionally drained from the day's events and the fire was dying down, so they decided to try to rest as best as they could. Reed and Dru snuggled together in each other's arms and kissed each other good night. Teera and Eve saw the boys kiss and looked at each other, smiled in understanding. They shifted to their wolves and laid down with their fur pressed against the boys' backs kept them warm, before they fell asleep.

Teera awoke in the middle of the night as more people made their way into the clearing. Teera acknowledged them and pointed to the dying fire, watched as they added wood to the fire before they quietly laid down and fell asleep in the little group.

In the morning Dru, Reed, and Eve awoke to discover their group had grown. Four more lycans and two more humans laid sleeping along with them in the clearing. Teera stood looking at the growing pack and wondered how many others would soon make their way to that spot. She noticed her new pack now consisted of four male lycans, two male humans, two human females, and two lycan females.

Teera asked the group, " *Does everyone know this place?"*

One of the women spoke up, *"Most lower-class do as we use to come here to gather berries for the pies."*

Teera soon realized, while crying and hugging them, happy that some of her people had survived the massacre. That the fresh raspberries she had always been treated to, were gathered from this place.

Teera called the pack together, *"We need to find a safe place for you all to hide, before I seek revenge for my family and the people that were killed in the massacre. Silfer and Dukut took more from me then Asslam ever did and I will make them pay."*

They moved on and after a week of traveling, stopping only to hide from passing troops. Exhausted and in need of rest they found a recently destroyed town. That had been burnt to the ground except for the blacksmith's shop which had been built of stone. The roof was missing having been claimed by fire as well. A pile of bones laid in the middle of the town where a pyre had been built, for apparently all of the residents of the town had been slaughtered.

A baby's skull laid at edge of the mixture of bones as testimony to the violence of the crimes that had been committed there. Teera broke down and started weeping uncontrollably while holding the tiny skull. *Had this been her baby son's fate?* she thought as she sat rocking back and forth crying, *"Joel, my poor baby."*

The others watched, tears fell down their faces as they felt their queen's pain and for all they had lost. They vowed to avenge her loss and the losses of so many others, for they all had lost family, friends, and lovers in the massacre at the castle.

Eve gently took Teera inside, with her still holding the skull as she had use to cradle Joel in her arms. She soon cried herself to sleep, rocking the skull the whole time. Eve covered Teera and slipped back outside.

While they let Teera rest, the others put a plan into place, where some would separate and gather more people to build an army to defeat the red cloaks and all the others that had participated in the slaughters.

Looking to Eve for guidance, Dru spoke up for the others and asked *"How shall we identify each other? Secrecy would be needed. Who will go forth to find others? How will we survive to build and hide this army of nine we have at the moment?"*

Eve, uncomfortable and unaccustomed to being asked for advice or looked to for leadership, unconsciously fingered the broken arrow brand on her thigh from when she had been an enslaved pet.

Reed noticed and turned to fire up the kiln to give all of them the warmth of the blacksmith shop as he started working with the tools. Meanwhile the others started searching the area for food and anything else that survived the destruction that they could use. An hour later, everyone met back in the blacksmith shop with their scrounged treasures.

Reed showed the brand he had made in the shape of a broken arrow. He had coated it in some silver he had found in the old armory. Teera woke with a start to the smell of burnt flesh and felt the pain that came from her new pack. She rushed out, still in a dream like state, shifting to save her people. She found everyone in her pack with tears flowing and holding their right thighs with watered rags and gritted teeth. Each member wore a duplicate of the brand that Eve wore. Eve had even renewed hers as a sign of unity. Teera felt their pain, pride, and determination, shifted back to herself.

Eve looked at Teera and smiled proudly, announced, *"We are the Broken Arrow pack. We will be your army and recruiters. Together we have formed a plan to grow stronger. Some of us will separate and find more members for our army. Only those that accept the branding and have no red cloak scars will be sent here to our new home. Reed, Dru, and I will remain to help you, our queen, and aid in rebuilding the town."*

Teera stared in stunned disbelief at what her new pack had planned and done. She hugged them again saying, *"Thank you,"* to each of her new friends. The nine of them embraced then ate the meager provisions before resting for the night.

In the morning the Broken Arrow pack set about to bury the bones, and searched the village to salvage what then could in the day light. They set about to rebuild the blacksmith's roof and town. Eve and Teera pitched in, before long Eve noticed Teera growing weak and in pain from her still not fully healed head wound. Eve called a break for everyone, they sat and rested while they formulated plans for the new pack.

Teera told them, *"If we could get to the valley, I could save you and you could live in safety away from these cruelties."*

Eve asked, *"Could we come and go as we please?"*

Teera replied, *"No, it opens only on full and new moons."*

Eve spoke up, *"We could not get an army together to help us fight if we hide away!"* All of the others nodded in unison and agreement at her words.

Days later, the town was cleaned up, the blacksmith shop rebuilt. They had found a pouch of gold that they divided among the four that had been chosen to travel and seek new pack members.

They decided, as Broken Arrow City was almost central, that the others would spread out from there to cover the most areas. Ryan, one of the lycan brothers, hugged his brother Brian and the others before heading West with a wave said, *"I'll see you all in a year."*

Brian said, *"Good bye,"* and hugged everyone before heading South. The other two lycans, Blane and Tom, also hugged their fellow pack mates. Before separating, Blane headed North and Tom headed East, both vowed, *"We'll return or send new pack members within a year."*

After Teera's break down, the infant's skull was kept on a stand beside her bed. Where Teera could be heard saying, *"Good night, and Good morning,"* to it every day as if speaking to Joel. The others worried silently about her speaking to the eerie reminder of her dead son. Several spoke of their unease to Eve who assured them that Teera was Ok, while silently worrying about her queen.

Teera and Eve hunted in the nearby woods for food for the small pack. Reed and Dru slowly rebuilt the town with the aid of the two sisters. Soon new towns people arrived that found their way through the forest.

Most drawn to the smell of hot food and looking for a safe place to rest. They decided to stay and help rebuild until, within a few months the town had grown, with more people gathering weekly. All of those that arrived told their stories of the atrocities of Lord Dukut in the North, King Silfer in the South, and the red cloaked monks that traveled all over the country, who were busy rounding up more to take to the arena. Over time, all of the town's people not only came to call Broken Arrow City home, but also became members, warriors, and family to the Broken Arrow pack, with their own brands solidifying their allegiance.

They set about building an inn for visitors and a barn for the animals found abandoned by the murdered farmers and others. They built a communal building, where the pack members ate and rested. Some started gardens, others tended to the expanding livestock until their small town was thriving.

The town's prosperity grew so much that the sisters started a bath house, that was built for the town and its visitors.

Everyone took time out daily to learn swordsman ship, archery, use of spears and defense so that every member of the town, from old to the young, were all part of the militia. In the evening everyone in the pack shared in a communal bath and meal.

As the town grew they stayed right on the edges of the woods. They did not clear cut the area for the town as was common, but left patches of forest between the houses and other buildings. Some buildings even had trees growing through them, until the town resembled less of a town surrounded by forest but more of a forest with a town built in it. The town kept growing as more and more people moved in.

✠ ✠ ✠ ✠ ✠ ✠ ✠ ✠ ✠ ✠

Brian, after a couple of weeks of traveling, watched silently from the trees as he saw two men at a farm. One threw a struggling woman to the ground within sight of a man's corpse, ripping off her dress in the process.

The second man growled at the first, *"Do not take too long we have to catch up to the others."* As he rode out of sight, Brian drew his bow. The first man lowered himself on top of the woman. Her eyes closed as she waited, trembling, for what she knew was to come. Her attackers body weight pressed her to the ground.

She waited and waited but nothing happened. She opened her eyes and was shocked to see an arrow head poking out of where his right eye should have been. Before she could scream, she heard a man whisper, *"Shhh, they can still hear you."*

Brian pulled the body off of her and cut off its head with his axe. Looking at her, Brian said, *"Run, follow, or stay it's your choice."* He walked back to where he left his pack.

She looked around and saw nothing left for her there, she retrieved a dress to cover herself and a small pack of things and decided to follow him.

Brian loaded up his pack. Looked at her, said, *"North, there is a town called Broken Arrow City where you would be safe. I am headed south to Arena City."*

She thought for a while before announcing, *"Thank you, I'm Rose, they killed my husband and took away my two sons. I will rescue my sons or die trying, so I will head south with you. What should I call you?"*

Nodding, he replied, *"I'm Brian. The road is long and hard. We do not know if your children still live. I will help you until the time comes that we must continue on our individual paths."*

They followed the caravan route south hoping to catch up to them. After a week of travel, they saw vultures circling and ran to the bend, still a mile in the distance. Rounding the bend just as the vultures seemed to land, Rose and Brian rushed the birds brandishing their weapons. They came to the bodies of twin boys, their backs lashed to shredded ribbons. Rose and Brian checked for life only to have their fears confirmed that the boys were dead, their eyes had been taken by birds or something else. Rose broke down, tears streaming from her eyes, as she brushed the hair from their faces while cradling their heads in her lap. Brian rested a hand upon her shoulder for a moment, before grabbing his axe and started getting wood for the pyre.

Hours passed and Rose had to chase off a few vultures several times while she washed the bodies with the water from her water skin. By dusk the pyre was built and Rose's grief is cried out. Brian and Rose put the bodies in the middle of the pyre and lit the fire. They sat and watched the fire lick the sky while Brian wrapped his arm around her and she rested her head upon his chest. When the pyre had burnt low and the sun had rose high into the sky, Brian and Rose moved on.

Rose vowed to avenge her family and Brian confessed, *"That is why I am heading to Arena City, for I too have a vengeful mind."*

As days turned to weeks, they got to know each other. Rose learned the truth of why Brian was headed south. That night Rose took the branding and became a Broken Arrow, promising to do all she could to recruit for the quiver that Brian planned to build in Arena City.

❂ ❂ ❂ ❂ ❂ ❂ ❂ ❂ ❂ ❂

Blane headed north, following the edge of the humans and wilds to avoid the bigger, more hostile, and suspicious towns where the red cloaks seemed to have a larger presence. The smaller villages seemed to take the brunt of red cloaks recruiting. While the wilderness creatures suffered the killing raids so that only the strongest, smartest, and luckiest seem able to scrape a living here.

One village had even progressed to the point of incorporating centaurs into the village. Many humans had edged closer to the wilds to avoid vampires, lycans, and red cloaks, preferring to take their chances with the uncontrolled wild and hungry creatures instead.

With the centaurs in the town, Blane decided to stay for a while. He wondered about the centaurs, he had heard rumors of them while living at Castle Black, hearing the occasional scout talk of encountering them. He was not afraid to show that he was lycan to the centaur that came out to challenge him, just as a red cloak entered the town from the opposite side of town with his apprentice.

Blane felt exceptionally cranky after having walked for months and drew his axe and offered the red cloak two options. He could stay in town but his head would sit on a stick outside of town, or his head stayed attached but he stayed out of the town. The monk chose the latter and left.

The centaurs approached him once more to challenge him, their bodies tensed until they soon recognized him as a fellow outcast. The leader told him, *"The humans were not part of the menu."*

He smiled and stated, *"I prefer to have them as friends and allies."*

He became slowly accepted over time by all in the town. Blane even took a human concubine that really enjoyed being taken by the large lycan and even loved the passion filled love bites.

Soon she even chose to wear a custom made collar styled necklace that showed off his bite marks claiming her as his.

Blane, with the centaurs help, had acquired just as many arrows, thanks to their mutual dislike of the red cloaks. They had centaurs, a naiad from a nearby river. The naiad, or as others call them a water spirit, always appeared as a beautiful woman that lived in and around rivers and lakes surrounded by trees. Friendly and mischievous, they controlled the currents in their domain. Many have lured men to be their mates or just to have a little fun. They were great allies when people traveled by water, but those that disrespected them often were soon found drowned. Having one join against a group of people was a true rarity and a true indication of the great crimes and disrespect committed. Bountiful supplies of humans, who all had encounters with red cloaks, also joined. Soon they numbered in the hundreds, all awaiting the call to fight.

⊗ ⊗ ⊗ ⊗ ⊗ ⊗ ⊗ ⊗ ⊗ ⊗ ⊗

Ryan headed east to the next biggest city and immediately went to work as a skilled fletcher and woodman, as the red cloaks needed a good bowyer for their militia and warrior training. Slowly, he became a valued and respected member of the town.

Ryan gathered information on the red cloaks and towns. He found out how many of the town's people put up with the red cloaks while building allies against them. No red cloak spy could sneak into the sweat lodge he built. The number of broken arrows started growing in the town. All of them laughed as the red cloaks began training them for militia while they ran their businesses.

Ryan's town sent out half of its highly trained broken arrow warriors as red cloaks under a red cloak commander to recruit others. It was not surprising that some red cloaks had started to think that Dukut, King Silfer and red cloaked monks had too much say about who lived, died, or went to the arena as entertainment, especially those that have lost friends and family to them. As the months passed more and more red cloaked warriors wore the broken arrow brand.

⊗ ⊗ ⊗ ⊗ ⊗ ⊗ ⊗ ⊗ ⊗ ⊗ ⊗

Tom headed west following the great sea until he came to

a village. He set up shop and plied his trade as leather worker and armorer. With his charm and skill, he soon became respected and in high demand, as the wilds were a dangerous place and good armor was essential for survival. He soon built a sweat lodge and bath for the villagers and travelers to use as a place to relax. It was not long that he became even more popular that he soon became the mayor of the village as it grew, so too did the broken arrows.

Tom recruited some rare shifters, a fox, a jaguar and a few others. Those rarities were sent to Broken Arrow City to meet the queen and join their ranks.

Tom found a group hiding out and invited them to join his village. They were fully grown people that were half the size of an average human female. They had moved to hide in the wilds after the red cloaks had slaughtered their villages. The red clocks had taken their women and children as playthings, so their masters could boast at the oddity of having a tiny slave.

So when Tom treated them like any other person and invited them to join his town for mutual protection, they agreed. The humans took to calling them half-lings as a group and it stuck. They could get into places and do things others could not, making them important and highly valued members of the western quiver.

❈ ❈ ❈ ❈ ❈ ❈ ❈ ❈ ❈ ❈ ❈

Brian and Rose arrived at Arena City, the site of Silfer's castle. With the gold they had they started up an inn with steam baths, thus The Broken Arrow Inn was born.

Rose, with her knowledge of plants, built a great herb garden. The inn became known for its relaxation, baths, and great food. Soon it expanded with it's newest employees, having pride and determination, even if they had to limp for a few days, as another quiver was created.

With everyone, male and female, naked and sharing the steaming bathing area, back scars and leg brands became hard to hide, therefore it turned into a great meeting place for the broken arrows. The sound of splashing water covered up quiet conversations.

Many people decided to use the pools and soon it was not uncommon to find red cloaks, average citizens, and broken arrows all sharing the pools. It came to pass that the red cloaks, instead of charging Brian and Rose to be allowed to run the business, offered a deal in which Brian and Rose allowed the red cloaks to use the facilities at a minimal cost. The red cloaks and Silfer's people told all that would listen that the monks, priests, and their soldiers were the poorest paid, contrary to what the rest of the populace believed.

❂ ❂ ❂ ❂ ❂ ❂ ❂ ❂ ❂ ❂ ❂

Every month, Broken Arrow City grew as more humans, lycans, red cloak warriors and other races came from the north, south, east, and west quivers. Their proof of loyalty proudly displayed on their legs in the steam baths. Messages constantly came and left between Broken Arrow City and the four quivers in the different regions of the continent.

The Search

During that time back at Castle Black, the pyre fire had continued to burn for several days, as Dukut had the castle cleared of all the dead bodies from both the massacre and his search for survivors that could tell the truth of how he had gotten his new rule. Soon the castle was cleared, with no more survivors found.

The secret passage in Dukut's office was left open, he sent in a dozen men to remove the bodies stuck on the traps and lost three more men to other traps. They found the exit for the tunnel and started the process of sealing it from any further use. Inside and out, mortar, wood, and stone were used to seal the passage.

Meanwhile, the search for Teera continued, Dukut's trackers had started at the secret passage following the red cloak monks. Finding Teera and the young prince Joel before the red cloaks would be of great advantage. After days of travel, Dukut's scouts found the monks trail had ran cold, while what the monks tracked seemingly became non-existent. The scouts returned to Dukut who was still tossing evidence of the old rulers, as well as all of the old occupant's possessions, on the fire, erasing their existence as the last of the bodies burned.

With fresh horses, the scouts restarted their search for Teera and Joel, as well as anyone harboring them, in ever widening circles. Dukut cursed Kenny for training Teera so well, while reveling in the challenge of the hunt.

Dukut could be heard muttering, *"Run Teera, hide Teera, we will catch you. Hiding in that valley of yours is only a temporary reprieve. When we break the seal, you will have nowhere to go. When we catch that brat of yours, you will come to me."*

Silfer looked around at the changes Dukut had already made to rebuild and assert his rule of Castle Black as he prepared to leave.

"Dukut, send out patrols to search for the rogues and heretics that have loyalty to the old castle rulers and anyone that fails to acknowledge my rule. Send the survivors to the arena pens in Arena City. I want to unite the whole territory under my rule, even if we have to do it with a show of force and ruthlessness," Dukut nodded in agreement to Silfer's plans.

The red cloaks monks were also sent out on search and destroy parties for any couples over forty and boys that looked about the age of three. Many villages and towns were decimated. It did not matter if they were human, half-ling, lycan or other.

Silfer arrived back at his castle and summoned his scribes, *"I want the public informed of the attack upon Castle Black and the continued hunt for the cowardly perpetrators of the massacre."* Silfer also said, *"I want all to begin a massive search to find Teera and her son. Announce that I am offering a large reward for information regarding the return of the new queen or her son to the throne."*

The search parties throughout the kingdom were given similar ordered, *"Find Queen Teera and any boys about the age of three that might be the young prince, Joel. Kill any couples over forty found wandering the country side. Any heretics were to be sent to the arena pens."*

During the months that followed Dukut had his troops expand his domain by taking over all that had once been James's area. He forced the nearby nobles and landowners to pledge their allegiance to King Silfer and Dukut. While still searching for Teera and Joel, he sent all couples found over forty from both the countryside and small towns in cages to Arena City where a fate worse than death awaited. He captured any boys about the age of three and sent them with the couples, heretics, and others who do not acknowledge the new King's rule.

The only places saved from the cleansing were Arena City, along with other large cities controlled by allied nobles or towns with a large red cloak presence, and the wilds from which hunting parties never returned.

Silfer and the red cloaks refilled their ranks with allied vampires, grudgingly, Dukut was forced into accepting vampires into his ranks to resupply his castle guards and to appease the red cloaks.

Keres vs Kenny

The witch Keres stayed close to Silfer, consoling him on the loss of Teera and Joel at Castle Black. Keres whispered, *"Finding Teera and making her your queen would legitimize your claim as king. If you and she had a child together, that would show that you are the true king. If you could find the young prince you as his guardian would rule as king in his place."* All the while Keres plotted to control or boil the flesh off the missing brat 's bones.

Keres often went to the pens to personally search for new victims for her amusement. Sometimes a wife, daughter, son, father, or mother would manage to make a deal with Keres for the newest gladiator's freedom. Everyone that made a deal with her soon regretted it and wished they had just left them in the arena to take their chances. It was safer and filled with less pain and sorrow than letting Keres get her hands on you in one of her deals.

Kenny observed one such deal where a young woman negotiated with Keres to free her love from certain death in the arena. Keres agreed to free him of all the pain he suffered and from the arena pens, if she offered herself to Keres's three lycan guards, who were also collared, while the young woman's love watched.

The young woman agreed and pricked her finger, signed the contract in her blood. Then the woman, full of tears and determination, stripped before her love and the lycans, pleaded for the lycans to take her and make her a woman.

Keres directed the scene, the magic of the contract gave Keres control over the girl and her lycan slaves. Keres made sure the young man was shackled and unable to look away, forced to view his love fulfilling her contract for his freedom. Keres used her abilities to coerce and enhance the need, wants, and desires of her contracted slaves. She made the woman's body fulfill her end with exuberance while her mind screamed in denial, but remained trapped in her passionate body.

The young man had tears in his eyes, because of what his love had to do to bring about his freedom, the pain obvious upon his face. With a sweet smile on her lovely face, Keres cut his throat right as the deal was completed, before he could utter a single word. Keres in her sweet voice said, *"The deal is complete, as agreed by in our deal; he has been freed from the pens and from his pain in payment for the services that you rendered."* Keres walked away, smiling even more sweetly, with her lycan slaves still pulling up their pants as they followed.

Kenny raged in silence as he covered the young woman with his cloak. The young woman was filled with shame and begged her love's forgiveness as she held his dead body in her arms.

Kenny swallowed his rage and threw himself into his work. He quickly became renowned for his great leadership and his fair but stern treatment of all under him. He became highly respected among the guards, peasants, and even the prisoners. Kenny did his best to keep Keres away as much as he could from the pens and areas he controlled.

More than once, guards went to Kenny to verify King Silfer's and Keres's orders as the young boys were painfully checked to see if they were of royal lycan lineage before being placed into the arena pens.

Kenny rescued the boys and girls from the pens and sent them to the orphanage he had built. He arranged for some of his warriors to start training the boys in the arts of battle and stealth, while the others started to learn trades to became blacksmiths, hunters, fletchers, armorers, leather workers, butchers. A few exceptional ones became apprentices' to apothecaries, merchants, and scribes.

None of the children were ever severely punished for practicing their stealth or acquiring money and items as long as the house was given the lion's share. If captured, they spent time in the cells equivalent to the number of times they were caught, with the same number of lashings. All the public lashings seemed to appease Keres and kept her from interfering, as she came to watch and gleefully applauded.

When the odd noble got mugged, there was a token search for the offenders, until someone previously caught, and heading to the arena already, confessed to the crime just to be kept out of Keres's clutches.

The nobles were always happy to have the offender caught and punished in the arena. They bet on their favorite gladiator to hand out justice within so many drum beats. Arena battles were doing so well that the nobles often made their money back. Often they would buy the gladiator and improve his life. The favored gladiators would often fight battles of honor among disputing nobles.

⊗ ⊗ ⊗ ⊗ ⊗ ⊗ ⊗ ⊗ ⊗ ⊗ ⊗

With a lot of the guards using the new bath facilities, Kenny went and visited the baths.

Brian bowed low in respect when the head of the guards arrived. He had heard from many of his customers that Kenny was one that all respected and trusted.

"*My Lord, Welcome to our pools. If you would undress in this private dressing room, I would see to it a private pool is made ready for you,*" Brian said.

Kenny looked around and saw others, including red cloaks, undressed near the larger pools where servants bathed them. He noticed that several seemed to wear a brand on their thigh and wondered about it, decided to investigate into the reason behind the brand later.

"*The larger common pool is fine and I'll leave my things on one of the benches near as the others do, I seek no special favors,*" replied Kenny.

Brian was astonished and said, "*Yes, My Lord, the reduced fee for your class is . .*"

Before he could finish Kenny interrupted, and firmly stated, "*I'll be paying the full price, not the reduced price when I come here. As I said, I seek no special favors.*"

Brian showed Kenny to a bench near the pool and motioned for a servant to service him. Kenny watched as the beautiful girl approached, admired her grace and wondered what secrets the gown she wore hid.

Rinette heard Brian call her name, she quickly grabbed fresh supplies before turning to see which customer she was to care for. She saw Brian standing beside a tall well-built man, his blond hair, which was held back by a leather tie, gleamed in the torches. She licked her suddenly dry lips as she approached feeling shy. Bowing low, she averted her eyes from his manhood that hung as if unaffected by the beautiful undressed women around him.

"*Rinette, I expect you to take good care of the Commander of the Guards, as well as personally see to all needs that he may have,*" Brian told her.

Rinette blushed and said, *"Yes, Sir."*

Brian said, *"My Lord Kenny, if you need anything Rinette will be happy to assist you."*

Kenny dismissed him with a wave of his hand, his eyes never left Rinette. He felt his shaft stir and thicken as she undressed and slipped into the pool. He tried to will the hardness away by relaxing back and allowing Rinette to bath him, which only succeeded in making him grow harder, he felt her start running the soft rag up and down his hard shaft. His moan of pleasure brought Rinette out of the trance she seemed to be in, causing her to blush deeper, at realizing what she had been doing. Kenny gently pulled her close, *"I seem to have developed a need that only you can take care of. Would you take care of it for me?"* He said as he captured her lips in a deep kiss.

"Yes," she whispered. He gently lifted and then lowered her onto his shaft. He moaned as her muscles gripped him tightly as if made for him alone. Leaning forward he took one of her raspberry colored nipples and suckled, loving the sounds of her purrs of pleasure. Both were soon lost in their pleasure, uncaring of the others around them as they both suddenly bonded in their mutual release. Kenny's eyes changed as he growled, *"Mine,"* just as he claimed her as his mate, marking her for all to see. Rinette responded by biting Kenny's shoulder in answer to his claim.

"I have a place for you away from here, Marry me. I want to be the only one you're with." Kenny said.

Rinette, as if in a daze, said, *"Yes,"* not believing that she had found her one true mate.

"I'll talk to your employer and arrange for you to join me. I forgot to ask, do you like children?" Kenny suddenly grew worried, about what he would do if she didn't like children, especially as his home was crowded with them.

Rinette smiled, *"I love children. I have always wanted a house full."*

Kenny breathed a sigh of relief, *"I'm glad because I have several children, actually my house if full of them, all ages. They were children I rescued from the pens. I started an orphanage to save all those I could. Would you be my wife and mother of my children?"* he asked her again, holding his breath. He watched as emotions played across her face just before she hugged him shouting, *"Yes!"* causing others to look their way.

Brian and Rose appeared suddenly, looking from one to the other before asking, *"I take it, My Lord, you found Rinette to your liking?"* Both Kenny and Rinette started laughing.

After a few weeks it seemed that Kenny had hurt his leg, causing him to limp for a few days as he fingered a broken arrow brand. Soon, many townspeople, and castle guards also acquired limps for a few days. In a few short months there were four score guards and five times as many citizens, all over the city, wearing the broken arrow brand.

Back at Broken Arrow City

To protect Teera and her seemingly fragile mind, at the suggestion of Eve and the other betas, Teera took up cooking at the inn for her people. It kept her out of sight of the occasional red cloaked monk, hunters, and scouting parties that came through searching for the queen. Only those that wore the Broken Arrow brand really knew who Teera was. She cooked for her pack, while she secretly ruled from the shadows. Most believed Eve led the town with Dru and Reed as her seconds.

Teera talked to the skull that she carried with her everywhere, and was sometimes seen cooing softly to it. Many believed that she was just a demented cook, while those closer to her knew the truth. While she cooked, Teera always placed the skull on a shelf near her, where she often talked to it.

Teera's home and throne were in the inn, so Teera never had to go anywhere. Yet her eyes flared with a frightening fire whenever a red cloak entered the town. Even newcomers, Teera held in suspicion, until they earned their broken arrow brand and were introduced by Eve to Teera showing their brand and had proven their loyalty to the queen.

The betas hid Teera until they assessed who or what the newcomers' motives were. News arrived regularly that King

Silfer still searched for the missing queen and her son Joel, with the promise of a high reward for them or the enemy that had caused the massacre at Castle Black if delivered to the red cloak monks. Dukut's scouts searched the area for bandits, heretics, and anyone harboring those loyal to James and Rizalle.

Those coming into the town to live always seemed to be between twelve and twenty years old. No others seemed to escape Silfer's encompassing net. The truth found its way to Teera's ears that all towns were being raided, the people questioned and only those that acknowledged King Silfer's rule escaped the trip to Arena City.

The small town grew over months and Teera stayed out of sight, while Broken Arrow pack met in the Inn. When Teera was not cooking she ran the town from the kitchen. She had the beta's find trainers for the warriors of the broken arrows. The red cloaked warriors that had been sent by Blane and were loyal to the queen, taught the advanced skills of their specialties bow, sword, spear, and shield. All trained for the day when the broken arrows would be called to war against Silfer and his red cloaks. The broken arrows consisted mainly of those that survived the cleansing of their homes. Most were hunters, gathers, or members of the militia of a town who had came back to find it empty of family and friends, the dead burning on a pyre.

A scout patrol went through town taking people to Arena City for crimes of heresy. The town's people moved out of their way, bowed and hoping they would not come back that way. As many towns were destroyed outright when a military party came through. Even though they hid in plain sight with red cloak warriors, the people knew Dukut's people might cull their town anyway.

That day as Teera picked fresh herbs for the roast beast she was cooking over the hearth fire in the inn, she overheard the passing men talking about the massive reward offered for her and her son. The men dismissed her as demented as she talked to the skull while she worked. Briefly her eyes glowed as she realized for the first time that her son must still be alive. The hope shone in Teera's eyes that had been absent for months. *"Joel LIVES, or else Silfer and the rest would have stopped searching for him. Where would he be? The valley! She needed to find him and protect her people at the same time."*

Teera made a plan while she gathered the fresh herbs, *"She knew the betas would argue amongst themselves about who would travel with her, or they may even try to stop her all together."* Once back at the kitchen, she placed the herbs on the roast and lowered the heat before she grabbed the skull and walked out into the forest. She shifted into a wolf, and carried the skull in her mouth. Her white coat was bright against the green when the light shone on it until she was shrouded by the trees and shade. Teera ran, putting many miles between her and the broken arrows before they even realized she was gone.

Later, Eve wondered where supper was. She went in to check on Teera. Eve's eyes were immediately drawn to the missing skull. *"Damn she's ran off,"* Eve sighed as she went to call upon fifty lycans to join her in bringing the queen back. Reed and Dru took over the broken arrows that stayed behind so the red cloaks wouldn't know they were missing fifty people.

The chase was on with Teera's royal wolf outdistancing her friendly pursuers by several extra miles a day. Eve and her troop, hid from Dukut's scouts and warriors that searched the area, exasperated by the delays as they tried to catch their queen. They were worried those warriors were heading towards Broken Arrow Town. Eve reassured her warriors the town should be safe from the culling, with the oldest gone from town and in pursuit of Teera. While those left were prepared to make a show of compliance. They would pretend that Broken Arrow Town was a prosperous town loyal to King Silfer, with nothing to hide from his enforcers.

Captured

After weeks of running west toward the mountains then north along the mountain range, the first snow started falling. Teera's coat finally started to blend in with her surroundings. The white blanket covered all, allowing her pace to quicken as she did not have to focus as much on hiding in the shadows when the light shone. It started as a heavy blanket of wet snow, it soon turned to soft fluffy snow that thickened the blanket, that aided in covering her tracks. The snow deepened as she got closer to the mountains and paths she knew so well.

Teera's excitement rose as she thought of her valley, her home, and where she spent some of the best times of her life with her mate, and forgot all about the loneliness that was her prison.

She only stopped to rest for a few hours during the day or to hunt a snow hare for a meal. Teera trotted as a wolf, the scent of hunters' faint and distant. She was excited because that night the moon would be full, she could escape into the valley for a while to rest and be with her son.

Her steps were a little bouncy with the excitement. Suddenly with a snap, a silver net picked her up and the surprise of the trap made her drop the skull, it disappeared from sight under the snow. The moon had risen and set as she sat and swung, unable to shift or even move as the silvery net burned. The silence of the forest was broken when the scouts arrived to collect their prize. Cutting the net from the tree, they dragged Teera in the net through the snow to Dukut's Castle.

She was dragged through the courtyard that she had not seen since her wedding day. Tears of pain started to fall and freeze in the snow, the pain was so raw from the memory of those lost that she forgot about the net.

She was dumped, like no more than a sack full of garbage, into a dungeon cell. Angry she remembered all that she had gone through to escape capture, just to end up in the dungeon as if she had walked in and gave herself to her enemies. She fell unconsciousness partially to heal from the pain of the net and partially from the exhaustion of her emotions.

Teera awoke in the dungeon, her arms and legs cuffed to chains. She raised her head and looked up as she heard a voice and saw a hazy figure that approached through her sleep filled eyes. She saw the hazy figure pull a lever that caused Teera's arms to be pulled up and away from her naked chest, revealing her ample bosom as she was lifted up off the ground. With another lever her legs were pulled apart, making her look like a pale naked star held in place by chains. As her eyes cleared they turned to flames as her hatred surged. She watched him approach and swallowed back the angry words on her tongue as she wondered what his next move would be.

"Finally you have arrived in my dungeon, Queen Teera," the last bit was added with a sarcastic sneer. Dukut circled her while flicking his riding crop lightly over her breasts, belly, buttocks, and calves. He smiled at how helpless and exposed to him Teera was. Dukut also enjoyed how her body blushed as she felt his eyes roaming her body.

Dukut sneered, *"Now my queen you need to be punished for disobedience. It took a while for me to catch you. For the trouble you have caused and the time wasted in hunting you, you need to pay."*

He struck her across her breast with the riding crop,

leaving a red welt. Teera cried out from the pain and shock before she could stifle it.

Dukut smiled at Teera's outcry and said, *"I am not sure when you got into and out of your valley. I knew if we set traps and waited long enough you would land in one."* He smacked her her across her thigh, then ran his finger along the newly developing welt.

"King Silfer had us running all over the land searching for you, while we worked to break the seal on your valley." Suddenly he smacked the crop across the other thigh and again he ran his finger along the newest welt. *"Don't worry when we break the seal to the valley we will get your brat as well."*

Teera's fear and exhaustion left as she realized, *"They thought she had hid him in the valley. Maybe Joel did make it into the valley. He was a resourceful child."* Teera's will to fight was renewed, *"All she had to do is hold out."* Teera was filled with hope as she briefly dreamed, *"of Joel hunting deer in the valley and sunning himself on rocks. She could see him playing hide and seek with Holy and Krap while Brenat watched them play as he chopped wood."* Teera's daydream ended abruptly as she came back to the immediate present when Dukut smacked her again on her breast.

Dukut smiled cruelly, *"For the long wait, you are to be punished for your disobedience to the king before he comes to collect you. The king has ordered that you are to be kept alive. So you will be used as my play thing. It is time for you to learn who is in charge of Castle Black now. This will bring much pleasure to me and my men, but not to you."*

As he threw cold water on Teera, Dukut watched as goosebumps covered her body and how swollen and erect her nipples got in the cool air. He dragged his calloused fingers down her welt covered back before he slid his finger between her thighs.

Teera snarled and tried to recoil at his touch, *"No touchy, your king said so, Dukut. Ha! You should have been named coyote, like the mangy mutt that you are. Your nothing but a glorified errand boy nothing but a lowly servant doing Silfer's bidding."*

With a snarl he reversed the levers and the chains went slack. Teera fell to the floor to her hands and knees. *"He said you had to be kept alive, and your face pretty for your upcoming public wedding, the rest of you doesn't matter. I think for starters you will service me with your mouth,"* Dukut snarled.

Teera, with a venomous look in her eyes, snapped her teeth and said with a sneer, *"Please do. I need some meat, even if it is flea infested."*

Dukut, with rage filled eyes, strapped a silver collar around Teera's neck and anchored it to a floor hook before he released her arms and feet. With a smirk he said, *"Now you shall be treated like the mutt you are, while you service me and my men. My Queen, you're no longer the pampered princess anymore, now you're just the royal whore."*

Dukut called in his personal guards, and he picked up the silver tipped cat-o-nine tails. He lashed her right buttocks, leaving nine bloody slashes, stark against her milky white thighs, again the lashes hit. Teera screamed in burning pain and moved her body away. Anchored to the floor by her neck, she spun from the painful lashes until she faced the wall, her face inches from the floor. When the lashes stopped she turned to face Dukut again, he struck her again, he laughed at her attempts to escape his whip.

He stopped and stood, admired his handy work. As she rested for a few moments, the deep bloody gashes begun to heal, leaving only the remnant of pain and bright red welts. Her nipples, arms, and legs were scraped and tender from the rough cold stone floor.

The guards arrived, saw the queen on her elbows and knees, her blood streaked backside presented itself for their inspection.

Teera felt their emotions, the burning hatred and lustful arousal of the leering men. Their lust and anger overshadowed the pain of the many bloody whip marks.

Her eyes were drawn to a childlike corpse shackled to a wall, her eyes flared with a calm vengeance as she vowed that she would bide her time until she could eat Dukut's and Silfer's hearts to avenge all those lost. Her mind focused on the skeleton, and the men became distant like a faraway storm, that barely registered.

With a sneer Dukut spat on Teera, his spittle hitting her right buttocks. Dukut nodded and stepped back, watched as his men started spitting on her back and buttocks until the slime ran down her sides, into her hair, down her legs, and between her buttocks.

The warriors laughed and sword belts dropped, as one after another penetrated her from behind, their seed dripping from her, while others shot their seed upon her back and buttocks. Teera, in shock and pain, could only count the number of them as they used her, *"one, two, three,"* more tears as the pain continued until she counted, *"nine, ten, eleven."* As the last one finished, they left, leaving her chained and laying in a puddle of their seed and saliva. Through the haze of pain, Teera looked at child sized skeleton chained to a wall as the tears of pain and humiliation turned to pure vengeance while whispering, *"For what they did to you, my family, and for every other atrocity they have committed, they all will pay. "*

Teera dropped her forehead to the cool floor catching a glint of something just in range. If she laid flat and stretched out her leg she could just reach it. Touching it, she felt the burn of the silver. Ignoring the pain, she pulled it closer with her foot until she could pick it up and see it better. She saw it was one of the cat-o-nine's silver claws. With determination she used it to pick the locks and free herself.

She smiled once freed then looked around. *"This is my castle I know the way out of the dungeon,"* Teera said as she remembered the secret passage Eve had told her about. In their over confidence they had forgotten to leave a guard at the cell door. With a little more work, Teera picked that lock too then headed down the corridor to the last dungeon cell. There she removed a stone and crawled into the wall. Pulling the stone back behind her, Teera walked through the passage that was covered in moat slime that had seeped in, until she reached the barred exit that was underwater. With the bars still loose, Teera removed them to slip under the water then swam through the gate into the moat. Once out she replaced the bars and swam beneath the water to the opposite shore. She stayed hid in the reeds until she came to the creek that fed the moat. The waters from the moat and creek washed the men's slime from her as well as covered her scent.

With all of the stealth and skills she had practiced over the months with her town militia, she slipped silently away. Tired and sore she shifted into her wolf. Her white coat blended in with the snow on the ground. Even in the brightest of the daylight she managed to distance herself from Dukut's castle before they realized she was gone.

Eve and her troops tracked Teera to where she had gotten captured. They moved north-east, skirted the castle, and stayed deep in the trees looking across the field of white, to where the creek intersects with the moat at the backside of the castle. Headed deeper into the forest they regrouped and started to plan on how they were going to rescue Teera.

"Come nightfall, ten of us will sneak in and grab Teera, the rest of you will attack the front as a diversion to get the troops to chase you. Each of you will head away from castle in groups of two and find a place to hide out for a few days, then make your way back to town. If you're followed, take your time and follow the paths we set out in the wilds. They are dangerous, but they are safer for us than for them. Everyone rest, we will take turns watching. We have an interesting night ahead,"

Eve instructed the others.

While the warriors rested, Eve watched the castle. Time and again she thought she saw something move on the blanket of white, until it came closer. Eve noticed the white wolf approaching and woke the others, who were ready to race out and protect Teera if needed. Eve stood, her foot tapped impatiently as she watched the white wolf approach with seeming slowness. She admired the stealth and grace in which the wolf moved. An eternity seemed to have passed as the group awaited the arrival of their wayward queen, their muscles and minds tensed like cats waiting to pounce at the first sign of alarm. Eve switched between growls of impatience and anger to smiles of relief and joy as Teera's agonizingly slow progress brought her ever closer. Finally, Teera came into the area where the Broken Arrows awaited.

Teera, once she escaped had headed toward the valley, keeping to the shadows and trees. She suddenly remembered all the traps, so veered away from her valley and instead turned towards the town of the broken arrows. Entering the trees, Teera came face to face with an obviously upset and scowling Eve and fifty of her best warriors.

Teera looked at the group and smiled as she said, *"Hi. Were you waiting for me or was this a planned assault you forgot to let me in on?"*

Sighs of exasperation could be heard from the warriors as she tossed off the situation as nothing. Eve gave a snort before she hugged Teera and said, *"Don't you ever leave like that again, we would die to protect you."*

Eve turned to face the troops, *"Since the queen has escaped from the clutches of that coyote. We have got to make sure she stays free. We need to proceed with the second part of our plan."*

Teera and Eve left first and the rest walked around in ever widening circles for five minutes. Before they left the group, they joined in a group hug with Teera and Eve at its center and the fifty lycans gathered as close as possible until it looked like a spiral of bodies. Then the spiral unraveled as they started peeling off two at a time for their designated hiding places.

Eve again warned them, *"We will see you all when you get back to town. If you are pursued, kill them or let them try and follow you through the wilds. Let it and its inhabitants do the killing for you."* Some headed off to deliver messages of warning to the small villages, while others just separated to confuse the trails more.

As the miles dragged on there was no pursuit, Teera's thoughts ran to that idiot Dukut and how he could not even ran a simple village let alone a castle. Then she started to fret, *maybe they found a way into the valley and were now after Joel.* With a dismissive scoff she thought, *No, if that was the case the castle would have been alive with activity and ruckus.*

Teera refocused her thoughts on the things she could control like killing Silfer, Dukut, and destroying Keres, along with her coven, before they broke the seal on her valley. After that, she was going to hunt down every red cloak and slaughter them like they did so many others. So her son, where ever he was, and others could live freely and happy.

That evening as they rested Teera and Eve sat talking around their fire, *"Eve, I found out that Silfer, Dukut, and the red cloaks are still searching for Joel. That means Joel still lives and is free somewhere. They think he is hiding out in valley so they are working to break the seal."*

Eve watched as Teera's eyes filled with such hope and determination. They started making plans, *"Teera, we need to try and figure out ways to take out Dukut first or Silfer and his witches. Dukut may make a poor castle leader, but when it came to matters of war, Silfer would let Dukut lead the war. In defeating Silfer, surprise will be the key. Then gaining superior numbers would help us defeat Dukut. Keres and her witches' coven are still an unknown factor. I am not sure how it would be best to destroy them and their power, or the red cloaks."*

Teera replied, *"So, what about sneaking into Arena City we could free the slaves and gladiators? We have no great weapons for siege warfare so we will need to use stealth and surprise to destroy Silfer from the inside out."*

Eve thought a bit then replied, *"So if we sneak into Arena City, free the slaves and gladiators to help in the fight we will add more to our forces. We could get all the Broken Arrows to start making their way into Arena City where Brian could help us plan our assault for the fall harvest festival, when the arena and games are in full swing. Usually it is just the once a month battles where nobles pit their gladiators against one another. With more people in the city for the harvest festival, we could easily slip our people in."* Teera and Eve continued to plan and strategize about their upcoming overthrow of Silfer until long into the night.

Plans Put in Motion

Eve and Teera caught up with several of their warriors and sent them with the new plans to all the quivers as they continued on to Broken Arrow City to finalize the plans to destroy their enemies.

Blane read the message and immediately, with his people having the furthest to travel, started sending them in groups of twelve to twenty. He sent out a few caravans every two to three days until more than several hundred troops were on route. The once massive town population was soon halved with so many leaving. Soon the town is left with only two hundred to thrive and prosper until the those that left returned.

Ryan, after receiving his message, formed a plan to move his quiver without suspicion from the red cloaks. He began commenting on the abundance of this year's harvest and, after paying for an early blessing for next year's harvest from the red cloak monks. Announced his plans to have a caravan leave for Arena City for the fall harvest festival, to sell the overage in order to gain coin to expand the town and monks' facilities. Many people paid and added their names to the lists of those that the monks had set up. The payments were for the warriors needed to protect such a large caravan. Ryan smiled as he watched the red cloaks organize and pay his troops to travel to Arena City.

Unknowingly they were giving their blessing to the trip that would bring the downfall to their allies and them, while more broken arrows added their names to the list daily.

Tom, his half-ling helpers, and other broken arrows had made friends over the last year with many of the wild inhabitants. The wild inhabitants all hated the red cloaks that had been trying to exterminate them for years. Most of the trouble always seemed to originate from the castle in Arena City. The Drucars, short and strong cave dwelling men though only four feet tall, could toss two hundred pound rocks thirty feet. The Treedins, fifteen-foot-tall men that resembled trees, had decided to take root in Tom's city for mutual protection, along with Centaurs, two headed men, and many others.

Upon hearing of the upcoming assault on the infamous Arena City, many more decided to join in the upcoming battle because not just humans, lycans and vampires had been sent to their demise in that cursed place. Tom thanked the Drucar for lending their mighty arms to the cause as well as the five score of troops of Treedins and the mosaic of races that had come to call Tom's town home. They all followed Tom's leadership and took his cause to be their own, for everyone had their own reasons to hate the red cloaks and those that helped them. They headed south towards Arena City immediately as they had a very long distance to cover to help in the upcoming war.

Plans Change

Dukut sent out his fastest scout with a sealed message to Silfer. *"We have captured Teera. She resides in our nicest dungeon cell. She is presently being trained to receive you properly. We await your arrival, Your Highness."*

Upon receiving the news, Keres and Silfer immediately set out with a silver cage in a covered wagon with their normal accompaniment of warriors to bring back Silfer's prize.

Dukut, after sending his correspondence to the King, had a drink of whiskey then headed to the dungeons to teach Teera more manners. He decided to stop first in the kitchen to grab a bite to eat before continuing to the dungeon. Humming around a bite of turkey leg, he came to the cell door laughing, *"My Queen, I am here to teach you more manners."* He nearly choked on the turkey before spitting it out, seeing the empty collar still chained to the floor. The turkey leg went flying across the room as he bellowed his rage. His men came running at his command.

His second in command arrived but did not even get to speak, as Dukut grabbed his head and smashed it into the steel door, leaving nothing but a chunky red smear. Dukut looked at the next man, announced, *"Congratulations on your promotion to second. Find her before the King shows up or you may find yourself in the arena or, worse yet, working for Keres."* The man visibly paled at his commander's words. Quickly he turned and rushed up the stairs, calling for the troops and trackers to assemble.

Dukut's troops headed out towards the valley after their search of the castle turned up nothing. No one knew Teera had many hours' head start in the opposite direction from the valley.

Meanwhile Dukut and a few of his more seasoned troops prepared the newest slaves and arena participants for the King's arrival. Dukut had a dozen men made permanent dungeon guards. With a stressful sigh Dukut sent for a few good scribes to help him with the castle's day to day business. He then mumbled to himself, *"Running a castle is not as easy as it looked. Maybe Keres could give me some witches to help with the day to day irritants of castle life as well as caring for my other needs."*

After days of travel, the king arrived and found that the queen had escaped yet again. It was suspected she was back in her valley with her brat. The scouts had found multiple tracks leading away from the castle and were following to make sure it wasn't the queen or her helpers.

Keres separated from the king and his rage to work her magic. Communing with the gaunts she inquired if Brenat was ready to hunt his wife and son down. The gaunts replied, *"No, he fought the change. Now he fights even harder, he will become food."*

Keres ordered, *"No, he will not be food, yet. Bring him to Arena City and put him in the slave pens. I will turn him myself for my needs. I have additional plans for Brenat, he will fight in the arena until he dies. Upon his death you can feast of the flesh from his bones."*

With a bow of acknowledgment to Keres's ghostly presence, the gaunt replied, *"Your bidding will be done, witch."*

Keres showed her sweetest smile as she approached king, *"I have arranged for Brenat to be delivered to the slave pens. I have a plan that will make the queen a little more agreeable when she's captured again."*

Silfer, with a sly smile pulled Keres in for a kiss, *"Wonderful you can share your idea with me on our return trip."*

Silfer directed a cold stare at Dukut and ordered, *"Find Teera and bring her immediately to me when you do. Search all the areas again. If she is harbored by anyone, bring them as well. You had better have that valley trapped so that not even a rabbit can get through until we break that spell."*

Leaving the queen's silver cage, Silfer and Keres headed back to his castle with his new slaves taken from Dukut's dungeon, in tow.

Brenat Tortured

During this time Brenat had awoke strapped to a table with a pain in his right hand and a red cloak interrogator gnawing on his pinky finger as if it was a piece of gum.

"Glad to see you're awake," the red cloak said as it removed its hood and the gaunt's visage was shown. *"We're going to have a talk,"* it said as it pulled a stool closer to Brenat's head. The gaunt smiled a bloody smile, *"Well let's get this out of the way. How you hid your royal lineage from us, we do not know, but we will find out. Had you died of your wounds or been a normal lycan, we would have eaten you outright. Now that we know you're a royal, you will join us as a gaunt. The change is slow and painful. The more you resist the more painful and longer the process, but you will change. As a gaunt there is just hunger."*

Another gaunt entered pulling in a young pregnant woman that both gaunts chained to a wall. The new gaunt told Brenat, *"When you turn, you will eat her starting with the unborn child."*

The young woman fainted in terror as both gaunts turned to leave. The first one looked at Brenat coldly and announced, *"The pain will start tomorrow for you. Oh, Brenat, you were very tasty."*

Brenat noticed his finger with the first knuckle missing. Shivering, he realized the gaunt was still chewing on his first knuckle.

The next day his finger was still healing, but was far from whole when six red cloaks arrived and woke the girl, trying to feed and water her. She shook her head in fear. The gaunt calmly told her, *"If you, or your baby, die before he is ready to eat you. We will eat you and bring your pregnant sister in to replace you. If your baby lives and is born before he is ready, your child will be freed to your family."*

She stared at him then asked, *"You would let my baby live?"*

The gaunt coldly replied, *"Yes, so you have hope for at least one of you. Would you eat and drink now?"* With fearful resignation, she ate, not for herself, but for her baby.

Once their future food had been fed, the gaunts turned their attention on Brenat. The smell of putrid flesh assaulted Brenat's nostrils as it was tossed upon the coals and cooked just like roast beast, the gaunts salivated over the smell. Each took a nail and sliced into Brenat's flesh and started lapping up the blood, their tongues felt like scalding silver where they lapped. Once the meat was seared, they stopped and pulled the hot flesh from the coals. They tossed the hot meat onto Brenat's naked body and they started eating, using Brenat as a plate. Occasionally he felt one of their teeth gouge into his flesh as they devoured whomever that rotting, putrid flesh had been before.

The girl, after eating and drinking closed her eyes, listened to Brenat's torment. She shivered in fear for herself and her baby, she hoped that the man on the table could last through the torment and avoid turning until her baby was born.

Days passed in pain for Brenat as his flesh was flayed as the gaunts peeled it from his body and eaten. Rarely did they detach all of it first, barely allowing him time to heal, so that his flesh was still pink and tender. They always offered to feed him some of the putrid flesh before they started again. His resistance slowly weakened as his body weakened and his hunger grew. The putrid flesh was the only nourishment he was offered other than water.

The young woman watched as more days passed with Brenat still refusing to eat, even as he started wasting away, without enough nourishment to heal anymore. They brought in some fresh meat and offered it to Brenat. From shear hunger and need to survive, he ate the meat offered with curiosity, wondering what or who he was eating. The torment stopped for the day as Brenat ate and healed. With the first bite he felt the hunger start growing within him along the coldness of death.

Brenat looked over at the girl, saw the fear in her eyes. With the gaunts gone he hoarsely told her, *"I will resist for you and your baby."* When she heard his words, she once again felt hope.

Days passed and the torment continued as it had been before. Every morning they offered him nourishment. When he resisted they feasted upon his flesh. Each evening, nourishment was again offered before they retired. If he ate in the morning, he got a daily reprieve from his torment. The routine continued until he started to eat daily yet still seemed to lose weight, becoming gaunt and ever hungrier. His eyes often went to the girl, clouded in pain and filled with pity. His will to resist gone, only hunger resided in his eyes.

Her hope faded and she too started wasting away, food and water no longer mattered, for she realized that the time when he would feast upon her and her unborn child was near. The gaunts freed his arms, and they all, Brenat included, feasted upon the putrid, maggot infested, uncooked meat while the girl watched. The toxic meat and steady supply of poison started to change Brenat's visage.

The gaunts smiled, *"In two days' time we will feed upon the woman's unborn child."* The woman watched Brenat as he licked his lips, and saw only hunger reflected back from his eyes. All her hope faded as she realized that he resisted no more and all hope was gone.

One gaunt told Brenat, *"When we finally find your son you can join in the feast we will make of him."*

Brenat nodded, his hunger filled eyes still upon the girl. The gaunts left and realization broke through his hunger. *"My son lives! They expect me to eat my son! Never would I turn on my son."*

The girl watched as Brenat's eyes changed from cold and hungry. They became filled with hope, determination, and rage. The longer he held out would offer more protection for his son. He started planning his freedom so he could kill the gaunts as well. The pain returned as the hunger abated, but he pushed it aside in his determination. The girl cried for Brenat as she watched him regain his will. She felt it was just another trick to torment him more.

The next day they brought the putrid flesh in for the feeding and released Brenat from his chains just as before, so he could join in the feast. Brenat grabbed the nearest gaunt and, without even shifting, bit out his throat, larynx and all. His lips closed tightly on the pumping, bloody neck and sucked it dry before the others could react. He started to eat the bloodless corpse, his belly distended from the gluttonous feeding, before the gaunts could save their compatriot. The gaunts then broke Brenat arms and fingers before chaining him back to the table. Brenat had eaten all life from the gaunt before they managed to finally re-shackle him. The gaunts looked at their dead member, then at Brenat. They then started to feast on the rest of their deceased member. Looking up at Brenat with a chunk of gaunt meat hanging from his maw one said, *"You did not leave us much to feast on, but there is enough for us to eat today and tomorrow."*

It chewed another bite before it continued, *"Brenat, you will have a single day's reprieve as we feast on our dead. The following days it will be your turn, until there is not enough left of you to heal.*

Your months for changing and torment are over, you will not survive the next month."

Brenat awaited more information, but his tormented mind made time slide by at a snail's pace. Still, it focused on the news that his son lived and that was more hope than he thought he would get out of this life. There was no mention of Teera, so she must be dead, as he could not contact her through their bond. He had always known that, sooner or later, his life would be forfeit at the whim of the gaunt controlled red cloaks.

The next morning four gaunts came down and release one limb at a time, shackling it to the other. Brenat smiled, *"I guess you are not taking any chances after I already took one of you out."*

They looked upon him with cold hungry eyes as one replied, *"True Brenat, but you are to be given a reprieve from filling our bellies. For the time being, you shall become the mistress's pet. Keres wants you in Arena City. Fear Brenat, for many have wished for ravishing hunger over Keres' s attentions. When you die you will be our food. For now, however, you go to Arena City to be Keres' s special project."*

Brenat noticed one of the gaunts shiver at the mention of Keres. While another looked upon him coldly and said, *"I would not wish to be you."*

Meanwhile Elsewhere On the Run

Sid and Elsie hugged the rocky mountain cliffs in order to leave as few tracks as possible while they traveled. They did all they could to hide from their pursuers while running and carrying their young grandchild.

Joel often cried in hunger, Elsie shifted one hand to a black, sleek paw and cut open her breast, feeding Joel of her hearts blood. Joel, while feeding, felt Elsie's gift and licked to heal the wound when he finished his fill, then licked her chin to show his thanks and love for his grandmother.

They steadily moved north, Sid and Elsie took turns carrying Joel. During one of their few rest periods, when Elsie felt weak, Sid shifted a single huge white paw, slashed open a wound on his chest for Joel to feed off him as Joel had Elsie.

After several days and nights of walking, they rubbed themselves down with pine, cedar, mint, or rose to cover their scent. Elsie shifted to her royal black panther then dragged the branches down the mountainside to hide the remnants in the forest. Sometimes she would drag them up the mountainside to be thrown in a chasm.

Elsie shifted to a wolf and followed the scent to catch up to Sid and Joel before she stopped and took a much needed rest.

Sid shifted to his royal white bear, pushed over trees to bring back eggs, honey combs, and other prey to feed themselves and Joel.

One evening, while they rested in wolf form to share warmth, Joel growled a low warning. Elsie and Sid looked towards Joel, saw his eyes change, as his body starting to shift. Elsie shifted to that of the great cat, pressed her body into the shadow of the shallow cave as she planned to ambush those that followed. Sid picked up Joel, interrupting his shift and continued on.

On the move, seconds turned into hours and the minutes seemed to drag on like days. Sid was always aware of a potential ambush and worried whether Elsie had survived the encounter.

What felt like hours later, Elsie overheard two red cloaks outside of the cave, as they conferred together, that the scent had moved northward. The red cloaks moved past the cave, following the scent. Elsie waited as the shadows grew longer and the sun set, before she slinked from the cave, ever observant, to follow the red cloak's scent. Within a few hours she caught up and observed them, testing the ground searching for more signs. The red cloaks tried to figure out if they went up the mountain or down, confused by their prey's trail. Elsie waited until one finally moved close to her shadowed form. The black panther's sleek and powerful form sprang with speed, all claws and teeth. Her front claws pierced the red cloak's neck, hooking under the jaw on both sides of his head. Her rear claws hooked on his rib cage as she leapt again, bringing his head with her, a fountain of blood cascaded as she leapt. The head in her jaws, she ran down the mountain into the forest and away from the path Sid took.

The second red cloak shifted into a gray fleshed, hairless wolf. Its mouth full of teeth that were more shark like than wolf, the eyes dull and lifeless. Its skin was taunt over the bones as if he was starving. He pursued the fleeing panther with mindless hunger.

Elsie ran with the speed and agility of the great cat, speeding away from the gaunt, adding distance, knowing the gaunts did not need to stop for rest. Elsie knew that when she would need a rest the gaunt would catch up. She headed to the scent of water and leapt in, dropped the head and shifted to her human form just as she hit the water. The head tumbled down stream by the current. She swam under water and against the current of the stream until her lungs screamed for air. Surfacing and gulping air into her aching lungs, Elsie tired from the exertion and pulled herself from the water on the opposite bank. She shifted into her wolf, raced up stream before crossing the river again in human form. Then she shifted into her panther form, pacing herself so as to catch up to Sid and Joel.

Elsie knew she had thrown the gaunt off their trail, even if for only a little while. She ran, enjoying the scent of the forest pine and a rabbit. *"Rabbit! A little hunt and tasty snack before resuming my long trek. MMMM so good,"* Elsie thought to Sid.

Sid laughed, and thought, *"See you soon, Love."*

Joel looked at Sid, *"Say "Hi" to Grandma for me."*

Sid looked at Joel, stunned, and just nodded and relayed the message to Elsie who nearly stumbled in shock and asked, *"How could he know we were talking?"*

"I don't know, Love, but I suspect our grandson is even more special then we all thought." replied Sid as they continued their steady pace northward.

By sunrise the next day, Elsie caught up to Sid, a sleeping Joel in his arms as he continued to press on. Elsie exhausted said, *"I must rest. I will watch Joel while you hunt."*

Sid shifted into his bear and headed off to hunt for some meat for them all. He knew they would need the extra nourishment as they continued on the run.

Meanwhile, Joel awoke hungry and Elsie fed him of herself

then watched, amazed, as his hair became sleek and deep blue black like hers while he licked the wound to heal it. His hunger was still there, but he instinctively knew she was too weak for him to feed fully. Elsie was shocked that he stopped before he could be full, as she knew he was still hungry. For someone so young, knowing when to stop feeding surprised her. She decided that she and Sid must talk more about their grandson. Yawning, she shifted to her panther and fell asleep exhausted.

Joel looked at his grandmother then shifted to that of a black panther cub and hid, snuggling in her shadow, quietly waiting his grandfather's returned. Sid arrived back carrying a mountain goat, its white coat almost hidden in Sid's white fur.

Looking around, he nudged Elsie, *"Elsie, wake up. Where's Joel?"*

"He was here when I fell asleep he can't be far," she sleepily replied.

Frantically they looked around, searching for Joel in a panic as they realized he was gone his scent lost. Just before they bounded off to look for him more, Joel appeared out of the shadows as a panther cub carrying a large rat. In mid stride he shifted back into a human, *"You're awake, grandma, I found you a snack. Look,"* Joel said happily as he gave his grandmother a hug and kiss on her cheek, then handed her the small snack he had caught her.

Elsie and Sid, startled, looked at Joel amazed at the new discovery. They looked at each other before Sid had an idea and pulled the heart of the goat. Turning to Joel he said, *"Let's play a game. For every form you turn into, we will give you a slice of this juicy heart and you will be able to eat it first."*

Joel's excitement shone in his eyes at the game his grandfather wanted to play, he went from child to black wolf pup to white tiger cub. Then he changed into a white bear cub, then into to black panther kitten. From the panther, he turned into a fiery red hell hound pup and then back to his child form. He retained one form only long enough to spin in a circle. Before Sid and Elsie could gasp in surprise, Joel was in a new form, shifting faster than either Sid, Elsie, or even Brenat had ever been able to.

Joel smiled at his grandparents and asked, *"Was that good?"*

Without a word Sid, smiled proudly and Elsie hugged Joel, telling him how wonderful he was. Sid sliced the heart into ten pieces, giving Joel six. Sid and Elsie were silent as they waited for the future alpha to eat first before they divided up the rest of the goat and feasted until they were all so full that they laid resting with swollen bellies.

Later as Joel slept, Sid and Elsie laid together and discussed their grandson's powers and abilities. *"Sid, do you remember the ancient legend? Do you think he may be the one it told of?"*

Sid pulled Elsie closer, *"Yes, I remember and yes he is, which makes him more important and special than just the precious miracle we thought he was for our family. In truth, he is the long sought miracle for our world. Our job has just become even more important and more dangerous than either of us thought."*

Weeks later they were only a little ahead of their pursuers. Sid continued guarding their back trail, bringing in the occasional food for them. Meanwhile, Elsie continued to feed Joel more of her blood on the ran north, with the gaunts slowly closing in.

Elsie looked at Sid, *"You know they won't stop. You could teach Joel to survive the north land. I could make them chase me to my jungle home in the south. We will meet again when he is ready for his fight."*

Sid nodded, knew Elsie was right, but unable to speak because of the goodbye that he knew was coming. With a loving embrace and tears in their eyes, Elsie and Sid let go of each other reluctantly. Elsie hugged Joel and tickled him with her body, arms, and face.

Elsie stopped one last time before bounding off ten feet away. She turned, shifting to human form. Elsie called, *"Joel please came give grandma one last hug."*

Joel rushed to Elsie and jumped into her arms, giving her a big hug and kissing away the tears on her cheeks, *"I love you grandma."*

She told him *"I love you, too."* She then tossed Joel back to Sid. Elsie looked at the tracks that Joel left in the snow alongside her own, shifted, and pranced off, her paws leaving deep imprints in the fresh snow. With a goodbye, she became a wolf bounded down the mountain and into the forest, she then turned southeasterly. Sid, with tears in his eyes but determination on his face, looked after her thinking, *"Goodbye. Until we meet again."*

Sid caught Joel and settled him on his shoulders, they continued their northward trek. Sid told Joel stories of his northern home where the sun wouldn't be seen for months. It was a place where the spirits and their many colors danced from the heavens to the snow awaiting their turn to be reborn.

Many hours later the gaunt came to the parting. Taking his medallion, he sliced his arm and let the blood ran into the symbols he drew in the snow. After a short chant, the ghostly visage of his master the chamberlain appeared. The gaunt relayed his findings, *"Master they separated. The male ran north and the bitch ran southeast the boy's tracks announce that he traveled with the bitch."*

Eon stared at his tracker before speaking, *"Wait where you are for me and our three brother gaunts to join you."* The gaunt sat down to build a fire, rest, eat, and waited.

The chamberlain left his second in charge during his absence as Eon with three gaunts climbed on the back of a griffin to fly to where the blood mark called him. Eon sent the griffin back with new orders for his second, *"Take four gaunts, follow then kill the bitch but take the brat alive to Cathedral City. There you can start the turning process. I will complete the ceremony personally upon my return."* Eon picked up the scent of the male, recognized it from his past, He also caught a hint of the boy and started tracking him northward. *"Sid may have a day's head start but I will catch him at world's end."*

Elsie stopped prancing when she got deep into the trees where the snow had lessened. Looking back at her tracks, she felt satisfied that they were deep enough to make the gaunts believe that she carried Joel on her back. She then rubbed hers and Joel's scent on a nearby pine tree with a smile. *"Now when Joel's scent lessens they will think I'm just concealing it better."* Picking up her pace, she started adding miles between her and the gaunts she knew would be following.

Sid talked on while he walked and Joel soon was deeply engrossed in the stories his grandpa told him. He told of how the northern wind talked with the whispers of the spirits, if you learned to calm the noise of your own beating heart you could hear what they had to say. There were stories about how the lights would show you the way around the hidden crevices if you watched with patience and were willing to learn. He spoke of how after you showed the wind you were strong and worthy enough to be allowed to share the living wind, that with a little thought you could pull the living wind and snow around you, insulating you from its cold. It could hide you from your enemies' sight and smell. Into the night they walked, the coldness of the wind surrounded them but did not touch them as Sid demonstrated the power of the wind and continued his stories.

The moonless night was still bright as Sid showed Joel the mighty Ursa leading her cub Ursa Minor. He told him, *"The heavenly milk that the cub fed on is made up of all the animals and life. They all appear in the milk of the heavens and the mighty Ursa taught her cub that every animal fed them but they protect and guard their little brothers and sisters. When our time comes we give our essence back to them."*

Joel, riding on Sid's shoulders, rested his head on his Sid's and asked, *"Grandpa, are Momma, Daddy, Gapa James, Gama Rizalle, Holy and Kwap with Ursa now?"*

Sid's eyes filled with tears as he thought about those they had lost and he replied, *"Yes Joel, they are watching over us with the mighty Ursa."*

Joel, in a small voice asked, *"Grandpa will you and Grandma join Ursa soon too?"*

Sid rubbed Joel's legs and said, *"One day we will join the spirits, but not for a long while. Even then we will always be with you, watching over and guiding you. You must continue on, grow strong, learn to fight, and lead."*

Joel hugged and kissed his grandpa cheek, *"I will grandpa I will."*

The further north they traveled the stars seem to shine just a bit brighter as they danced around Ursa, showing their respect. From the fish to the mighty whale, from the ant to the dragon, the stars seemed to flicker brightly then faintly as if saying *"Hi"* to Joel when Sid pointed out who was who among the night sky.

Finally, Joel fell asleep while Sid told the story of how man and beast were fused together by God to fend off the black void that wanted to destroy all the light and rebirth. Day followed night and night follow day while Sid told tales and taught Joel of magic. They rested and ate little, for the stars seemed to nourish their bodies and minds.

The trees got smaller until they disappeared completely and all that was around them was snow. The sun had not been seen in how long Joel could not remember. Sid kept him warm, as the dancing lights kept them entertained and magic kept them full. Sid's voice filled Joel's mind, while it kissed his ears with knowledge. Suddenly Joel, listening to the wind, started to growl and shift. Sid whispered into his ear and Joel fell into an enchanted sleep. Sid knew his former brother grew near and formed a safe burrow made of snow to hide Joel.

Sid, with a kiss on the cheek goodbye, whispered, *"Joel grow big and strong. When you are ready, your fights will find you. You will be a great leader one day and bring about a new way of life."* The wind started blowing hard and strong, ice crystals flew while Sid trekked on. Joel became buried under three feet of snow, safely hidden inside the snowy den where he slept.

Between two mountainous peaks of snow a veil of light danced between them from the heavens to the ground, the colors shifted across the rainbow as if rushing to find their seat for the nearing show. Sid shifted to his big white bear to sit and wait, his fur slightly ruffled. The living wind blew hard, snow and ice flew, moving like shards of glass trying to shred everything in its path. Night upon night the wind blew while Sid waited until out of the darkness and snow came a large gaunt, hairless bear wearing a red cloak made of dyed lycan flesh. The wind died, the snow and ice fell out of the air as all calmed. Both bears shifted to men of the same size and stature. Their eyes were the same crystal blue, their strong features were almost identical except that one was gaunt, hungry, and scowling while the other was alive, patient, and smiling.

The gaunt one snarled, *"What did you do with my little snack? After I kill you do I have to search every snow bank in this desolate cursed cold land?"*

Sid laughed, *"Eon, little brother, you know as well as I that only the most hearty and lucky could survive up here. The young could never survive up here without constant help. So you traveled all this way for naught."*

Eon snarled, *"Not for naught, for I will tear you apart until you are too weak to heal, then slowly this land you love will freeze you solid.*

The irony will be that your death will be caused by the land you love so much. Those spirits behind you can watch as I trap your soul in your frozen, broken, torn corpse to stop it from ever joining them."

They both shifted to their bears the wind picked up, circling them and carrying with it ice that glittered with the light of the stars. They circled, stalking one another; white fur and gray skin speckled with moving dots of light from the reflections of the shards of ice spinning around them.

Eon growled, his voice like gravel shaken around in pottery, *"After I finish with you I will go and get the boy. I will then eat him in a slow, glorious feast while I make your bitch watch before I have her service me and my minions. She will watch us eat every child she bares, before she is forced to service us again. When all hope has faded from her eyes we will eat her as well."*

Sid stepped forward with a paw swiping at Eon's face as he growled, *"You, nor your kind will ever catch my mate or my grandson, let alone kill them."*

Eon's own paw easily blocked the swipe, the impact sounded like the clash of two boulders crashing down a mountainside. Sid planted an upper cut that had Eon's head snapping back as a piece of his tongue fell bloodily to the once pristine white snow. Spitting blood at Sid, Eon barreled into him, pushing him to the edge of the swirling snow where the glittering deadly ice flayed Sid's back, adding a red streak to the circling snow around them. Sid spun to the center, away from the deadly ring of swirling ice. The snow packed and drops of blood slowly turned the ring of white to red, as blow after blow each brother added even more blood in their death match for survival.

Snarls and growls were heard as their bodies clashed against one another repeatedly like a mountain shaking free its boulders to crash in crevasses far below. Their claws struck against one another creating a flash of light and the clash of thunder. On and on they fought. Sid slowly weakened for he had not eaten in days and he had kept Joel fed of himself. Eon was stronger, having left a trail of half-eaten corpses tainted and poisoned so that any creature that partook of the leftovers, rotted from the inside out to became a ghoulish form of their original self. The new creatures would have a constant need to eat to replenish their bodies from the rot that would leave them nothing more than bones in a matter of months.

Like an unlucky wolverine, that now killed and ate nonstop just to keep the hole in its side from growing any bigger where its own stomach had eaten a hole through its body. The toxic magic that killed the wolverine, fed and kept Eon's strength up. After days of battling the wolverine was longing for death with only its front half not consumed by the magic. It dragged its intestines through the dirt in search of food even as it continued to rot away.

Sid swiped Eon's throat, blood gushed from the mortal wound, yet the wound healed instantly with his strength renewed. Sid just watched, astonished by the flash of unknown magic.

At that moment, many miles south, a fearful young woman gave birth under the eyes of a hungry gaunt. She watched as the gaunt reached for her newborn baby, just as the gaunt's own stomach, digested the gaunt in a matter of seconds leaving nothing but a mushy mess of stomach acid, bones, and a stink of evil magic. Around the world people watch as gaunts suddenly turned to mush, eaten as if by magic.

Every time Sid struck a blow, gouged or shredded flesh and spilled enough blood to mortally wound Eon, he seemed to heal rapidly under a flash glow of magic. Sid's claws opened up Eon's stomach, spilling his intestine while his other swipe tore out Eon's throat again. Yet before Eon fell he healed again. He came back up slashing and gouging with no finesse or skill just a mindless need for destruction. Eon's mind occasionally broke the haze of hate and wanton destruction of his brother, to remind himself to block some of the time.

Sid continued to be worn down as time and again he swiped a killing blew onto Eon, yet Eon always recuperated. Sid battled on knowing that the more damage he did the weaker Eon's protective magic became. Joel would have to gain strength to defeat even a weaken Eon when the time was right. Sid's arms and legs grew heavy with fatigue and the circle of snow was packed down so they battled in a three-foot depression from where they started their fight. A tired and worn Sid slipped allowing Eon to grab his arm and bite off Sid's paw then spit it to the far side of the ring. Sid's essence of love, honor, and compassion burned Eon's tongue like acid. Sid again took another swipe, landing a killing blow, disemboweling Eon and causing another gaunt from across the continent to be turned to mush as the magic swallowed it to heal Eon yet again.

Sid's body mass shrank as the bear's fat was consumed to regenerate the lost paw. Sid, exhausted beyond endurance, stopped moving to trade blow for blow. Eon smiled as he was healing because Sid could not. Sid in exhaustion fell to his knees, the wind stopped and the ice fell. Looking up from the three-foot depression, Eon looked upon the dancing lights and laughed, *"When I am finished, even you will be extinguished for no more souls will come to you, sharing of their light and no more babies will be born for you to fill to became reborn."*

Eon looked upon his brother and said with a snarl, *"You have damaged me much more then you know or will ever be able to tell and now you will suffer greatly before you die."*

Eon started ripping Sid apart, tossing a paw over here, then another paw there, as he listened to Sid scream. Sid's body shifted several times, trying to heal the damage so that a human hand appeared at one side of the ring, a wolf paw at the other, and a bear paw in yet another spot. Sid screamed as he was slowly dismembered as Eon continued tossing his severed parts;

a forearm flew here, a calf there, a shoulder tossed over to one side. Eon pulled out Sid's intestines, using them to make a mystic symbol that surrounded Sid's dying body. Sid died slowly as Eon chanted, but the agony remained.

Finishing his chant, Eon laughed at his brother, *"Your soul is now trapped in your heart so that when it freezes solid your soul will fade. You will never join with those cursed lights you favor so much. When I catch up with the child I will turn him and together we will eat until no more life exists. I will also get him to eat his father just as I did our father."*

Eon wrapped himself once more with his cloak, climbed from the three foot, bloody depression that was surrounded by pure white, then turned his back upon the lights as he did a very long, long, long time ago. He headed south to find the bitch that had so foolishly loved his brother, as he dreamed of the feast he and the brat would enjoy.

Alone

oel awoke after the magic storm abated. He dug eventually digging himself from the snowy den. Smelling the air, he growled and shifted, the scent of distant evil making Joel salivate. His eyes burned with a hidden fire. He stopped and listened as faint gentle breeze blew, guiding him to the valley of light where he saw a bloody mess three feet below him with a barely recognizable human hand and wolf paw, where something no longer distinguishable moaned.

Joel climbed down, going to the familiar smell that is so permeated by an evil, that recognition was near impossible as it was trying to distinguish what body part was what. Joel approached and noticed an eyeball still attached to something that moved to looked upon him. A clawed hand attached to an arm that was more bone then flesh, tried to move. Joel knelt next to the bloody remains of his grandfather and helped the arm move to reach into what was left of its chest where it pulled out it's still beating heart, then placed it in Joel's hand. With that the body died but the heart still beat as it rested in Joel's hand. Joel looked at the dancing lights and stars. He was confused, alone, and hungry. Starting to feel the chill, Joel sat focusing on the heart beat that was not his own as the gentle wind whispered, *"Eat and stay strong."*

Joel lifted the beating heart to his lips, tentatively took a bite, as he did he felt Sid's essence fill his mouth. Tears filled his eyes as he felt Sid's memory of the first time he looked upon a beautiful black panther that shifted into the most beautiful woman that Sid had ever seen. Joel shared in a sample of the love he felt toward her and the joy they felt when they rescued the girl and baby boy to raise as their children. He felt how much Sid enjoyed sharing the magic of his homeland with Joel as they traveled into the snowy lands and, finally the battle between both brothers.

Joel fed upon Sid's heart feeling Sid's desire to nourish Joel with the last of his life. Joel was able to watch his grandpa's soul join with those of the rest of his family in the dancing lights. Joel waved good bye to the ghostly image before he headed south. He knew not what awaited, he only knew that if he found half of Sid's happiness he would be truly blessed.

With no real guide, Joel shifted to a white bear, growling when he picked up the evil scent and started to follow it. The wind picked up, pushing Joel. Every time he stepped forward, it caused him to slide back, the snow and ice stung as it slapped at his face. The cold northern wind sucked at his heat while the heart that resided in his belly warmed him. Joel fought on as the wind blew harder until Joel had to use his claws to anchor his steps in the ice beneath the snow. Joel pushed on until he began to think, *"Maybe I should burrow into the snow until the wind forgets about me."* Sid's whisper came to him hidden among the howl of the wind that tried to hold him back. *"Fight on, walk on, make the wind give up before you. Tame the wind and make it yours."*

With that feeling Joel steeled his determination against the living wind. The wind blew against him for nights as there were no days, just endless nights. Suddenly the wind tired and shifted, first one way then the other. It pulled at his fur then pushed, striving to blind him with snow. When he lifted his head to smell a path the wind filled his nostrils with snow causing Joel to sneeze in order to clear them. The wind reached under him, trying to pick his claws from the ice below then pounded him from the top trying to make him cringe and hide under the snow. The wind swirls around him trying to dump him ass over face, then to his right and his left, then back to his face. With every step he still pushed on slowly but undeterred.

As Joel stepped one paw at a time, he suddenly felt nothing in front of him just as the wind reversed, trying to push into the crevice in front of him. Anchored and unmoving, he stepped right following the edge of the crevice with the wind pushing him and working to defeat or end him.

Joel stopped to roar a challenge as he knew the wind would blow but it would never win. Again he moved until he almost pranced as he defied the wind and its goal; he walked between two mounds of snow that towered over him. Suddenly, the wind stopped causing Joel to hesitate. In the calm he climbed to the top of one of the snow towers and howled at the wind, *"Friend where have you gone, I'm not done playing yet."* With that the wind slowed to a gentle breeze kissing and tickling at his ears, its wrath and fight blown out. The light on the horizon glinted off of the snow as the sun slowly rose.

Soon there was light all the time, the sun never set, it just got higher in the sky as it circled him. The snow was soft under his paws and at the smell of a rabbit nearby Joel crouched, waiting, nose and ears twitching as he quietly listened and watched the hare. The hare sensed no danger and went back to digging in the snow for some lichen. Joel pounced, his jaws closed upon the rabbit crushing its skull in his teeth, and then it fed his hungry belly. Looking up he saw the soul heading north to join its fellow lights. Joel honored his brother hare with a howl of thanks for feeding him this day and left a little on an open patch of ground that he cleared the snow away, so the hare's sacrifice may feed more than just him. Every day that Joel ate he howled his thanks and left a little for another. Even if his meal was but a mouse, he left some for another.

His ears picked up the sound of something hidden under a snowy mound and Joel pounced, crashing through the mound in a puff of snow. Backing out, he pulled a seal from the mound, his jaws clamped on the seal's neck, breaking its spine and ending any suffering. The blood coated his lips as he tasted the essence of the life that would nourish his. He sensed every scar the old seal acquired as it survived again and again, the glorious fish that it had eaten, the many pups it had sired, and the full life it had led. All flooded into Joel's mind as he once again howled his thanks as was finally able to eat his fill while he still left some for others.

He looked back at the mother Snow fox that had followed him for a long time. She came forward with her kits when Joel called to them and shared in the feast. Joel rested as the mother fox cleaned his face of excess blubber and blood while the kits ran over him. Standing, he nodded his goodbye to the fox and her kits as they headed back to their den. With a little of the meat left, Joel reached out and his mind touched that of the snow owl not far away. He called it to a feast before he continued traveled south.

He traveled day after endless day, for night never seemed to come this way, before he saw small trees on the horizon. The snow begun melting and flowers started blooming in green grass that showed between snowbanks. With the snow nearly gone the big paws of the bear were no longer needed to keep him from sinking in the snow and his white coat was beginning to warn his food he was close before he could get to it. He shifted to a wolf the size of the large bear cub, but with a pup's soft fur. He moved into the trees. He was now far enough south that the days were broken up with nights.

Evil Stalks the Land

Eon traveled south grumbling about losing many good pets and minions in his battle with his brother. He shrugged, *"Oh well there were always more filled with a gluttonous hunger for power, greed, lust, and hate that he could convert to fill the vacancies that the battle had created. There were so many with malice want that would gladly join his fold of gaunts to get what they wanted."*

Coming to a small farm, his red cloak gave him his right to join the family for an evening meal. The family were too afraid to turn a red cloak away after remembering the rumor that the last farmer to have done that had his eyes pulled from his corpse before he had even stopped breathing.

The family slew their pregnant sow at Eon's order and cooked it up, the embryos separate from the sow, just for his meal as ordered. Sitting down, they prayed as was their habit while Eon scarfed down the embryos. He talked to the father, *"I will offer you ten pieces of gold for the use of your wife for the night."*

Even though it was more gold then either parent had seen in their life time, the father answered with a polite, *"No."*

Eon said, *"I will make you the same offer for your oldest girl."*

The father, angry and afraid, again replied, *"No."*

Eon looked at the mother, *"You would starve rather than give me one of your children, even your least favorite? Your sow is dead and there will be no piglets. You could even offer yourself for the gold that would feed and care for your family for years?"* The mother declined the offer three times.

With a wave of his hand sugary treats appeared upon the table and he left gold beside the pig. *"We all know who the favorite child is and with one less mouth to feed it would be much easier on the family. Which one of you two sisters would come with me so your family could survive the harsh winters."*

Both girls hugged one another and answered in union with a polite, *"No, neither of us will go with you."* As a family they had survived hard times and would do so again.

Though the laws forbade kicking a priest out of their home, the father did just that. Eon left under the watchful eye of the father. As he left, the strength of the hearth fire where the love and power of the good family no longer bound him, he called upon his power and sent in a poison that he had pulled from the embryos that he regurgitated. Smiling as their prayers went unanswered for his evil killed them in mid prayer. He waited, unable to enter until the hearth fire went out completely, then entered to trap the souls of the family in the meat. He left the gold on the table, for he knew sooner or later someone with a hunger, would come along ignoring the warning to steal the gold or would devour the meat, then he could have pulled that one to him with his callus greed, and start corrupting them.

With his keen sense of smell Joel smelled a faint evil and hot coals of a burnt out fire. As he followed the scent on the breeze he came to a farm house quiet and still. Smelling something wrong, he hid in the bushes in the shadow of a great tree, watching the farm. Joel stilled the beating of his heart so he could hear the whispers on the slight breeze that barely moved a single leaf in front of him. Slowly, his heart traveled from a strong steady beat to that of a slow thump with a long, long pause, then a thump followed by even a longer pause. Between beats he listened as the wind whispered that evil had been there and left a great wrong. Nature cried at the atrocity trapped inside and of how the dead were unable to rest or move on.

Joel crept to the house and noticed that, even the insects had moved from the building, skirting it by a foot. Cautiously he nudged the door that was left slightly ajar and listened to the creak as it pushed open. The sound and smell of the house was like that of a crypt. Entering he shifted so a boy appeared where the wolf was a minute before. He walked to the table where a mother, a father, and two children sat as if praying at their evening meal in front of empty plates. All were lifeless and there was meat resembling a pig sat on a platter in the middle of the table. It smelled like it had just been freshly pulled from the oven, yet stank of an evil touch. On the table also sat a pouch of gold and sweets that also stank of evil.

Joel grabbed a knife, cutting the meat open, the souls of the family burst free, but remained tethered to the meat. The souls cried about their capture and tugged for their freedom at the tethers binding them to the meat, like men pulling at their shackles in a dungeon. The souls noticed Joel watching them and started all jabbering at once. Joel could see them but was not able to understand them, yet he could feel their torment at being trapped.

He washed the bodies and faces of the family with fresh water and wrapped them in blankets found in the bed rooms. The spirits calmed watching him cut the pig into four pieces and placing each piece that trapped a soul onto the corresponding body it came from.

With care he placed wood from the wood pile around the mother, father, and children to make a pyre. He blew on the coals and fed it some kindling until a good hearth fire ignited. Joel sat and cooed to the spirits, not knowing two large wolves watched from a distance at the strange human talking to the tainted corpses. When the sun set Joel looked up to the starry night and spoke aloud, *"Accept them home so they may have more in the next life."*

Walking into the house, he grabbed a well burning log and lit the remaining beds on fire, then lit the pyre as he saw the spirits lay upon their bodies restful as they awaited their peaceful rest. Joel stepped out of the house, watched as the flames engulfed it, then sat watching as the evil burned away. All night Joel sat and watched their departure, while the two wolfs sat watching Joel as guardians.

With the morning light Joel shifted to his wolf and the two wolves, a male and female, came to him, each nuzzling the pup whose size rivaled that of their alpha. Joel had never been so exhausted, the pair laid with Joel until he was rested. The two pack guardians took Joel to their den, introducing him to the alpha and den mother. The wolves knew he fixed a wrong in their territory and accepted Joel into their pack. The mother cleaned him while he rested. Even the other pups decided to stop playing to rest against him, sharing their warmth and heartbeats with him.

✾ ✾ ✾ ✾ ✾ ✾ ✾ ✾ ✾ ✾

Eon stopped traveling as he felt his spell on the family of farmers was suddenly just gone as if someone or something just washed it clean. Filled with rage he spent days retracing his steps only to find the farm house had been burnt to the ground. Eon searched for days looking for clues as to who destroyed his spell and which way they went. He was angry that all the clues were washed away by the recent cleansing rains. With a growl he resumed his hunt for that bitch and the boy she protects.

❂ ❂ ❂ ❂ ❂ ❂ ❂ ❂ ❂ ❂ ❂

Elsie on the run through the forests, headed south moving slowly through the day. She rested at noon high in the trees. She always stayed in the shadows at night picking up the pace. One day, resting in an inn, having a meal, and just being human for a change, her breath caught in her throat as she felt her bond with Sid break and a great emptiness was suddenly inside her followed by a great sadness as Sid died. Not knowing what had happened to Joel, she suspected that he was either on his own or dead. With the deep sadness of the loss of her bonded mate came an even greater anger, Elsie decided to become the hunter instead of the hunted.

She began leaving false trails and killing those that hunted her. Elsie's thoughts roamed. *If Joel is dead I will exact my revenge for my son, my husband, and my grandson. If Joel lives he will need me to kill as many of the red cloaks as I can, which would have them putting more effort into hunting me then him.*

She started tracking red cloaked monks often for days waiting for her chance, always knowing that the gaunts followed her. As the panther she was able to hide when needed. She killed using speed, stealth, and well planned ambushes. As a result of her cunning and skills, she managed to bypass many traps that were set for her. The gaunts were forced several times to back track when hunting her, and more than once came across one of their red cloak brothers killed with their insides ripped out, the heart and liver missing.

Her passage was also sometimes marked by the occasional lone red cloak that she had ambushed, shredding its back and ripping its head off leaving the head upon a stick stuck in the ground, the corpse nearby. Soon the red cloaks started traveling in larger groups of four or more with at least one seasoned warrior.

The red cloaks started a rumor that was whispered at night around the fires, that she was a vengeful spirit that ripped off the heads of all travelers. It was said that if you walked alone in the trees, the ghost would hunt you down, tear off your head, then eat your brains and heart before it stole your soul. Even though the truth was that it was only red cloaks and their spies that she killed.

She always took the red cloak's pouches of money that they carried, then she stopped in a town to buy the odd item here and there. She also payed generously for rumors and something for the children of which ever town she was in. When she found a priest, monk, or red cloaked warrior sleeping indoors or out, they were found the next morning disemboweled and decapitated in the street. She did all of that while running from the gaunts that hunted her. As time went on the rumor of a black shadowed woman who killed those that traveled alone by decapitating them soon became a legend of a shadow woman that ate the brains, hearts and souls of lone travelers, disobedient children, and unfaithful husbands.

In an inn Elsie relaxed knowing she is about two days ahead of the gaunts. She sat eating as she listened to the story being told of the shadow woman stealing children around the age of three. A bounty of one gold piece was offered for confirmed sightings of her so the priests could capture her to save the towns and their children from her. Her eyes narrowed as she watched a red cloak warrior drink heavily instead of guarding the priest as he should have been. She admired the priest for his story telling about how malicious she was to the listening town folk, who were trembling in fear of such a vicious woman. Elsie sat and listened while she decided whether she would kill one or both of the red cloaks tonight.

Elsie's eyes fill up with tears as she felt the emptiness of Sid's absence and the death of all of her family. She smiled at the rumors that the red cloaks were still hunting for Joel and her. So Joel must be alive, which means as long as she kept hunting there was hope. With hope she would continue to hunt the red cloaks while they hunted her. She knew she was saving the towns and the world one red cloak at a time, whether they be gaunt, priest, monk, or warrior. She took extra pride in her wins when a child apprentice threw away his or her red cloak and started the long trek home. Suddenly her mind came back to the present as she again watched the priest and drunk warrior.

❈ ❈ ❈ ❈ ❈ ❈ ❈ ❈ ❈ ❈ ❈

Joel awoke when his new brothers and sister started to nurse. With an open teat close to him, Joel nursed as well, but straight wolf milk was a light meal for him. Its essence told him of nurse mother's happiness and sadness that of the six pups, only three survived the hunters that had killed half the pack and three pups before they could be moved to another den. Mother wolf growled at him, kicked him off the teat, for he was too big and must leave the milk for his adopted siblings.

Joel, making himself useful, hunted down a few rabbits, he ate one for his meal, then brought back the other two to mother and the pups. The alpha gave him a warning growl for not giving him first choice, but that was it for a reprimand.

Joel decided it was best to follow the guardians and learn so that he made no more mistakes. Joel impressed his guardians with his stealth and patience, for while his size was confusingly large, his scent said he was a pup. Joel followed them to learn, so they tested his endurance to find out if he could keep up, which Joel did easily.

Joel watched as the pack found a herd of deer and

surrounded them and chased them closer to the den. They cut the herd several times and ran and ran. When one wolf got tired or the deer started to outpace a pack member, another one leapt into the chase to take over. Joel watched them do this for miles again and again, forcing the deer to run and never allowing them to stop running. The pack so focused on running the deer to exhaustion did not know that Joel watched from in front of a large buck's path hidden in between rocks among some tall grass.

Joel, seeing his chance to help his pack, sent a silent thanks to the heavens for the upcoming meal. As he leapt out the buck reared out of surprise with Joel's teeth clamped upon it throat. The strong buck kicked out, catching one of Joel's legs and breaking it. Through the pain Joel hung on tasting the buck's life as it flowed past his tongue, accepting the pain in exchange for the pack's feast and thanking his brother for his nourishment.

While the pack was slow to react, for that was not their target, they noticed Joel with the buck. The pack quickly joined in, taking it down under the combined mass. The first wolf barreled into it clamping his teeth down on flesh tearing open another bloody wound followed by another. Their teeth tore out the hamstring; even as the deer fell more wolves clamped on. When the deer finally fell Joel got his three good legs under him he and tore out the deer's throat to end its suffering before limping away to let the pack eat while the deer's life washed through Joel with its blood. With a great feast so near the den, the whole pack came to the kill instead of it being carried it back to the den.

Joel laid licking at his broken leg while all the wolves howl their praise of Joel's first kill, before any realized he was seriously wounded. Mother wolf arrived and knew right away that he was injured. She gently licked his leg then cleaned his muzzle as she became sad thinking she would lose yet another pup. All ate well with the mother bringing him some meat so he did not need to walk to the kill. As the pack went back to the den, for the pups were too small to stay in the open for long, Joel stayed where he was. The two guardians stayed with him through the night so he would not be alone when he died. Through the night Joel shifted through several forms to encourage the healing of the leg all the while under the watchful eyes of the pack guardians.

Joel was fully healed the next morning, the guardians now knew he was not a regular wolf and took him to the alpha. He was praised well as a pack member, but the alpha knew that this was not his life and sent him under the watchful eyes of the pack guardians to the edge of their territory where a village of man resided in the distance. There, the two wolves nuzzled him in farewell, hating to see him go but knew he must.

Joel smelled the air and was compelled to be closer to the people. He felt sadness at being sent away but realized that the alpha was as wise as he was strong. Joel proceeded to the village, hearing the wolves howl a farewell and a welcome to come home after he had learned and had enough of men.

Joel Captured

Nearing town the scent of evil was strong and Joel snuck forward watching. He calmed his heart while he searched his mind for what he saw and it came to him that soldiers were killing the old. He shifted to a boy about the age of eight. His anger was apparent as he walked up to a lycan, pulled out his dagger, and plunged it into the murdering soldier's leg. Calmly, with seething anger at the soldier he had just stabbed, Joel said, *"If they were not food there was no need to kill them."*

The soldier was furious that a boy would dare attack him. He growled and tried to back hand Joel. Joel more angry than smart, dodged the back hand, pulled out the dagger, and plunged into the soldier's leg again.

The other warriors laughed at the soldier because a naked boy was beating him. Then, out of nowhere, a big silver studded club smacked Joel in the side of the head and all went black.

Joel woke up in a cage filled with men and boys. The cage that followed was filled with women and girls. A few in the cage with Joel scowled and cursed at him, *"If it was not for you, boy, most of the town would have been left but now we're all to go to the arena and slave pens."* Joel had a pounding headache and took a moment to realize the men in the cage were talking about and to him with open hostility.

The caravan stopped and a guard with a limp snarled as

he stuck his face against the bars, *"You alive boy?"*

Before he could say anything else, he smelled the stink of evil which was strong on the soldier's breath. It caused Joel to stick his fingers up the soldier's nose while head butting him through the bars. The head butting added to Joel's headache and the soldier fell back with a broken nose. The soldier got up to the laughter of his friends and drew his sword only to be stopped by his commander, *"He has more value in the arena. You're lucky he did not grab your sword while your nose was that close and run you through. Stay away from the cages, Haroc, before I let the boy beat you and put you in the cage."* Joel was oblivious to the danger he was in from both in and out of the cage. He glowered at the one they called, Haroc.

The commander sensed that the boy had enough spirit to end up dead in the cages for the men thought the boy would get them killed before they arrived, so he ordered the boy to be pulled out and shackled behind the last cage. The commander looked at Joel and said, *"Maybe walking would pull some of that vinegar from your spirit and give you some humility."* Shackled and pulled behind the wagons as the caravan continued, Joel's eyes were drawn to an older red haired woman whose eyes met and held Joel's.

During the trip Haroc was in charge of giving water to the slaves and he made sure every slave got a ladle full until it was Joel's turn. He spilled his ladle on the ground, stating, *"One ladle a person. If you spill it that is your problem."* Joel went thirsty the first day because every time Haroc had to deliver water, he dumped Joel's out and smiled. Joel could feel Haroc's evil and went to say something, but the red haired woman, put her finger to her lips to shush him. Joel stifled his growl and followed her direction that night as it rained and the caravan stopped for the night. Joel lifted his face to the rain and enjoyed the drops that fell from the canopy to his dry lips.

Haroc, during the rest stops took to going to the back of caravan, every time Joel went to sit down Haroc brought out his whip and lashed Joel's back. If Joel looked like he is about to fall asleep while standing up his back was laid open again. The only one that even seemed to notice was the red haired woman who Joel could see flinch every time he yelled out.

The slow trek south took them through many small villages. Haroc came after Joel again during another rest stop. In an attempt to avoid the painful whip Joel fell against the women's cage, his arms grabbing the bars. Haroc moved in to whip him again. Joel turned on Haroc but tripped in the mud, falling down while Haroc laughed and started whipping Joel again. Joel, in anger, sunk his teeth into Haroc's foot, biting off a toe and causing Haroc to hop around howling, *"The brat bit my toe off."*

The other guards laughed saying, *"It serves you right you were told to leave the boy alone. He has beaten you three times now. He is naked while you wear armor. You have a whip while he is chained to a cage and he still got you."*

The captain chuckled as he watched Joel stick a toe out of his mouth at Haroc before he continued chewing. The captain locked Joel's arms through the female's cage bars before looking at Haroc and saying, *"There now, the boy cannot hurt you, Toe-less."*

The name soon stuck and Toe-less was made to walk beside the male cage and another guard was assigned to hand out the water to the prisoners.

The women were warned to leave him tied or they would suffer, so they could only watch and feel sorrow for the boy. When the new guard with water approached and before he gave Joel water, he said, *"If you behave I will give you water and if you don't you will go thirsty do you understand?"*

Joel looked at the guard sensing him dutiful but not evil, nodded and said, *"Yes, sir."* When the guard gave him water Joel nodded and said, *"Thank you,"* which stunned the guard.

The captain was following and noted the politeness of the boy and how only Toe-less and the caged men seemed to have a problem with the boy. The commander chuckled to himself, *"He stuck the toe out at Toe-less; that was just so funny. If any have a chance to survive the arena I would put my money on the boy, if he survives the trip."*

The next town was Cathedral City, a training town for red cloak warriors, the red haired woman slid over to Joel in a hushed whisper said, *"Do not say or do anything regardless of what happens."*

He nodded, *"Yes."* Joel was weak from hunger with only a toe for nourishment. After many days of walking, his legs faltered until he collapsed and was dragged through the town.

The captain called Toe-less over and stated, *"You stay here to get extra training, maybe we will pick you up on our way back."*

Toe-less was shocked and angry at his dismissal. He glared at the boy who he suspected was the reason. Eon noticed the hate flowing from Toe-less and licked his lips. Then following Toe-less's glare, he looked at the still exhausted, naked boy with whip marks on his back and his legs who was bleeding from where he fell and was dragged through the city. He wondered what happened to make Toe-less hate a boy so much before dismissing the caravan without another thought, turned his attention to the hate of a potential new convert.

Joel felt great evil near, but was so exhausted from the trip and so much blood loss he was barely even able to stay conscious. The caravan moved through town with Joel hanging from his arms, his legs dragging.

The caravan was resupplied, three dead slaves were dumped from the men's cage, and the rest were fed a scoop full of porridge. The red haired woman cut her finger, feeding a little bit of herself with a bit of her porridge to Joel. Less than a thimbleful of her blood was what she squeezed from her finger, letting him nurse off it. Joel could feel her strong beautiful essence as he faded in and out of consciousness as the caravan continued south until nightfall. The next morning the guards checked for any dead, Joel being the first checked with the guards having placed bets on when the boy would die. After weeks of travel the prisoners were thin and starving. The only nourishment they got was a thin piece of meat with a cup full of porridge once every three days, along with what they could eat of the dead that died before the guards tossed the corpses to the side of the road. The prisoners also ate the bugs that crawled in the cages or the lice that feasted upon them that they picked off of one another.

The red haired woman picked the parasites off of Joel nightly while she fed him from her finger. Every night she used a new finger. After he suckled his little nourishment, he dreamed of a beautiful jaguar running free, hunting, and watching as vampires ruled the towns by night, sucking the life slowly from the town, then by day as the red cloaked priest took away the children. The number of babies born became less and less, only one in ten babies born managed to make it past age five and of those over two thirds were taken by the red cloaks. He dreamed of not just humans, but lycans and many other races with the same thing happening as the red cloaks came through. When a vampire followed fewer babies were born. The animals near the towns were hunted to near extinction. The extermination of all was slow and insidious, bit by bit.

Always the jaguar watched and helped from the shadows killing a red cloak here and a vampire there. Soon the jaguar moved on because other towns needed her as well. Every five years the red cloaks came to test and round up the children that were five to eight years of age. As a town or city grew, a vampire would move in and, over the following years, the population of the town would slowly decrease.

As the days passed Joel learned more of the jaguar's

knowledge but only by a thimble full at a time and even that was achieved only in a dream like state. The royal jaguar Solana, had planned to escape, but for some reason the young, foolish boy called to her heart and every day they traveled she fed him just to keep him alive but did not know that she was feeding him her knowledge as well.

Day after day this continued until they came to Castle Black where the slaves were pulled from the cages barely able to stand after being cramped for so long in the cages. The cages were cleaned with buckets of water. The slaves were also cleaned the same way to eliminate the stink. Many slaves opened their mouths to catch some extra water as it drenched their bodies.

The slaves were inspected and fed more porridge. The captain and Dukut visited like old friends and soon the story of Toe-less began to surface. Joel found himself repeatedly inspected and talked about. Many noticed how the weeks of walking had made the boy's feet tough his legs long and lanky. The boy's hair had taken on a reddish tinge similar to that of the woman's. The boy's tenacious personality was believed the major factor as to how he had lived so long and the captain collected on many of the bets placed.

That night a storm raged. The drunken soldiers took a few of the slaves to share among the guards and even offered them extra food. Solana was taken, among others. During this time, Joel was chained to the wheel, finally able to sit or lie down while the rain fell. During flashes of lightening, some noticed a big raven, that landed and fed Joel a mouse, but it was passed off as a trick of the light. The next morning, the caravan moved towards Arena City, leaving Castle Black behind. The rains turned hard for three days and nights. The roads were soon nothing more than muddy ruts. The caravan was almost forced to stop until the storms blew themselves out, but the caravan plodded on as it was too far out to turn back to Castle Black. The slaves were allowed out of the cages to help push the wagons out of the ruts and for their work they were fed a cup of porridge a day instead of every three days.

Every night Joel was brought a mouse, rat, or rabbit by the raven. Every night after the guards slept, Solana let Joel nurse on a finger. Joel, with that help soon worked his way back from death's door. When the sun shone, the days became warm and the roads started to dry up. The caravan was loaded and packed once more. It started to move at their regular pace. The guards became edgy as more and then one commented that it felt like the forest had eyes. The only thing anyone ever noticed was a raven high in the sky lazily circling on the air.

Before long it was back to the same old routine. The prisoners were given only one ladle of water per day and every third day a thin tiny piece of meat with their porridge. Solana picked the lice from Joel's hair and gave him a thimble full of her blood. The raven continued to circle the caravan as if watching and following. The sun soon dried the roads and the pace picked up. When Joel was unable to walk, he was dragged behind the cage. Every morning the cages were checked for any dead who were removed and tossed to the side of the road. A new guard was put in charge of the slaves, he stayed back due to the stink and just whipped Joel to get him moving. Every day Joel's reaction to the whip was to announce, *"I still live!"* A sigh of relief from both the guards and slaves alike was heard when Arena City came into view.

The Orphanage

Kenny watched as the caravan entered the city. The single naked boy tied to the end of the caravan caught his attention. His legs were bloody from all the times he had been dragged and his back a mass of scars and welts from daily whippings. With silent rage Kenny wondered what one young boy could have done to deserve that type of abuse. Grabbing two bottles of whiskey, he went to the pens where the slaves were about to be lined up and organized into the auction or arena pens.

Kenny arrived and talked to the captain, *"The slaves can wait until morning join me in a drink and tell me of your travels."*

As the bottle ran low, their brains became fuzzy and Joel's story came out with much laughter at Toe-less' expense. Kenny asked, *"What was Toe-less's name before?"*

No one could remember, but Joel in his haze of exhaustion answered, *"Haroc"*.

The only one to notice that Kenny's question had been answered was Kenny himself. Kenny caught out the corner of his eye as a red haired woman fed the boy blood from her finger when she saw no one was watching, before she appeared to fall asleep. The guards started passing out as the spirits and the trip's end seemed to had finally caught up with them.

Kenny noticed the boy was near death and not likely to

survive as a lot of the bloody welts seemed to be infected and had forgotten how to heal. He knew that the next few days in the pens would likely kill the boy. Kenny seemed to accidentally cut his hand upon the ladies' cage, while he inspected the ladies, allowing his blood to drip onto the boy's lips with no one noticing but Solana who pretended to be asleep. Kenny spent a good five minutes inspecting the ladies, while his blood continued to nourish the boy long enough for him to survive the pens. Kenny thought, *"This boy will make a great addition to the orphanage,"* which actually had become a rather profitable business.

Kenny left Joel with his wounds healing rapidly as he went to make plans to get the boy transferred to his orphanage as soon as possible. Kenny worked the boy's story through his mind. *For a boy so young to defeat a warrior, even a weak dumb one, three separate times, unarmored, once with a weapon stolen from the warrior, once while caged, and then again while shackled, is impressive. That's not even taking into account he survived the trip.* Kenny walked away in thought, *The boy would do well in his orphanage.* Solana watched Kenny disappear, and saw the guards were asleep. She used one of her claws to cut the bindings on the cage door and slipped out, quickly retied the twine bindings. She wiped blood from the now sleeping Joel's lips and kissed his forehead one last time before shifting to her jaguar form and following the shadows to disappear into the night.

Joel awoke groggily in the morning weak but more alive than he had felt in weeks. His hair had grown seemingly longer overnight and if he was cleaned one would almost say he acquired a blonde mane. The next morning the guards were hung over, they struggled to do their jobs. More from habit then need they whipped Joel just to see if he still lived, then separated the slaves into those that were to go for auction and those that were to go to training for the arena.

Before the slave branding and Keres's inspection took place Kenny had arrived and purchased Joel. He had him moved to Kenny's personal holding cell to be later delivered to his orphanage along with a couple others he purchased for the orphanage. The paper work signed and the payment complete, Joel was fed and finally allowed to truly sleep.

Keres arrived with her guards and inspected the new slaves. She shivered as seemingly cold fingers ran up her spine, though strange, she ignored the feeling and went about her business. She watched and smiled as guards and slaves' alike cringes as she walked by, she thought how much fun it will be teaching the newest slaves how to fear her properly.

At the supper time meal, the boys and girls of the orphanage gathered, there were twenty total. The boys outnumbered the girls four to one, the youngest was a girl of six and the oldest was a boy of twelve. Everyone turned to look as two of Kenny's guards carried in a boy whose legs seemed to move even in his sleep, two more children followed them. Rinette, the madam of the house and Kenny's wife, motioned for the oldest girl to see to the new arrivals, while she motioned the two guards to carry the boy upstairs. Once she saw her orders were being carried out she proceeded the guards up the stairs. The other children of the house, being naturally curious, followed wanting to find out more about the naked boy being carried between the two men. The guards hauled him up the stairs and placed him onto the cot that she motioned to.

Rinette asked, *"Where were his clothes?"*

The guards replied, *"He did not have any."*

They laid him face down so his bleeding back and scars were left to the air. At the sight she turned to the cabinet and pulled out a salve to treat his wounds while asking the guards, *"What is his name?"*

The guards shrugged, *"We do not know, we call him, Boy."*

Rinette asked, *"Do you have any useful information for me about the boy?"*

The guards replied, *"No, but we do have a funny story about how the boy renamed a warrior, Toe-less."*

She looked at them with a curious scowl before she sent the guards on their way. She saw all the children at the door and ushered them off to finish eating and to do their nightly chores. *"You can investigate your new house mate later,"* she told them. Then she put more of the soothing salve upon Joel's legs and back, wondering what he had done that caused him to be treated so cruelly.

The children, after they ate and the evening chores were completed, went up to bed, each looking at the boy who was sleeping fitfully, before they went to sleep. Later that night, the youngest girl woke to a tapping at the window, and then she heard tapping at another. She opened the window and looked out seeing nothing. She suddenly heard the tapping at yet another window and went over to check it out. While looking out the window she heard a flapping sound in the room behind her. She turned around and saw a raven taller than her standing beside Joel's bed, trying to roll him over with its beak.

The girl stood beside the biggest boy's bed and shook him awake. Mike groggily asked, *"What is it Sallem?"* as he noticed her shushing him and pointing. The raven looked at the two and seemed to motion for them to help turn Joel over. Moving to stand on the far side of Joel's bed, opposite the raven, they turned him over and watched as the raven peeled bloody flesh from a rat then placed the bloody meat on Joel's lips. Sallem gathered her courage and opened Joel's mouth so the blood from the meat could enter his mouth more directly. Joel came to, semi conscience, and was able to chew. With Joel fed, the raven devoured the rest and flew out the window to the stunned looks of all the children, as all had awoken to watch the scene in stunned silence. Joel fell back into a deep healing sleep.

The next morning when all of the children woke, Sallem noticed a bloody stain on the floor where the rat had been and quickly cleaned it up. Joel woke and tried to sit up but seemed stuck, *"Help, I'm stuck,"* he said. The children rushed over to help by pulling him upright. Tears of pain flowed from Joel's eyes as the sheet pulled away, reopened the wounds where the scabs had healed overnight into the fabric of the sheet. Joel did not even flinch for it is nothing compared to what had caused the wounds in the first place.

Then the questions and the child inquisition started, *"What's your name? Where do you come from? How did you get all those wounds?"* The children all asked different questions at the same time, until Sallem asked, *"How did you get that raven?"* All of the children grew quiet and listened as they nodded in unison. That was the first question they wanted answered. Joel thought a moment, his mind just starting to clear, *"I am Joel. I was captured a long time ago, in the very, very, very far north, and what raven?"* That got the children started telling him about the raven that visited the night before and how it had fed him a bloody rat and how they had helped it.

Joel stopped and thought a moment, *"Aah, the raven, just stops by sometimes when it thinks I need food, like a friend who just stops by when it has time and is near."* The children nodded and introductions took place from youngest to the oldest, Sallem .... Mike.

Just then Rinette came in, *"OK, children get your chores done. We have got to get some stuff for the house."*

The children said, *"Bye"* and were gone, leaving only Rinette and Joel.

Rinette looked a Joel and smiled, *"I think we need to get you a bath and some clothes, plus I imagine you might like some food. Then I'll show you around before Kenny gets home. Do you know your name?"*

Joel politely replied, *"Yes, Ma'am, my name is Joel."*

Rinette said, *"Your parents taught you very good manners, that's a nice change from most of the children that we get here."*

She got Joel a bath, some cloths, breakfast, and showed him the house.

Kenny arrived and called the children out to the yard. Joel followed the rest of the children. Kenny called Joel over having found out his name from Rinette, said, *"Joel, I want you to tell me and everybody about your encounters with the Toe-less warrior."*

Joel stopped and thought, tracing his memory back. *"Well Haroc was killing people just to kill them for fun. So I walked up behind him, grabbed his dagger, and plunged it into the back of his leg,"* Joel pointed to his calf. *"Then when he turned and tried to hit me I stabbed the front of his leg,"* Joel pointed to his thigh. *"Then I woke up in a cage. When Haroc came to talk to me with his stinky breath while I was in the cage, I stuck these two fingers up his nose and rammed my head into him. I then got tied up to the end of the girls' cage. Haroc whipped me and I tried to get away but I was right against the cage. I got whipped again so I charged him and fell. Before he could whip me again, I bit him as hard as I could and got a toe out of the deal. That was when they tied my hands to the cage and I stuck his toe that I had bitten off out at Haroc."* Joel showed what he meant by sticking his tongue out at Kenny. Kenny, his guards, and the children that were listening and watching, then began to laugh.

Kenny looked at Joel, *"You were reckless, disorganized, and haphazard. You have great speed, toughness, great endurance, and, even better, warrior instincts. With some training you would be a great warrior with much respect."*

While Kenny talked to Joel he noticed the children talking quietly to each other. Then saw them sticking their tongues out at each other giggling while a few other children could be seen hopping around on one foot. Before the unruly bunch unraveled into fits of stomach holding laughter, Kenny sent them to get their wooden practice swords and had them practice blocks, parries, and deflects.

Over the next few weeks Joel healed, trained and made friends with the other children. Both Kenny and the guards that helped train the children, were surprised at how skilled Joel was with the sword and how quickly he learned.

Joel's was working on his skills in the courtyard and regaining his strength when the raven landed and called to him. Looking at the raven, he followed knowing something was wrong. Still carrying his wooden practice sword, he ran. There, ahead of him, was Mike and Sallem, coming back from the market with food, surrounded by five much older boys. Three were kicking at Mike as he laid on the ground curled up in a ball, trying to protect his head, while two boys held the crying Sallem. The food laid scattered on the ground. Joel without even slowing down, smacked a kicker in the head with the sword, while he body checked another kicker into the third.

The five boys turned on Joel, he then stabbed a boy in the stomach with the wooden sword, knocking the wind out of him as he back handed another boy. One boy drew a knife and swiped at Joel. Joel put the training he had to use as he deflected the knife and punched the boy in the nose with a satisfying crunch. He hit one then moved to another, smacking them with the sword; punching, kicking, and head butting. Every boy that went down got stepped on or kicked. Joel did not stop until the boys ran away. Even the last boy to run got kicked in the ass. Sallem stood stock still as she watched Joel swing, punch, and kick around her and Mike, without one of the bullies even laying a finger on him; not one of the attackers ran away unscathed.

He helped Sallem to pick up the groceries while Mike picked up the damaged fish that had been stepped on by someone more than once. Cleaning it off, they then looked around at the people that had not even look up at the scuffle, but kept walking by. Joel stepped into the alley and called to the raven, giving it the fish with his thanks. The raven flew off to its nest on the roof of the orphanage as the three worked their way home.

When asked what happened Sallem told the story while Mike was having his broken ribs wrapped. Rinette asked Joel, *"How did you find out they were being attacked?"*

Joel replied, *"Raven told me."*

Rinette asked, *"Who's Raven?"* Sallem opened the window and the raven appeared when Joel called. Rinette a little shocked announced, *"It does not stay in the house and what does it like to eat?"*

Joel said, *"We know, it has made its nest on the roof."* Joel looked at the raven very intensely then looked at Rinette and said, *"His favorite food are the small silver fish about the size of your finger."*

Rinette, a little startled said, *"Sardines?"*

The raven nodded and Joel looked at her saying, *"I guess that is right."*

Rinette sat on the bed, *"It understood me?"*

Joel shrugged, *"Yes."*

Rinette shivered said, *"I hate sardines but what is one more mouth to feed? Joel, it looks like you and raven are the guardians of the others. It also looks like a few more trips to the fish market will need to be made each week unless some of you want to take up fishing a couple of days a week."*

Two boys jumped at the chance as they exclaimed, *"We will do it but we won't have time to do the breakfast dishes if we are going to be there when the fish are biting."* Everybody laughed as Chris and Chad were always looking for a way out of doing dishes.

The next morning Joel walked everyone to their destinations, carrying his wooden sword and when he was not walking someone to and from their destinations, he trained. Raven flew over the city in lazy circles watching the children, especially the two fishermen. Joel went and picked everyone up and walked them home in the evening. He did this for all, but six boys who often showed up with a wound or bloody nose along with a good supply of money and items.

When Joel asked, *"What do they do?"*

Sallem shrugged, *"I do not know but you could ask Tyrone."*

Tyrone replied, *"Shush we are the secret here. When asked we do odd jobs like today we were financial assistants to some wealthy merchants."* Some boys chuckled as Joel looked a little perplexed. Tyrone replied, *"Like today we helped and assisted a merchant improve his finances and got well paid. We also assisted our finances from another wealthy merchant by having him make an involuntary donation to the house."*

Joel said in wonder, *"You get paid to steal and mug?"*

Tyrone smiling said, *" Basically, yes."*

Brenat Arrives at Arena City

everal weeks later, Arris arrived with a whispered message to Kenny. Kenny told the warriors to take over training the children as Arris and Kenny left.

Keres and her guards, along with King Silfer, were standing around when Brenat was delivered by the red cloak gaunts. When Kenny arrived he looked around at the fan fair, *"So this is the important prisoner we have been waiting on, are there any special instructions to go with this prisoner."*

Kenny barely recognized Brenat and wondered if he would live long enough to be rescued. He barely held back a gasp at Keres's instructions for his care.

Arris wrote the instructions down while Keres announced, *"Every night after he is fed one ounce of human blood mixed with an equal amount of vampire venom, two ounces of his blood is to be drawn and put into these magical jars then brought to me immediately. Every morning he is to be fed two ounces of manticore blood and two ounces of Medusa venom. Afterward two ounces of his blood are to be drawn again and placed in the jars and immediately brought to me. In the afternoon he is to be fed three ounces each of hell hound, humanoid meat and an ounce of spider venom with three ounces of pixie blood. Then three ounces of his blood is to be drawn and brought to me."*

Keres continued, "*I had four slaves blinded, to gather the Medusa venom. The manticore is chained in the cell next to her. The last mortal that made a deal with me to become immortal has gotten her wish granted and is chained in the cell next to the manticore and she shall supply all the venom I need for eternity.*"

Arris, prudent in his job asked, "*Humanoid meat, is anything special about that?*"

Keres walked over to him and said, " *Human, lycan, slave, any sentient mortal meat. If you have problems finding any,*" she reached over and grabbed hold of his hand then broke two of his fingers, "*You could feed him your useless fingers.*"

Arris cried out in pain and everyone watched as Keres's smile grew sweeter. Kenny pulled Arris aside and ordered him to go get his fingers tended to. Inside, Kenny's hatred grew towards Keres.

Brenat opened his eyes at the scream, he was confused and his blood had been drained to near death, he was shackled in a cage. He overheard a scribe say, "*Kenny, a few of the new slaves have the potential to survive their first fights in the arena if they don't die in their cages first.*"

Kenny replied, while looking upon Brenat, as he tried to figure a way to keep him alive until he could be rescued, "*Then clean the pens, attend to all wounds, and see that everyone is fed properly.*"

Then Brenat heard a guard was saying, "*Rumor has it that Queen Teera has been rescued from bandits and once she is well enough she will marry King Silfer.*"

Kenny replied, "*Don't believe everything you hear,*" as he walked from Brenat's cell.

Brenat's eyes cleared, *Teera lives? Joel still lives, as they have not mentioned him and the gaunts still search for him.* Brenat laid thinking *I still live, there must be a reason. They still hunt for Joel, so I need to live and resist so I can rescue Teera and kill those that hunt for Joel.* Brenat fell back into unconsciousness once again.

Brenat awoke to tormented screaming, before he realized it is his own screams he heard. Keres, with a lovely smile said, *"Brenat, I am so glad you have awoken for our little time together."* Keres then ran her wand down Brenat's chest to his scrotum, just as pain exploded through him. Brenat realized why he was screaming as his screams filled the dungeon.

Keres, with a musical laugh said, *"Brenat, I heard you resisted the red cloaks torment even when they ate your living flesh right from your body. That is impressive, now I will get to see how much fun I can have with you. I will teach you to obey my every order, just as I will teach your body that your arousal or impotence will be strictly at my command."*

With a gentle touch, Keres stroked and encouraged his arousal, no matter how hard he tried to fight it, until his body moved in her hand. His body ached with the need of release. Then she showed him what looked like a bear trap missing its middle teeth, before Brenat could shrink from the sight and thought of its use, Keres had clamped it around his testicles and shaft. Making him feel like he was in a vice, unable to shrink from the pain or release the pent of pressure as she continued to stroke his aching shaft.

Keres kissed down his chest to the mushroom head as it throbbed and grew with every kiss and flick of her tongue. His shaft filled and seemed to stretch as every heartbeat added more blood, but the trap allowed very little to escape until his body could not decide if it was torturous pleasure or pleasurable pain.

Keres stood and dropped her clothing then guided him into her waiting warmth where her muscles clenched then released as she reached around him and pressed the enlarged tip of the wand against his anus. She released the trap causing Brenat's seed to begin to flow in a powerful release just as a jolt of pain flowed from the wand, in an explosive release that made Brenat's hips buck in an uncontrollable seizure. Keres screamed her pleasure as Brenat's seed filled her and she bit his lip, leaving bloody teeth marks as she claimed him as her newest toy.

Keres smiled as she pulled herself off of him, *"Your seed will create a child of power within me and your wife Teera will be witness to your voluntary seeding of my womb, before I cut off your manhood and feed it to the gaunts as you watch."* Keres got dressed and left him in his cage, shackled and sore. She turned back, *"Oh by the way Teera will get the same treatment before she marries Silfer and bares him a child, which she will do after she watches you betray her with your lust for me. I will see you tomorrow for more training."* Brenat threw up all over himself. He heard Keres order the guards, *"Clean him and the cell up before I return tomorrow."*

In the morning Brenat was awakened to cold water splashing over him, followed by a bloody potion being forced down his throat. Then there was a rough soapy scrubbing and more cold water as both he and his his cell were cleaned.

Keres arrived with her two huge lycan body guards who were naked except for the collars they wore and the belts that held their weapons. With a lovely smile and sing song voice Keres caressed the side of Brenat's face. *"How is my good boy this morning?"* Her hands slid down his body to hold his tightened scrotum before she ran her nails along the underside his shaft to scratch the very tip of his sensitive head. *"Ah, is my pet up for a little training?"* Keres kissed the nipples on Brenat's chest before biting them again leaving bloody teeth marks around each nipple, as she manipulated his shaft in her hand, it grew hard against his will. All the while, his testicles were trying to crawl up and hide in his clenched stomach.

One of the lycans came over putting a collar around Brenat's neck. The tiny silver spikes pierces and burned into his neck. The other lycan brought over a cushioned, leather covered table. Keres started tapping her wand upon her palm, Brenat's body reacted to the memory of the pain that flowed through him the day before. Keres watched his shaft lose its hardness, *"Well, Brenat, would you like me to use my wand on you again today?"* Brenat without thought just shook his head no as his mouth became dry with memory of the pain.

Keres nodded her head, *"If you perform well for me today, I will not use the wand on you."*

Brenat's thoughts went to the last time he was with Teera and his arousal sprang to life.

Keres nodded with appreciation, *"Well done, my pet."*

Brenat struggled to maintain his thoughts of Teera as Keres undressed then laid upon the table, her legs open and ready for Brenat.

Keres smiled, *"Come on lover, show me the kind of man you are."*

Brenat's chains were loosened so he could approach and mount his mistress. With slow steady strokes, his body reacted to her gripping body and the magical scented oils that one of her slave guards poured onto his body and rubbed in. Brenat's movement became vigorous as the potion worked its magic and his eyes filled with lust. Brenat heard Keres snap her fingers, then he cried out as he was filled and stretched by the guard's arousal. Brenat's body and mind recoiled from the invasion, the other guard rubbed more of the oils onto Brenat which did their magic. Before long his movements were mimicked by the guard, while his body swelled with even more pleasurable pain then before. Soon Brenat released his seed in an explosive thrust, just before he felt his bowels swelling from the slave guard's release.

Keres bit Brenat's lips again remarking him as before. Her fingers scratched rivets into his back as her body gripped him through her release. The slave guard pulled out, leaving Brenat gaping and bleeding. Brenat's chains tightened as he was forcefully removed from Keres and pulled tight against the stone wall. Keres got dressed and she smiled at Brenat, *"Well done, Lover. See, I always keep my promises, I never used my wand on you."*

Keres left, the slave moved the table off to the corner of the cell. Brenat vomited upon himself once again. The slave cleaned him up then in a whisper said, *"Beware of any gift Keres offers, they are always worse than the punishments."*

The days moved on with each day filled with a nightmare whether awake or not and the torment became worse. Brenat began to remember the treatment of the gaunts with fond memories.

❂ ❂ ❂ ❂ ❂ ❂ ❂ ❂ ❂ ❂ ❂

Brian and Kenny sent out a secretive message to all the arrows in town just before a public announcement was made, *"A large red cloak caravan came through delivering Brenat. He had been captured and placed in the pens of Arena City. Keres has taken a personalized interest in him. It is a trap to catch Teera and those that hide her."*

A week after the large red cloak caravan arrived, the public announcements went out, *"We have captured Brenat, the leader of the Castle Black's massacre, the bandit who killed, raped, and pillaged many of the smaller villages. He will be battling in the arena until his crimes against the king and the people are paid for in full. Come and see the murderous coward get his just rewards for his crimes at the Fall Festival Event."*

Joel listened to the announcement like everyone else and his mind started whirling as he sat down hard. His thoughts racing and troubled by all he had heard. *My dad is alive and here, I have to save him. Why are they saying he did all that bad stuff when he fought against the bad ones? My dad is good not bad.* Sallem watched as Joel went pale as he sat down hard, asked him, *"What's wrong?"*

Joel looked at her, *"That was my home. My Gapa James was the king. They lie, my dad was defending Castle Black. The red cloaks are evil they were the ones that killed everyone at the castle."*

Sallem looked confused asked, *"What are you talking about?"*

Joel answered, *"Brenat is my dad. Grandma and grandpa thought he died when momma, Gapa, and Gama died while protecting Castle Black."*

Sallem shushed him as some red cloaks started walking by and said, *"Let's get home."*

Joel took her with him to go get the rest of the children safely home. All the children talked of their day over supper while Joel was his normal quiet self. After Rinette sent them off to bed after evening chores, the six children that shared Joel's room snuck out onto the roof like spiders climbing up a wall. They sat as the raven came and stood behind Joel, resting its beak on his head. Sallem elbowed Joel and gave him a nod.

Joel sighed and started his story again, *"Uh, what the town squire was saying about Brenat was wrong. Brenat is my daddy. My daddy tried to save my momma, Gama Rizalle, and Gapa James. I saw my momma get shot in the head with a crossbow bolt. The red cloaks attacked my daddy and killed everyone in the castle. My Grandma Elsie and Grandpa Sid ran away with me from the evil red cloaks that followed us and later killed my Grandpa Sid after he hid me in a snow den after Grandma Elsie tried to lead them away. I think she is dead too. Since then I have been in one of my animal forms until I got captured and brought here."*

Mike interrupted, *"Animal forms? Like what? Would you show us?"*

The raven stepped back as Joel stood up then shifted into a white bear cub, then turned into a black wolf, then to a lion cub, next a jaguar kitten, then to a white tiger cub, on to a hell hound pup and lastly into a black panther cub before resuming his eight-year-old looking human form. Once done he sat down again the raven moved forward and rested its beak back on Joel's head in a reassuring presence.

The children stared in wide eyed in awe. They all asked, *"Could you teach us to do that?"*

Joel stopped and thought, his mind roamed to the dancing lights before he answered, *"Only your animal spirit can help you change. All I can do is help you find your guiding spirit."*

The children nodded, that made sense, as some of the children asked, *"How do we get in touch with our animals?"*

Joel said, *"I'm not sure. I would have to ask the spirits of the lights."*

The raven cocked its head and let out a little squawk. The children grew quiet and listened as they heard Rinette moving around and checking the other children's rooms. She told those that were still awake goodnight and to get to sleep. The children climbed down and snuck back to bed just before Rinette came in and checked on them. When they heard her head to her room, they climbed out of bed and gather again in a circle.

Operation Rescue

Sallem elbowed Joel, *"Tell us more about your dad."*

Joel relayed his story to all the children.

Willie asked, *"What are we going to do?"*

Joel answered, *"I am going to rescue my dad, I just don't know how. Would you help me?"*

Tyrone excitedly exclaimed, *"Now we're talking. We're good at sneaking into places and getting things."*

He looked at his crew, *"We have never gotten a person out of the pens before, this will be fun."*

Tyrone looked at the rest of the children, *"Are all of you in for operation rescue?"* All of the children nodded and said, *"Yes."*

Tyrone looked at their friends, *"Bill, Tye, you need to find out where Brenat is being held and the locks we will need to pick."* Tyrone looked at Willie, *"You organize and talk with the other children, see what they can supply to help in the rescue. We will need a wagon for the goods and a way to cover the goods. We will need tools and maps so we can plan the best way to do the escape. Then we are going to need a hideout big enough for an adult as well as medicines, bandages, and food for him."*

Sallem pointed up at the attic hatch overhead.

Tyrone replied, *"That is a great place. We can take care of him there. Now we just need to sneak him out of the cages and in here without anyone catching us."*

They made plans with Tyrone organizing everything. He assigned Mike and Joel, as they were the biggest of the boys, to be the muscle of their group. While that was going on, the raven sat quietly as if watching and listening. It suddenly let out a squawk. Tyrone's eyes lit up, looking at the raven. He told it, *"You could be the lookout and advance scout, showing us the best way around the adults when we make our get away."* The raven nodded and hopped on one foot, as if sharing in the children's excitement.

They heard Rinette call out, *"I am coming up and everybody had better be in bed."* They all rushed to their beds as the raven flew back out the window to its nest.

The next morning the children's excitement was high as everyone finished breakfast and their morning chores in a hurry. Rinette knew they were up to something when Chris and Chad stayed to do the breakfast dishes.

Rinette looked at them, *"Have fun children."* All she got in response was a, *"Yup,"* as they all rushed out the door.

Everyone went to their jobs, and over the next couple of days. The smithy apprentice went to the blacksmith where he managed to get some lock picks and bolt cutters. Larry, the leather worker's apprentice, managed to get a cart and he also collected all the scraps of fur and leather. Chris and Chad went fishing. Ken, the apprentice to one of the storekeepers, got some old moth eaten clothes. Mary, the apprentice map maker found some maps on the arena and pens.

Joel, Sallem, and Mike ran around collecting the cart and other supplies that the other children were supplying. They met with them and snuck around during lunch. Willie, Bill, Tyrone, and Tye gave their reports, *"Seems to be guards and people around morning, noon, and night. We may succeed either just after lunch or after his evening potion feeding. That, or we would have to wait until the evening after bed time. But the night guards seem to be more regular in their checks. Brenat is even called their special prisoner. He is fed a special potion twice daily and they take his blood. Plus, he is kept chained to the wall. They say Keres the witch has a special use for him and visits him regularly in the mornings. The best time is when they are busy just like when we sneak from the merchants, the busier they are the more time we have, but the more people around that can see us."* Tyrone plopped down, eating an apple and offering to share his supply with the others.

Joel asked, *"What about the window."*

Tye answered, *"Sallem may be able to fit, but that is it. We would never be able to get him out it."*

Joel asked hopefully, *"Could I see him from the window?"*

Tyrone replied, *"Sure, that is a great idea. Let's all go have a look, when you get back we will make our rescue plan."* Everyone nods yes, except Mike and Tye.

Mike and Tye replied, *"Nah, we will stay with the cart and eat our apples."*

Sneaking up to the window they let Joel see first. He looked in the window, through the bars and saw his dad sitting on the floor, head down like he was sleeping. His wrists were chained to the wall above his head and there were scars on his chest, arms, and legs. He backed away from the window reluctantly, so Tyrone, Willie, Bill, and lastly Sallem could look. Joel started walking back towards the cart when there was a holler, *"Hey, you children, get away from there."*

Tyrone yelled, *"RUN!"* and they all scattered.

Joel turned around to watch as everyone scattered in every which way just as Sallem ran right smack into a guard and got dragged inside through the guard entrance. While the guard yelled at her, Sallem just started crying in fear. Joel sighed and walked back to help Sallem. Tyrone saw the commotion and realized it was the break they needed to free Brenat. He motioned to the others to follow Joel at a distance.

The guard stood screaming at Sallem, who was hiccupping through her tears, in fear, as Joel approached the guard. The guard looked over at Joel, *"What do you want kid? You're not supposed to be here."*

All the scribes disappeared as they found something more important to do. Joel walked over, *"It is my fault sir, I wanted to see the man that was being talked about in town. My little sister just came along."*

The guard said, *"You could get whipped for that."*

Joel walked past the guard to where the whips were hanging on the wall and grabbed one nodding, *"Ok sir, but as this was my fault I will take her whipping too."*

The guard's eyes followed Joel, stunned, as he held out his hand for the whip. Joel turned his back on the guard and faced the closest cell with a deep sigh and told Sallem, *"Go home; Sis, I'll be home soon."*

Sallem scurried outside, racing past Tyrone and Willie and ran to the cart crying, escorted by Bill. The guard turned his back upon the entrance. Willie and Tyrone watched and saw that as the opportunity they needed.

Willie snuck into the pens and into a nearby door, seeing lockers and a chest. He decided to take a look into an open locker when there came a loud snore, close by. Willie grabbed the first tunic he saw, just as a helmet started to fall, he caught it and froze, looking at the back of the snoring guard. The guard continued snoring and Willie started sneaking back out as the guard rolled over. Willie dropped to the floor and hid under a table, bumping it, he heard a crash as something fell over. He froze, hoping the guard did not wake up. Feeling something wet land on his neck, Willie wiped at the liquid then smelled it and wrinkled his nose at the ale's sour smell. He put the helmet over him like a bowl, to stop the foul smelling liquid from landing on him, then snuck back out the door before the guard awoke.

The guard told Joel to put his hands on the bars. Joel removed his shirt as the guard took the whip from the boy, admiring his loyalty and strength of responsibility. He also admired his courage, as he stared at the mass of scars on the boy's back, wondering who had beaten the boy so badly.

While the guard's back is turned, Tyrone never being one to pass up an opportunity snuck the keys off of the desk. Going down the hall towards Brenat's cell, he motioned for Willie to follow.

The guard said, *"Five lashes for you, five for your sister, five for your friends, and I want you to count."*

"Yes sir," Joel replied and he gripped the bars tightly. A loud snap was heard, followed by Joel calling out, *"ONE!"*

Willie and Tyrone opened the cage and snuck in. Another snap and Joel hollered, *"TWO!"*

Tyrone unshackled Brenat, took the large tunic from Willie, and slid it over Brenat's head and arms. Tyrone whispered to Willie, *"Help! Don't just stand there."*

Willie put the helmet on Brenat's head and both boys recoiled from the smell as the foul liquid poured down Brenat's hair, face and tunic. *"THREE!"* came a holler from Joel following another snap. Tyrone and Willie each wrapped an arm from Brenat around their necks and walked down the hall. Tyrone and Willie heard another snap and both winced as the heard Joel holler, *"FOUR!"* Both boys knew their friend must be hurting and knew more were to come.

The guard noticed the two boys carrying out an obviously drunk guard from the smell and look of him. The guard turned back to Joel with another snap and Joel yelled out, *"FIVE!"* Tyrone tossed the keys at the table and missed, they jingled as they hit the floor, the guard turned to look at the boys.

The boys froze and looked at the guard, while the guard said, *"Tell him if he misses his shift tonight it will come out of his wages and to stay away from the female slaves, Kenny has ordered the guards to use a brothel, if caught with the slaves he'll join them."*

Tyrone answered, *"Yes, sir we will,"* and continued out the door. The guard noticed his keys were missing and shouted, *"Hold on!"* The boys stopped, then the guard noticed his keys just under the desk said, *"Never mind, get him home."*

Kenny's eyes were drawn to the pens by something familiar. He saw two boys' half dragging, half helping a drunk guard home. He made a mental note to remind himself to limit the amount of spirits allowed in the guard room then turned back to his captains and their daily reports.

The guard snapped the whip and Joel hollered, *"SIX!"* Admiring the boys strength, he decided to forgo the rest and told Joel, *"Ok, boy, that is enough now go home. If I ever catch you here again you will get the rest owed you plus any extra you have earned."*

Joel replied, *"Yes sir, thank you sir."*

Joe straightened as best he could against the pain and left. Once he got away from the pens he started running and ran to catch up with the others. He arrived to help the others get Brenat into the cart and as they started covering him up, Joel asked, *"Who is the stinky?"*

Tyrone replied, *"It's your dad. We snuck him out while the guard was busy with you."*

Sallem wrinkled her nose, *"Could you have found less stinky clothes for him?"*

As they started back to the house along the docks, Chris and Chad showed up and stepped back. *"Wow, that smells stronger than the fish we got. We are going to have to wash him, before we can even think of sneaking him into the house, without being caught."*

They took him under the docks and dumped him in the

water, removing the helmet and tunic as they dunked him again. Sallem stood back, sniffed, and shook her head, wrinkling her nose at the smell. They threw the tainted smelly furs into the river with the helmet and tunic. After three more dunks, they pulled him out and looked at Sallem for approval. Sniffing the air Sallem nodded and they squeezed the wet, still unconscious Brenat into the cart again, covered him with the leather that only smelled like leather. Chad and Chris gave Sallem their fish to hold, as they climbed into the cart with her. The three of them sat on top of the leather and Brenat munching on apples, while the bigger boys pulled the cart home.

Sallem, Chris, Chad, and the younger boys carried the fish into the house. Rinette taught them to clean then fillet them, while all the leftovers were taken out to the court yard to feed Raven. Joel, Mike, and Tyrone carried Brenat in the back door and up the stairs, while Willie stood guard, watching Rinette as she started to cook up the fish for supper. He motioned for the boys to hurry, Tye ran up ahead to open the door to their room. Once in the bed room, they looked up at the eight-foot ceiling, Mike inquired, *"Now how are we going to get him up there."*

They hid Brenat under one of the beds and the boys started moving furniture around to try and make a way to get Brenat up into the attic. Rinette came up stairs, observed the not so innocent looking boys and asked, *"What are you children up to?"*

"Nothing," came a unified reply.

Rinette walked away saying over her shoulder, *"I am watching you boys."*

Mike told the others, *"I don't know how she does it but she always knows what's going on."*

Tyrone whispered, *"I hate when she does that. It feels like she throws her eyes in the corner somewhere and just watches from where ever she is."*

Joel started looking in the corners, Willie could be heard

talking to Rinette. Tyrone watched down the stairs. Mike finished moving the furniture back to where it was. After checking every corner Joel announced, *"No eyeballs!"* and heard Rinette stifle a laugh from the nearby vent. Joel placed his fingers over his lips and walked to the window, motioning the boys over, *"I think her ears are in the vent, though."*

Tyrone whispered while they stood at the window, *"If only we could get the ladder from the barn, but there is no way we could sneak it up the stairs without Rinette catching us."*

Joel replied, *"Then we bring it in through the window."*

He stripped then shifted to a black panther and jumped out the window to the tree and climbed down the tree like a shadow, then headed to the barn.

Joel, the boy, carried the ladder back to the tree and stood the ladder up against it. Joel then climbed the tree, sitting on a thicker branch, and pulled the ladder up to him. Then going hand over hand, one rung at a time, the ladder moved closer to the window until Tyrone and Mike could almost grab it. Rinette started coming up the stairs causing Willie to let out a yell to distract and warn the others.

Tye left the room and went down the stairs, *"Rinette, could you get this sliver out of my finger for me?"* He showed her his finger as he pulled it from his mouth, giving Mike time to catch and balance the ladder on the ledge just outside the window.

While Joel waited for the boys, Rinette looked at the spot suspiciously, *"Hmm, looks like you got it out already."*

Tye replied, *"Thanks, your great,"* and gave Rinette a hug, then wandered out the front door. Rinette walked upstairs to see Mike and Tyrone standing in the middle of the room looking innocent.

Rinette asked, *"Where is Joel?"*

Both boys answered in unison, *"Barn, crapper,"* and knew

they were busted.

Suddenly Joel hollered from downstairs, *"The fish smells great. When do we get to eat?"*

Rinette looked at the two boys and told them to wash up as it was time to eat. The boys rushed off to wash. Rinette looked around the room and seeing nothing out of place thought, *"I wonder if I could whoop them for something I have not caught them at yet. No matter how many hugs and kisses I get, those boys are going get it. I know they are up to something, I just don't know what, yet."* Then she hollered as she headed back downstairs to the kitchen, *" Everybody had better be washed up for supper!"*

After supper as they went to clean up for bed, Rinette tossed some towels to the boys and noticed Joel's back was cut open with fresh lash marks. Rinette stopped Joel, *"What happened?"* she asked while she inspected the lashes. Joel hung his head and the other boys rushed from the room and up the stairs.

Mike and Tyrone pulled in the ladder that rested precariously on two tree branches just below the window ledge. With the help of the other children they struggled to pull Brenat through the hatch and onto a quickly made pallet. Then pushed the ladder up there as well before Tyrone, hanging by one arm, moved the cover back into place and jumped down.

Joel said, *"We went to the pens to look at the prisoner that everyone is talking about. We all ran away when the guard came but he caught Sallem. So I went back to rescue Sallem then took hers and my whipping."*

Rinette said, *"You all are to stay away from the pens, do you hear me?"*

"Yes ma'am I will I am sorry," replied Joel.

She added a salve to his back. Rinette sighed and thought, *"So that is what they were hiding."*

Suddenly a loud commotion was heard as Brenat's escape was found out by the guards who had went in to give him his nightly potion and bloodletting. Kenny was ordered to have the trained hell hounds brought out and an all-out search began. The guards and scribes were questioned that were supposed to have been on duty watching the prisoners.

Just before bed Kenny and his guards arrived escorting a red cloak priest. Kenny called all the children into the common room. After all the children gathered, Kenny told the two guards to go check the barn, yard, and house. *"Those of you that went to the pens today stay, the rest of you get to bed, NOW,"* Kenny ordered.

Kenny looked stern and very official, *"Ok, now tell me why you were at the pens?"*

Joel steps forward, *"We went to see the prisoner that everyone in town was talking about."*

Kenny after a moments pause asked, *"And, what did you see?"*

Sallem spoke shyly, *"A man was chained to a wall with whip marks. Then a guard chased us off."*

All the boys nodded except Sallem who's lower lip trembled. Kenny sternly looked at her and Sallem said with tears in her voice, *"I was not fast enough and was caught. Joel had to rescue me, sorry Kenny."*

Kenny looked at Joel, *"Then what happened?"*

Joel replied, *"I was whipped so Sallem could go free and for us being there and was told not to come back."*

Kenny asked Sallem, *"Where were you when Joel was being whipped?"*

Sallem replied, *"Joel told me to go home, but I ran back to Tye and Mike crying and they gave me an apple to eat with them. While we waited to help Joel home."*

The guards came back, *"The Barn, yard, and house are clear. The hell hounds have found no trace of the prisoner here."*

Kenny looked at the red cloak with a sneer, *"Satisfied, and where do you want to look next?"* The red cloak nodded, *"Let's check the other guard's housing next, I believe we need to find that drunkard."*

Kenny looked at the children, *"You children stay away from the pens, do you hear me!"*

All the children replied in unison, *"Yes, Kenny."*

"Now go to bed" Kenny ordered as he turned to leave with the guards and red cloak.

Rinette looked at Kenny, *"What is this all about?"*

Kenny replied, *"That criminal Brenat escaped we suspect sometime this afternoon, we suspect some guards helped him. So I may not be back until late tomorrow."* Kenny kissed Rinette good bye.

Arris was sent to notify Keres while Kenny was busy. Keres put on her sweetest smile at the interruption and her collared lycan guards shivered. Arris swallowed as he delivered the message.

Keres nodded as she listened to the report then asked, *"You are the head scribe at the pens and Kenny's personal aide, Yes?"*

Arris nodded yes, his mouth to dry from fear to speak. *"You failed Kenny by not keeping your scribes on task and, by not properly checking on and reporting to Kenny any lapse in his guards' attentiveness., Three guards missing and three scribes were missing during this time."* Keres counts off on her fingers for every error she believed made on Arris's part. *"That's ten errors on your part and you won't be of much use as a scribe with all your fingers broken since you already have two still healing. I would have to work on your toes but then you would not even be able to walk around to do your job and give a verbal report. Kenny would be better off with a new scribe,"* Keres mused out loud.

"Well Arris, I think you shall keep your fingers and toes while

you deliver a message for me."

Arris sighed with relief.

Keres told her guards, *"Take him to the new poles I just had installed, he can have a use by teaching others what will happen to them if they do not do their jobs correctly."*

Arris's hands and feet were shackled together around a greased fourteen-foot pole that Arris had to grip with all his might. His body is set right over top of an eight-foot tapered pole that widened at the base with a spear like sharp point at the top. Keres smiled sweetly and in her sing song voice said, *"Hang on as long as you can Arris, I would not want Kenny or the scribes to miss out on the lesson."*

Arris slipped a little and the spear point pushes into him lubricating the pole with his blood Arris flinched in pain and gripped the other pole even harder. As the night wore on Arris's arms and legs grew tired, causing him to slip further down the pole. The pain renewed his strength, but for only a short time. Arris thought about his two choices, let go and die quickly or hang on and hope Kenny could rescue him. Arris held on tighter until exhaustion sapped his strength again and he dropped another inch, his bloody bowels coating the shaft. Hour after hour Arris held on hoping Kenny would arrive to save him until his strength waned from blood loss and exhaustion, he lost his grip, to fall as his screams filled the night.

Kenny arrived back at the pens from his all night search and found Arris dead. The tip of the tapered pole's spear poked out the top of his head, blood and feces slicked down the tapered pole and pooled at the base. Kenny shook in rage as he had his friend removed from the pole, while vowing to kill Keres to avenge his friend and the others she had killed.

The Family Grows

That night after Rinette tucked the children in and added a fresh poultice to Joel's wounds before she too retired for the night, knowing Kenny would not be home that night. Joel got Mike and Tyrone to help boost him up to the attic as he needed his dad. Remembering how the jaguar, as well as, his grandparents had kept him alive, he cut his finger, letting the blood seep past Brenat's lips into his mouth. He watched as his dad swallowed it even in his sleep. Then taking the poultice that Rinette had used on him, he applied it to Brenat's black seeping wounds. He curled up with his dad to sleep after closing the hatch like the young boy he really is.

Early the next morning Joel opened the small window that was normally locked on the inside and crawled out onto the roof saying, *"Good Morning,"* to the raven before he snuck back through a window into his room to get ready for the day. After breakfast Rinette handed Sallem a note and some money with instructions, *"Go to the bath house and give it to the bath master, Brian, only. He will hand you some scented bath salts to bring back to me. The note will tell him what kind I want."*

Mike, Joel, and Sallem after dropping the other children off at their respective work sites went to the bath house. As this is Joel's first visit he started looking around at the scents and at all the fancy jars. A shop attendant offered him a jar of scent to smell. He opened the lid and smelled, closing it fast as he started sneezing and shaking his head from the potent smell. Mike and Sallem laughed at the funny look on Joel's face. The attendant asked Sallem, *"Is there is something you were wanting?"*

Sallem said, *"I was sent to see the bath master, Brian."* The attendant went to fetch Brian while they waited, a few others try to help her, but she politely said *"No thank you"* and the children continued to wait. Mike and Sallem told Joel about the place as they waited for the master.

Soon a big man came out smelling cleaner than fresh snow falling on your tongue. He announced with a gruff kindly voice, *"Sallem, Mike, nice to see you again. Who's your young friend and what can I do for you today?"* Sallem said, *"This is Joel, he lives with us and protects us from the bullies. Rinette sent us to bring her some special bath salts."* Sallem reached into her pocket and pulled out the money along with the note. Brian read the note, frowning at its message, *"I would like some SPECIAL bath salts that let me ESCAPE THE PRISON that the children seem to keep me PENNED up in. Last night my SPECIAL scent ESCAPED and went MISSING. I would like a suggestion while you SEARCH for my SPECIAL scent. We were WONDERING if YOU have any NEW SPECIAL scents that KENNY and I would like to HEAR about."*

Brian went and mixed up a small jar of bath salts, while the children watched him moving from jar to jar with a measuring spoon getting a scoop of this and adding a bit of that, before sealing the jar and handing it to Sallem with a hand written note of special instructions.

Brian invited Rinette, Kenny and all the children to come this Sunday to the bath for a pig roast, if they could make it. Rose came around the corner from another room and kissed Brian. Rose said, *"Hi Sallem, Mike, who's your friend?"* Joel announced, *"I am Joel, you smell likes roses."* She smiled at him then replied, *"That is because my name is Rose and my favorite scent is roses."* Brian handed Rose the note, *"Brent escaped!"* she exclaimed reading the note before covering her mouth and running from the room, leaving everyone to watch after her.

Returning home with the bath salts, Sallem told Rinette of the invitation for everyone to use the bath house and hands Rinette the note, *"Three pinches in your bath water. NO new SPECIAL scent in my store but if I FIND or HEAR about some I will think of you and KENNY first."*

Mike helped Joel sneak some broth and bread upstairs to his dad. Mike boosted Joel up then passed the food and water up before he rushed off to do the rest of his chores. Joel looked at his dad's scars and how pale he was. Sitting there Joel started talking, *"Please dad don't die, I need you."* Then he cut his finger, sopping up the blood with bread and broth, slowly feeding his dad. He told him to chew, and watched him swallow then gave him a little water. Meanwhile Brenat believed that he was in a wonderful dream of being with his son. Over the next several weeks Brenat slowly sweated out the poisons, venom and other toxins his body had been forced to ingest while in Keres and the gaunt's hands. Brenat's mind was stuck in the poison induced nightmare, as he struggled to answer his son's call for help, while running from the gaunt's gnashing teeth, the vampire's hunger, and Keres's magic.

Tyrone's crew stayed close to home watching as red cloaks and warriors searched house by house, business by business. Stabbing hay stacks with sword and spear, checking every ship as the hell hounds lost the scent at the docks. This went on for many days before the search headed out of town and everything could go back to normal. Joel spent as much time with his dad as possible sneaking in through the attic window. Joel continued feeding Brenat his blood slowly and watched as his dad's wounds slowly healed. He watched as his dad got color back in his skin right after a little feeding, before he started to sweat profusely and went gray again.

With the search moved out of town the whole orphanage went down to the baths the following Sunday. Where they saw some servants tending to a slowly roasting pig, Joel watched the excitement of the other children as they stripped down and jumped into the pool where they splashed, romped and laughed. Sallem swam in the water with true grace as if she was born to it easily avoiding the splashing and dunking.

Mike lounged in the water, watching everything including Joel. Joel looked at a familiar red haired woman lounging in the adult pools, who looked at Joel briefly. Joel stripped down and jumped in the water and dog paddled over to Mike where they sat together. Joel felt eyes staring at his back all the time as if they were counting the scars on his back. Feeling uncomfortable at all the eyes seeming to stare at him, Joel climbed from the pool, got dressed and went to get some food. Only to be joined soon by Mike, Sallem, Tyrone and the others of their small group. Tyrone asked, *"Joel, what is wrong?"* Joel explains, *"Nobody here trusts me, there is a lot of anger and hatred directed at me from all but Rinette and the red haired woman. You all stay and have fun, I will go back, I want check on raven and the attic anyway."*

Sallem, Mike, Tyrone, Tye, Bill and Willie all stated they would go with Joel back to the house. Rinette saw them leaving and asked, *"Where are you all going?"* Joel explained about the distrust and told her they were going to check on raven. Solana came from the bath house and watched as the children left before she too walked away.

Back at the house all the children sat and watched as Joel fed his dad a little of his blood. Sallem asked, *"Why do you feed him blood?"* Joel shrug, *"When I was being brought here a woman fed me blood to help keep me alive, my grandma and grandpa did as well when we ran north. Something in it gave me strength, knowledge and helped heal."* Tyrone nodded, *"Like our blood brothers bond."* Tyrone, Tye,

Bill and Willie show off their matching scars. Sallem asked, *"So would more blood help your dad?"*

Joel shrugged, Sallem grabbed the knife then cut her finger, dripping the blood into the tin cup, followed by Mike, Tyrone, Tye, Bill, Willie and finally Joel. They started dripping the blood in Brenat mouth, they watched as even more of his color came back before it again returned to the pale gray.

Joel showed how he could heal by shifting his head to that of a wolf and licked the wound on Sallem's finger as they watched it heal. Joel felt the awe, confidence, and kindness in Sallem along with how she wished she could do what he had done. Then Joel licked Mike's wound closed, felt his pride and protectiveness over his friends. Joel healed each, tasted their differences, Tyrone's strength and leadership. Tye, Bill, and Willie's cunning, stealth and mischievous. They all watched as Joel's eyes flicker with inner lights and how his wolf ears flicked at an unseen noise.

Shifting his head back to normal Joel looked upon his friends, *"I could taste your animal that resides in you."* Excitement ran in their eyes as they asked, *"Who's what animal? How do we talk to them? Would we be able to turn into them like you do?"* Joel said, *"Let's let my dad rest while we talk."*

Tyrone said, *"Let us become blood brothers and share in each other's blood so each of us can be linked by blood."* Sallem hands on hips, stomped her foot looking at Tyrone, *"and sister"* Tyrone added quickly.

Tyrone looked at Brenat then at Joel then at the others and saw them looking at Brenat. Sallem sat and ran her fingers in Brenat's hair as if drawing comfort from him. The others too seemed to be trying to touch Brenat to feel the parent they had lost.

Tyrone said, *"Joel, we no longer have dad's. Since we are sharing to help with yours could we adopt him as our dad? When we are all blood brothers and sister he could be our blood dad."* The others looked towards Joel in silence. Joel saw the longing and hopes in each of their eyes and faces as they awaited his answer. Joel smiled, *"That's a great idea we would all be family then."* Using the knife and cup, Joel cut each of them, they watched as the blood ran into the cup then they fed it to their dad. They watched as his color returned then after cleaning the gray sludge off his arm they drew some of Brenat's blood. Each one took a sip of his bright red blood to blood bond with their dad, then they watched as his color again started to fade as gray sludge begun to drip from the cut.

After climbing from the attic and checking to made sure no one had come home yet. They went out to the court yard before they realized they had forgotten the knife. Joel shifted his head to a wolf, bit his arm the blood drained into the cup before he licked it closed. They each held their arm out for Joel to bite. He bit fast each yelped in pain before they to added their blood to the cup and Joel licked each of the bites closed. Joel's head shifted slightly as he tasted each of their essence even stronger than before. He stirred the blood with a single claw before handing the cup to Sallem who took a sip, while watching Joel whose head started to resemble a bear, his head shifted to each of their animals as they were revealed. She heard Joel's thoughts in her mind, *"Bear meet Sallem, Sallem meet bear you share a body as we share our blood."* Joel turned to Mike who heard Joel's thoughts, *"The lion in you calls to you Mike, you share a body as we share our blood. Tyrone, your wolf is glad to be home as you share a body just like we share our blood. Tye your panther has snuck in and now shares your body as we share blood. Billy your tiger had found you now you both share a body as we share our blood. Willie your jaguar has found its body to share just as we share our blood."* They all heard Joel's wolf howl, *"Welcoming his pack home."* They felt each other in their minds, as if hearing them speak aloud. They knew they were a family more than before when they heard their animals speak to them.

Suddenly they heard Joel's alpha order commanding them to shift. Sallem cried out screaming in pain as her bones broke, and reformed as she shifted. Her body skin stretched and grew fur. She heard her bear say, *"You will be ok. Soon you will be you and more. The pain will lessen each time."* Suddenly there stood a black bear cub, where once the girl had stood. Sallem looked at her paws, claws and touches her teeth. While noticing all the new smells. *"Will it hurt to turn back?"* she asked. The bear answered, *"Yes, but you are strong and confident. We will never have a problem and the pain will lessen the more we shift until it disappears. Remember I will always be with you."*

As each turned, the family support made the shift's painful transition easier to take. After the lion, the wolf emerged next, his pack there with him the whole time reassuring the young beta. The tiger, jaguar, and panther shifted with speed as one almost as if racing to see who was fastest the race ending in tie. The pack soon stood before Joel, all fully formed and strong. The only witnesses to the forming of the new pack was Raven from the roof top, and a lone jaguar hiding in the bushes that disappeared down an alley soon after.

Brenat heard his children scream and his mind struggled to consciousness at his children screams of pain. Briefly confused at having seven children not one, he reached out seeking who was hurting his children. As he felt their familiar bond, he felt their pain from the shift. In a cloudy memory he remembered the same pain at his first shift and sent each a warm hug with his love and told them, *"Daddy is here."* A smile formed as they returned his love and hugs, before he once more slipped back into the nightmare of running from Keres's smile.

Teera sat talking to Eve, Reed and Dru about who in the town was next to leave for Arena City. When she felt a faint hug and feeling of love from her mate, then she heard, *"Daddy is here,"* before she lost the contact again. She caught her breath as she realized both Brenat and Joel were alive. At the loss of contact she breathed as if she had been holding her breath for months. Eve, Reed and Dru looked towards her, worried at her strange actions asked, *"What's was wrong?"* Teera looked at them and smiled her face coming alive in her happiness, replied, *"Brenat and Joel are alive."*

All the children went still and quiet as they each felt their dad as he sent them each a hug, his love and heard him as he told them, *"He was there,"* before he was gone from their minds. They looked at each other whispering, *"Did you hear and feel daddy?"* Each smiling in happiness as this confirmed they were a family.

Looking around at each other they noticed their cloths were ripped in places and a little tighter in others. They heard Joel in their minds, *"That is why I wear loose fitting clothing."* They sat in a circle laughing at each other's new and wonderful experience.

Rinette went out to the court yard and saw the seven of them smiling from ear to ear, giddy with happiness, wondered what they were up to. She called them in from the yard and stared when she saw the state of their clothes, wondered how she could have missed them growing out of their clothes so fast.

Teera wanting as well as needing to get to her family started packing to leave right away. Eve grabbed Teera, *"If we don't stop Silfer and Dukut there would be no home for you, Brenat, Joel or anyone. There are fewer and fewer towns and people every month, we need to stay with the plan."* Teera growled at Eve, *"My family needs me and I need them"* she sat crying, as she knew Eve was right.

The newly formed pack snuck out to the surrounding forest to practice with their new senses, claws and teeth. Raven watched them and scouted from above. She sent a warning, Joel heard the raven squawk, and he quickly sent out a mental command to his pack to hide. They all found a shadow, bush or tree nook to hide in. Joel watched raven following the path of the red haired woman, Solana that shifted to a jaguar as she entered the forest. Joel sent his pack a warning to beware a jaguar shifter that was coming towards them.

Joel using Raven's eyes observed glimpses of the jaguar until she stopped moving hidden in the trees as she too waited and observed. The pack growing impatient Tyrone sent a mental message, *"Lets surround her and see what she wants."* Tyrone moved his people into position, then they sprung and shredded the bushes, but found no Jaguar. The pack regathered into the clearing confused by where she could have gone. They shifted and got dressed then headed back to the safety of the city. While the Jaguar watched the children fifteen feet from their clumsy attack on the now destroyed bush.

She watched as the children leave with the raven following as their eyes in the sky. She waited until the children went into the city before heading deeper into the woods catching a meal of a nearby rabbit. Then wondered how she could teach them to fight better as a unit, while staying hidden, which was becoming tougher now that Joel was learning to use the raven.

The pack on the way home, some still looking behind them for the unknown visitor to their practice site, started talking about learning to fight better as a group in both forms animal and human.

Going back into the city, the pack headed to the guards' barracks and asked for Jason, but was told that he was up at the pens. They headed up to the pens and were startled as Joel stopped short and started to growl in a low deadly way. He struggled not to shift, his eyes flaming red as they stalked the movements of someone in the distance. The pack looked towards where Joel was starring, saw the beautiful witch Keres and her guards. They felt Joel warn them, *"She is evil, and cruel. She helped kill our mother and family*" then he told them of her dangerous nature. Tyrone feeling the danger she posed to Joel and the rest of his family ordered the pack to retreat and surrounded Joel while he and Mike pulled Joel with them back home.

The pack went up to care for Brenat, while Rinette was out and before they were needed to get the other children. The children took turns feeding Brenat blood of themselves, bread and bits of meat they had stolen away from supper. All the while talking to their dad about themselves, knowing they needed help to fight the evil that ruled, they begged Brenat to, *"Please wake up and come help us, we need and love you."* Always one pack member stayed with him washing him as the sweat became more like gray ooze, that clung to Brenat's body as if it was trying to get back in.

Busted

One night as he laid with his dad, Joel started feeling exceptionally stuffy. He opened the window, all the way open and sat there looking at the full moon. Brenat stirred as if trying to fight mystic bonds that trapped him. Joel feeling that the unusual stuffiness of the attic must be bothering his dad, he pulled his dad, who had gained some of his weight and color back, to the open window, so he could rest easier. Unable to lift him through the window, Joel stripped then climbed through the window, then shifted to his bear for the enhanced strength. He then pulled his dad through the window and sat him up against the chimney. Joel shifted back to his human self where he sat holding Brenat under the light of the full moon while a light breeze blew. While a jaguar watched, gasped and covered her mouth with her paw, as she noticed how father and son backs have almost identical scars, when their backs were towards her as Joel positioned his father. The Jaguar scoffed at herself for acting so human, continued watching the boy share the moonlight with his father.

Brenat stuck in his nightmare and feeling suffocated, suddenly felt a strong mind he recognized helping him as the moon's light pushed back the demons. A light breeze washed over his skin, chasing away the evil bonds that held him. His freed soul ran from the nightmare in his body, until it found the one it sought. Drawn to his love like a beacon, he stood mere inches from her wanting to caress her, needing that which only she could truly give him. Teera's healing light washed the gray poisons from his soul and body as it had healed him so long ago when he was hurt.

Teera saw Brenat's soul through the mystic bonds that shackled him as they had when they were younger. They sat together in the light of the moon, slipping into their old ways, until the bonds flared and he was gone from her again. Teera knew he was far away and needed help, but she knew he was alive, getting stronger, and they would be together again.

Joel felt his dad jerk and convulse a bit, Joel laid him back onto the roof and bit his arm, he fed his dad more of his blood. He then watched as gray ooze seeped from Brenat's body and it seemed as if it ran for the gutter to escape from the light of the moon. After a while Joel tried to get his dad back inside and was unable to do so, he called his pack, who came to help get their dad back inside.

While Mike, Tyrone and Willie pulled to get Brenat back inside, Joel, Billy and Tye lifted and pushed from outside. Sallem fretted below the attic hatch, heard a noise, looked over to see Rinette standing in the doorway looking from her to the open attic. Sallem said and sent an, *"Oh oh"* to her brothers as Rinette poked her head up into the attic to stare at the boys in fury. She climbed up into the attic and helped the boys get Brenat back into his make shift bed. Then ordered the children to bed saying, *"Shush, we will talk in the morning."* The children hung their heads mumbling, *"Yes Ma'am"* each dreading what was going to happen in the morning.

In the morning with breakfast complete and the children at their respective jobs, the pack returned home to see Rinette and Kenny sitting drinking tea having a polite conversation as if nothing was wrong, caused the pack to stop short. Kenny stood up looking at each then said, *"You children have some explaining to do."* Joel stepped ahead of the others and drew his wooden sword, *"I will fight you to protect my dad from going back to the pens."* The pack stepped forward with a unified, *"We."* Sallem added with pleading whisper, *"If we have to."*

Kenny stood shocked as the knowledge sunk in as to who Joel really was. Angered at how they challenged him warred with his being proud that the children would challenge him to save Brenat. Then a sense of proudness and anger again washed over him, not only had they snuck the ailing near dead Brenat out of the highly guarded pens, but they also managed to hide him for several months in Kenny's own home. If Rinette had not awoken because she was feeling ill, they still would have gotten away with it.

Rinette watching tensely as seconds passed then told the children, *"Put your weapons away and sit down so we can all talk about this calmly."* With a gentle hand she pushed Kenny back into his chair, handing him his tea while his mind raced. Rinette gave her mate a hug and whispered, *"You must be proud of what they have done. I don't know many well trained adults that could have pulled off that heist and then to have hidden it from you as well as from the red cloaks, witches, hell hounds, and all the broken arrow members in town."*

Rinette looking at everybody gave all the children a cookie off the plate full on the table said, *"First we need to get him into a proper bed then get an apothecary to look at him since Keres and the red cloaks have had him for so long. Joel, you will be allowed to spend as much time with him as could be arranged."*

Sallem cleared her throat and said, *"We want to be with our daddy too."* Rinette confused asked, *"Sallem, explain what you mean?"* Sallem proudly said, *"We all shared blood with Joel and can touch our animals, we are a pack now. We also shared our blood with daddy to help him get better faster."* Rinette looked around at all the children, *"Yes, time will be made for all of you to spend time with *your father.*" Rinette looked at Kenny sending through their bond, "*Pack? That means they are all Lycans. How could that have happened? They were all tested and were declared humans?*"

Kenny looked at the children, "*Since you chose to challenge me and have a lot of training to do before that would have a chance at being successful, you will train from noon until supper every day. You will learn to add, subtract, read, and write after supper, while doing your chores between breakfast and noon.*" Sallem asked, "*What about our animals?*" Kenny looked at Rinette they both looked at the children, "*Time will be made for you to show us and to train with your wolves?*" They said thinking the children were just human children or at most normal lycan wolves, "*Show us your wolves.*"

The children looked at each other, then at Joel, at his silent command they all shifted. Kenny and Rinette gasped in surprise as a bear, wolf, tiger, lion, panther, and jaguar now sat in front of them their loose fitting tunics now snug on their animal forms. Kenny leaned back stunned said, "*But you were human children, you can't be royals. The red cloaks would have known when you were tested.*"

Joel spoke up, "*No, they just needed help touching their animals after they hid from the evil ones and now we are a pack. My father is theirs for our blood is shared and mixed. We will fight as one and for one another with our lives.*" Kenny and Rinette shocked asked Joel, "*What is your animal if you lead this pack?*" Joel answered, "*ALL, I am all of them and they are all of me.*"

Kenny's eyes went wide as he realized that not only was his lost godson standing in front of him but Joel is the embodiment of the ancient legend. He is a three-year-old child in a ten-year old's body with an ancient soul that was now standing in his kitchen eating a cookie and asking "*HIM*" what should be done.

Kenny shook his head, "*Ok, part of your training will be learning your animals but only shift in secret in the court yard and your trainers will be hand-picked by me. No shifting where anyone can see you unless I give the ok."* Kenny asked Joel to show him his animals. Joel shifted to the white bear to a white tiger then to the black panther on to a jaguar then a black wolf followed by a fiery hell hound and last into a golden lion that both Rinette and Kenny knew so well, before he turned back to a human child. Kenny sighed and thought, *"Finally, I am no longer the only lion left. Joel will need a lot of training so he can fulfill his destiny to bring back the guardians."*

Almost a month after Teera had visited with Brenat's soul, a rider arrived looking as if he was about to fall out of the saddle followed by a train of exhausted horses. The horses soon were stabled, he headed to the bath, stripped down with only a pouch around his neck, his broken arrow brand in plain sight as he lounges back into the pool. A naked woman came to him and started bathing the travel from his weary bones. She guided his hands to her own brand, while she satisfied his growing arousal with gentle hands. After which from the pouch he handed her two coins after she found him a lounger to rest on. She quickly took the coins to Eve, who took the note hidden from between the coins, handed the coins to the woman then dismissed her. Eve unfolded the paper that read, *"Brenat captured and in Arena City pens. His debut in the arena is to be the Fall Harvest Festival if he lives that long. He is the bait for a trap set by king Silfer so he can marry Queen Teera when she is finally rescued. He has been in the pens a week before we were able to send this out."*

Six days later, another messenger arrived at the pools. This message's transfer completed within sight of a red cloak priest and his two warriors, as the rider's bath came to completion. Eve read the note, *"Brenat four days ago escaped. Friends and enemies alike are searching for him. No one knows who helped him escape if anyone. Search continues for his where about."*

Eve laughed as she took the note to Teera, shook her head

as the information was over a month behind, Teera already knew that Brenat and Joel were alive and were together free of the pens, as she had briefly gotten a visit from Brenat on the full moon.

Teera looked at herself in a mirror hardly recognizing herself because of the cooking grease and soot. On her face the soot and grease exaggerated the bags under her eyes from sorrow filled sleepless nights. Only now were her mornings filled with hope and laughter. Teera read the note that came in and wondered if she would have time to have a bath before she saw them or if that message would arrive a moon cycle behind too.

Brenat was moved into a spare bedroom by Kenny and Rinette with the packs help. A trusted apothecary was due to show up to heal him or at least try. Rinette lifted her dress revealing her leg and thigh so the children could see the brand one hand's breadth down from the hip bone. She told them that others with this mark could be trusted as long as they don't have these special back scars. Gently she turned Brenat over to show them his back and the scars there. Sallem said, *"Joel has those scars just like daddy does and we trust him. They are exceptions to the rule"* Kenny said, *"But only if we say so understand? Also never talk openly about your shifting abilities or about your dad to anyone even to the other children."*

Tyrone said, *"Duh, you adults are always trying to interfere in our fun"* then looking ashamed apologized, *"I am sorry Kenny and Rinette."* Kenny replied, *"I will overlook that one, but you mind your manners and show respect from now on understood."* Brenat briefly woke from the pain of the move looked towards Kenny then to his kids told them, *"All of you children mind your god parents."* The pack answers as one, *"Yes sir."* Once more Brenat passed out, leaving seven children starring from their father to their new aunt and uncle, while Kenny and Rinette stared at Brenat. Rinette said stunned, *"He made us their god parents."* Kenny replied, *"I was made Joel's god father with Arris when he was born, looks like Brenat trusts us with all their children."* Sallem looked from her father to her new aunt and uncle said, *"Our family is getting bigger."* Rinette with her hand on her belly replied, *"Yes, it is"* to which Kenny pulled her closer to him.

The apothecary showed up to examine Brenat, when Kenny revealed the diet he had been on in the pens, the apothecary whistled in exasperation and stunned disbelief. Said, *"He should have been dead long before now so whatever you were doing keep it up. Also could you tell me what were you doing so I could add that to my books and see if there is anything I could do to assist after I have done some research?"* Joel answered, *"We fed him bread, water, some scraps of meat from our meals and we each gave him our blood daily. When the gray ooze seeped from his body we washed it away as it tried to go back in if we don't and it made him sicker."*

"Where did you learn that?" They all look at Joel who answered, *"I have been fed blood since I could remember, with and without meat. My parents did it, my grandparents did it and so have others to save me."* He looked at Kenny who remembered giving Joel blood when he was first brought in he also remembered Brenat feeding both Joel and Teera his blood when Joel was born and Teera was dieing. The apothecary said, *"I should be back in a few days if not sooner with more information and keep doing what you're doing."*

As Brenat got stronger he was able to reach Teera and the children with his mind for a few minutes each day before he passed into unconsciousness once more.

Training Begins

Jason showed up, showing the children his wolf then his warrior lycan humanoid that had teeth as well as claws but could carry weapons and wear armor, his warrior form. The pack eyes alight as he had each one shift to the warrior form which they did with ease except for Joel who's many forms struggle for dominance. Joel shifted his head to that of a lion, one arm to that of a bear; his other arm of a tiger with retractable claws on the body of a wolf, was the combat form he could hold longest. Jason told Joel to quit trying and to just be human and only shift as needed.

It soon became evident Joel's easiest shift was a wolf head and bear arms with retractable claws with cat legs on a human body. Jason told him, *"That should be kept secretive and stick with the all or nothing do not shift single body parts for there are beings out there that have been specially trained in hunting you so the more secretive the better. Fight as human or as animal nothing in between unless absolutely necessary."*

The rest of the pack learned the in between or lycan form. They learned that be it witch, lycan or vampire tearing out the heart and beheading it is the best way to kill everything mystical or not. Also learned the touch of silver would burn the lycan, vampires were affected by holy wood, holy water and silver the same way although it was very hard to behead a vampire with a wooden sword. But water collected from consecrated ground was devastating to vampires as was prolonged exposure to direct sunlight.

Jason said, *"That is why we cut off their heads and burn the bodies for Vampires are easy to hurt but hard to kill remember that. Bows and crossbow shots to the head and heart only, anything else would just slow them down so be prepared to finish them off. Lycans biting their heads off and eating their hearts seem to be just as effective as anything else, but vampires could do the same to us so always remember vampires are extremely dangerous be very careful when fighting them."*

The pack under Jason's and Kenny's tutelage learned to fight as human, animal and lycan. Learned how to block, parry, deflect as well as where the cuts, slashes and piercing only slow your opponent down until you could make the killing blow by piercing the heart and severing the spine where the neck met the head.

They practiced trying to pierce the string attached to a balloon that blew in the wind with a rapier. Then on to wooden dummies wearing armor with a pig spine and heart where the jointed arms swing wooden swords up or down until they learned to defeat them. They fought each other wearing leather armor and leather neck pieces. Bruised and sore they came in discussing their feats of grandeur and strength, their missteps and loses with laughter. When Mike brought up while they were on discussions of tactics said, *"Remember a good toe bite could win the day"*, had everyone laughing.

Brenat Wakes

Every evening after they got cleaned up, eat, did their schooling, and soothed their bruises with poultices, the children spent time with their dad taking turns feeding him. Then each one would told him about what they had learned and done that day, they told him about their training and their adventures. Every Sunday they were allowed off from training and schooling to play.

Brenat was unable to answer but the stories helped to chase away the nightmares. He listened to his children with growing pride. At first his confusion at not remembering any of his children except Joel upset him but soon that faded as his bond and love for his amazing children replaced any confusion.

When the apothecary came back the next day with a poultice to be placed on his chest nightly with instructions for him to be given three drops of a healing potion every night. *"Brenat's recovery should speed up as the spell weakens and the poisons are pulled from every inch of his body bit by bit when he sweats. The gray ooze would be sucked up by the poultice which is then to be peeled off his body and burned."*

By the end of the week, Brenat woke for fifteen minutes, allowing him to tell the children of his pride in them and how their talking to him had helped to keep the nightmares at bay. He thanked Kenny, Rinette and Jason for saving them and keeping them safe before he fell unconscious again.

Every day he stayed awake longer than the day before. The children told him of how he was rescued and what had happened since. They sat down with him, feeding him solid food slowly as he was still so weak. Each day he made a point to show each one how proud he was of them and how much he loved them. *"Rinette, Jason and Kenny, I want to Thank you again for saving my children and for keeping them and me safe. I know this was a great risk, I owe you a debt that I could never repay."* Kenny looked at him, *"Brenat you, Teera and the children are family."*

By the end of the following week Brenat was walking again as well as rebuilding his strength and went out to watch the children training. Kenny and Jason discussing tactics with the children asked Brenat, *"Would you like to help in their training?"* *"Yes"* he eagerly said, *"I'd love to help teach them tactics but I am still too weak to do any sparring yet, I thought you both had best do that while I watch for now."*

Brenat taught the children about how cold iron worked on witches and other creatures just like silver did on lycans. He also taught them little tricks like stabbing people in their foot, pinning them to the ground, while you got behind them for a better killing blow. If they were faster than you, how you could slow them down by tiring them by bleeding them out with little cuts all over their bodies. Also to always know where your feet were going, as you could lose a fight just by slipping on some blood or water. If you could make sure your opponent walked on treacherous ground, it could slow them down just a hair. That could be the difference between you getting cut or them, for a simple misstep could cause a downfall and made one vulnerable to attacks. Kenny and Jason reminded themselves to add that to their troop's training regimen.

He then taught them to watch out when fighting red cloaks, for they were the ones that taught him and some use magic as well as sword. Joel showed the pack a little of his magic, making Brenat decide to teach Joel the magic he knew. None of the other children seem to have the affinity towards magic. Brenat told them they took after their mother as she could not use magic either.

While he taught the children all that he knew. He did his own training while they trained to get his strength back. One day Joel and Brenat were standing beside each other shirtless drinking water while the other children finish the obstacle course, Jason motioned to Kenny to look at the backs of the other two. They stared at the identical scars, it was as if each whip mark Brenat had received, Joel had received as well. Jason and Kenny wondered at what it meant and why one so young had been made to suffer so harshly as they both knew Joel was only now four even though he looked older.

Teera laughed as almost two months after the last message, she received a message that Brenat, Joel and their six other children were safe and being guarded by the Broken Arrows in Arena City. She smiled as Brenat and she have been talking through their bond on every moon cycle when his soul traveled to her. He had shared with her the pride he had in their children and the stories they shared with him as well as how their training was going. At first she had also been confused as to how they could possibly have seven children not just the one she remembered them having. But soon she too dismissed it as just another miracle. They both laughed at how a couple not supposed to have any children now were the proud parents of seven very special children, six amazing boys and their little girl, Sallem.

Brenat passed on to each of the children the hugs and love Teera sent to them. Joel, his brothers and sister were shocked when Brenat told them that their momma sent them her love. Joel stared at his dad in stunned disbelief, *"Momma is alive? I thought momma was dead, I saw her shot with a crossbow bolt while*

I was being carried away by my grandparents." "Yes, Joel, she is very much alive and she told me to tell each of you how much she loves you." Suddenly Joel hugged his dad in happiness as he excitedly asked, *"Where is momma? When can we go to her or is she coming here?"* The others were equally excited as they thought they only had a dad, now they have a momma too. They like Joel bombarded their dad with questions, *"Momma really loves us? And is proud of us? When can we see her?"*

"Yes, your mother and I both love all of you, you are our miracle children. Soon you'll all see momma as we'll be together soon. Your mother, the Queen wants to be with her family as much as we want to be with her." The newly formed family grew even more excited as they learned they were soon to be together.

At hearing their momma was the true Queen, Sallem became serious then asked, *"Daddy, does that make me a Princess?"* Brenat acknowledged with a smile, *"Yes, it sure does."* Sallem smiled and skipped off. Brenat relays the question and Sallem's reaction to Teera, who started laughing causing those around her to ask, *"What's so funny?"* Teera smiled and replied, *"My daughter, the future Queen."*

Plans Are Made

Brenat and Teera started making plans for the reunion of their family and for taking out Silfer, Keres and Dukut.

Teera, Eve, Reed and Dru made plans over the next couple of weeks for Teera and Eve with the rest of the two hundred warring broken arrows to leave on the next several caravans. Dru and Reed along with a hundred others would stay back to protect the town, as they continued to recruit and help the town thrive. With the logistics and supplies taken care of they should arrive a full moon cycle before the solstice festival. Teera's sadness at missing another of Joel's birthdays was over ridden by the excitement of seeing her family. The excitement was high for all in the caravan until three days into the trip when a red cloak priest and three of his guards joined the caravan.

As the days turned into weeks, the priest was heard to mention that at least the peasant's cooking had improved, with a polite smile and a thank you from Teera for the generous praise. With a red cloak priest and three of his personal guards traveling with the caravan, Teera made sure she looked like an unkempt peasant. Changing her appearance by keeping her hair greasy and black with soot from the cook fires, her eyes were red and swollen from constantly blowing and tending the coals to keep her stew warm as she rode.

As caravan upon caravan headed to arena city for the

upcoming festival, Dukut's troops were spread thin as they stopped them to check for heretics and to see if the queen was hiding among the traveled populace.

On one of these searches, as the soldiers stopped the caravan, Teera started dishing out the warm stew to the servants, so as the red cloaked priest along with his guards got served first, then the warriors, and caravan guards, then the rest of the caravan populace while they were stopped.

Dukut's guards searched and poked their heads in every wagon as well as checked every person. One captain entered Teera's wagon spent a good minute just staring at Teera, her eyes and face down cast as she recognized him from having seen him during her time in the Castle Black's dungeon. The captain ordered her to look at him just as he stuck his hand into a bowl of the thick meaty stew, she had prepared for the red cloaks, tasting it, he spat and dumped the bowl she was holding into her face, growling, *"If you cooked for us, you would be lashed for this slop."* Teera looked down again, hiding her smile as a piece of gravy covered meat rolled off her nose. The captain angrily left the wagon looking back at her one more time before moving on to the next wagon.

The red cloak priest and his guards left with the captain to go back to Castle Black with the patrol. Agreeing with the captain that the cook's skilled were atrocious as she always added too much salt.

Teera smiled as she heard the comment, for she had been dishing up a special dish for the priest's meal, of half a scoop of stew, added two pinches salt, added another half scoop of stew then added a handful of salt, stirred and served. All those that rode with the red cloaks get this same dish. Every day the priest's guards changed so that while the ones furthest away from the red cloaks got a little spice for flavor, the closer they got to the red cloaks the saltier the meal became. While all the guards loved their rotations to the front or back of the caravan those that moved closer to the middle became more and more miserable. The guards that walked alongside the caravan, moods improved as their rotation cycle moved them away from the red cloaks, while their moods slowly got worse as they rotated to walk beside the red cloaks.

The priest could be heard to comment that her cooking had improved, for when he had first joined up it had tasted like shit. Teera smiled as she remembered the third day into the trip when the red cloaks had invited themselves to join the caravan. She had started adding some horse paddies to their bowls with extra salt only stopping when one of her people had almost eaten from the wrong bowl. After the patrol and red cloaks left. The caravan continued and everybody's moods as well as meals greatly improve.

❂ ❂ ❂ ❂ ❂ ❂ ❂ ❂ ❂ ❂ ❂

One Sunday, the pack was given a task to go practice their stealth and pick pocketing. With the one that collected the most would get a double helping of pudding and an extra cupcake.

Sallem, Joel and Mike walked along watching for guards and people, using their pack bond they helped each of the others get more than they ever have before even raven got in on the fun by pointing out shiny items. They came back with coins, silk scarves and jewelry from the wealthy. While the peasants lost a fish here or a pastry there.

Joel bought a flower for Sallem's hair saying, *"Every princess should have something pretty for her hair."* Sallem giggled and Mike smiled.

Returning home they found the bath master Brian and his wife Rose sitting with Brenat, Kenny and Rinette. The children soon unloaded their loot when asked who won they said, *"Raven as she did better than all the rest."* Raven had added the shiniest items to her nest and had done it without any help from the children. Everyone laughed as raven started giving Rinette all her stolen stuff until there is a large pile on the table and they all agree that raven had won the contest. As a prize Rinette gave it extra of its favorite fish.

Rose hugged Joel and the rest of the children, told them she is their dad's sister. Sallem the first to have the knowledge sink in asked, *"Aunt Rose, does this mean we can come swimming more?"* Brian laughed while nodding Rose answered, *"Yes"* Joel looked on quietly at this exchange, went to stand close to his dad. The pack, sensing his unease, moved as one to stand close to him protectively while also offering him comfort. The adults watched silently at seeing how protective the young pack was of their young alpha.

Brenat sensing Joel's unease asked, *"What's wrong?"* Joel told him, *"I don't want to upset my aunt and uncle or my pack. But I can't go back to the baths."* The adults asked him, *"Why not?"* Before Joel could speak Tyrone said, *"It's because the last time we went the people at the baths saw Joel's back and believed him to be a spy for the red cloaks."*

Brenat told Joel to remove his shirt and stared at the scars that look like his own. Rose gasped at the marks of an elite that were on Joel, just as they were on Brenat. Brian seeing asked, *"How could this have happened? We know Joel is not an elite."* Kenny told of Joel's capture and punishment at the hands of Toe-less and the other guards. Brenat's eyes flamed and silently added Toe-less on the to be killed by him personally list.

Brian watched as Brenat's eyes flared and said, *"There will be others that would ask too, so I need to know how do we really know that he is who you say he is? We could not take any chances that this is another trap to capture Teera or us. The baths would be ripe with more suspicion than normal when or if either of them show up.”*

Brian and Rose remembered back to the pool of how some of the broken arrows had talked about the scars on a young boy and the week long arguments that had followed. Brian reported that most of the arguments had been on the same thing, *“Everyone knew that red cloak's recruited young but none knew just how young one had to be, to be made an Elite such as Brenat was. With new broken arrows coming in weekly we may have to calm many until trusts are built. Kenny had announced a trap many times. Kenny, you have told us of the amazing things Joel could do. Also the children were tested and they tested as humans yet now they are royals and they claim to be Teera and Brenat's children. Also they are pack bonded to Joel who is claiming to be their alpha and brother. We ALL know Joel was only a one-year toddler when the massacre happened yet this boy looks to be ten. How do we know that this is the real Brenat and Joel? How do we know the real Brenat and Joel were not killed as believed and these are not imposters? Rose, how do you know this is not an imposter that was fed the information tortured from the original Brenat? There were many more arguments going back and forth that day for they trusted in the Brand, Teera, and their individual leaders. We had trouble regaining order.”*

Joel steps forward, *“He is my dad, our blood rings true.”*

Brian stood and said, *“What proves you are who you say you are? Now everyone is endangered if they are spies. We all knew that the red cloaks would use our hopes and dreams against us.”*

Sallem said, *“Joel is real, we share his blood.”*

Brian said, *“I have no doubt that you believe that child, but this is bigger than children's belief.”*

Looking at the Brian, Brenat stated, *“You are prudent, only one can verify me and that is Teera. Kenny has seen me only twice and believed I was Brenat, but now doubts rises in his eyes. Only if you accept Joel as your alpha and share of his blood will you have a chance at seeing his true self. Again the red cloaks have mastered the art of leadership and deception. Even while I talk with Teera through our bond, you would not know until she arrived. Whether it be distance or the poisons I was fed we are still only able to talk on new moons and full moons. So Joel and I will stay in the house under arrest. Kenny, one guard is insufficient for many times I have easily killed three superior well trained lycan guards in my career. While the next full moon is several days away yet. I do not know what I can say to her that I could relay back the next morn that you would believe."*

Tears flow down Rose's cheeks as she struggles with Brian's suspicions and her hope of having her brother back.

Kenny knew he could verify by sharing of Joel's blood, but he dared not show his royal self, he had not survived this long by taking chances. Instead he said, *"You will have two guards around you all the time Brenat and one on Joel. These are more for your protection and for show then for any other reason. You shall be under house arrest and train until Brian could verify with Teera. Even if I believe there is more at risk then just my life here."* He reaches his arms around Rinette his hands resting protectively on her stomach.

Rose tears falling hugged Brenat, *"I believe in you too. We will find a way to get the proof we need or a way for Teera verify you."*

Joel asked, *"Is my pack free to go around as normal?"* Brian nodded yes and watched Joel as he directs his pack, *"Now it is up to you all to take the children to and from their jobs and protect them. You are the Guardians now."* The adults shivered as that statement rings of magic, both Brenat and Kenny stared at Joel as he called the meeting with his pack to an end and all the children nodded their heads before they hug their dad and brother then headed to bed without a word.

Imprisoned

Brenat and Joel were moved to a windowless room, when not training in the courtyard with a guard outside their door and two others spaced out down the hall. Brenat tested Joel, to see how much magic ability he had, by teaching Joel the spell of the zephyr, that allows his feet to hover an eighth of an inch off any surface. Which allowed him to walk and make no sound or tracks even over the softest of snow or dried out leaf. Joel excelled in less the thirty minutes by walking across the bed and not even ruffling the sheets. Brenat shook his head in awe as he remembered it had taken him a week to be able to hover and another to walk and fight.

Brenat then taught him to shadow, how to gather shadows from around you and deepens them so that others could not see into them but you could see out. Joel once again in minutes hid in the deepest of shadows. Brenat shook his head as he realized that Joel had more power then he even thought he had. Brenat's eyes barely caught a shadowy movement and was stunned that Joel was able to move and keep the shadow spell on him. Watching as the deep shadow moved across the bed not ruffling the sheets. Brenat eyes open wide as he realized Joel was holding two spells while moving something that even the most skilled priests and elite were unable to accomplish.

Joel dropping the spells excitedly said, *"What is next this is fun?"* Brenat taught him another spell, magic deflection. Brenat pushed a wind at Joel and watched as Joel's hair did not even flutter but the wooden chair behind Joel slid along the floor away from Brenat until it hit the wall. Joel's eyes widen with excitement as he imitated his dad, and both were surprised when Brenat flew back hitting the wall. Joel stopped concerned as Brenat shivered and stood brushing the ice off that had formed on his chest. Brenat looked at his son, *"Where did you learn to do that?"* Joel worried replied, *"From you, I just saw what you were doing and fixed it, was that ok?"* Brenat hugged his son and laughed, *"You do whatever you need to do to fix my clumsy attempts at magic. I'm sorry son, I have no more magic to show you."*

Joel replies, *"I can teach you one, Dad, that grandpa Sid taught me."*

Brenat, looked at Joel and asked, *"What spell did your grandpa teach you? When did grandpa teach you? Where are your grandma and grandpa?"*

Joel had his dad join him as they sat on the floor in the middle room, as Brenat sat down he felt a warmth. Then as he watched ice begin appearing on the walls, yet he still felt warm. He watched as the chair, bedding and other items began circling the room as if in a tornado, yet he felt no wind. Joel began, *"Grandma left to lead the red cloaks away that were following us. Grandpa and I continued to the land of ice. He told me about Ursa and her cub. When I awoke and crawled from the snow, I followed the scent of evil and found grandpa torn apart, by his brother, Eon. Then I helped grandpa's spirit join with others in the dancing lights."* The door splintered into the wind, and added its shattered remnants to the swirling mass, as the guard standing at the door, tried to force his way in but ended up part of the circling mass. Brenat seeing this told Joel to stop the spell before someone got hurt. Everything fell as if dropped by a hand. Everything inside the circle with Joel and Brenat was normal, while everything outside the circle lay in a circular mess. The guard picked himself up and looked around as he brushed himself off, looked at Brenat as he was leaving, *"You're going to need another room."* Brenat got up and walked to the hall way to see if anything else was damaged, but was surprised to find that nothing had been effected but their room.

Brenat looked at Joel, *"I think instead I will teach you of the people you could meet. Like the Anniste, a witch with four arms and steel like skin that cast spells that capture their prey so they could eat them alive, the Centaur half man half horse he did this all the way to the zombies. Making special notes on what to watch for to identify them and any unique abilities they have like spells or extra tough flesh, as well as any weakness they have and how to kill them."* Looking at Joel he said, *"Watch out for the Gaunts they have spells, a vicious hunger, are great fighters and trackers, along with other things I do not know."*

This all took place while Joel and Brenat were locked in their room alone. The rest of the time they trained in the courtyard with and without the pack. Raven was sent out to check on the children, if one got into trouble, Joel using his bond sent the pack to rescue and guard that child. When Jason came to guard Brenat they often sparred and train against one another, while Joel trained against another guard or practiced his magic. With Brenat's strength back and the pack with four trainers, the individual member's strength, endurance, speed, and skill excelled. The whole pack learned to fight as a great unit through their bond.

Soon the full moon was due, Brian, Rose, Rinette, Kenny sat across from Brenat after an early supper. Brian told Brenat, *"If Teera tells you who leads her four quivers and who her second is then we could include you into the plans as we would know you are really you and not imposters."* Rose interrupts, *"And it would stop this foolishness and we could let you come to the bath house. The distrust of new members we could deal with at that time."* Brenat looked at his sister, *"Rose, this is not foolishness, this is serious and I am glad it's being done. If we were imposters it could be death sentences to lots of people including Teera. We have to remember this all started because we trusted to easily at Castle Black."*

Off to bed they all went, the pack hugging their father good night, while Brenat and Joel went to their new room that now had a small window. Joel after snuggling up to his dad and asked him to say hi to mom for him before he went to sleep. Brenat relaxed and caressing his son's head laid back thinking of Teera, soon his soul followed the pull, he found her on the road in a caravan.

Teera smiled and told Brenat to give the children hugs, kisses and to tell them momma would see them soon. She listened with growing pride as he told of how well their training was going and he told her of Joel's incredible powers. She laughed with Brenat as he told of how Joel had gotten him with the wind spell by changing it to freezing ice. As he told of Joel's amazing growth she felt a twinge of regret for the time lost with her baby.

Brenat hesitated before telling Teera of the scars on Joel's back that were identical to his. At hearing the hesitation Teera, pushed him to hear the bad news she knew was coming. With a sigh, Brenat told her, *"There are scars on Joel's back that are so identical to mine that people are mistaking them for red cloak elite training marks."*

Her rage was so great that it was felt by all through their alpha bond that reopened in her intense anger and rage. Her tigress surged to the surface, guards and drivers alike had their hands full trying to calm the frightened horses as the great cat roared its promise of death from among the caravan.

Eve woke with a start, grabbed her clothes to go help and exclaimed out loud, *"Damn, who's pissed her off this time, last time we lost a guard and a servant in the castle garden, now what will she do? I thought Brenat was supposed to be with her tonight that usually keeps her calm. I'll kill the fool or fools that angered her myself if she doesn't."* Eve said through gritted teeth as she tried to help calm a frightened horse on her way to Teera's wagon.

Kenny and Brian wake up as did everyone else that was

pack bonded to Teera, all those that remembered what happened last time she was this angry, trembled hoping it was not them, that had caused her anger. Joel's siblings felt their mom's rage through Joel and rushed to their dad scared and unsure of what was happening.

Kenny told Rinette, *"Damn, Teera is pissed, and last time she was this mad she killed those that did it and she was only a child."* Rinette replied, *"Oh No, who's made her mad this time?"* Kenny answered, *"I don't know but I pity the idiots that did it, as they have loosened her tigress."* Rinette whispered, *"She's not that mad over our locking up Brenat and Joel is she?"* Kenny swallowed suddenly, *"I hope not. My niece is dangerous when not angry, angered she is deadly."* Meanwhile Brian and Rose were asking the same question with equal fear.

Brenat finally calmed Teera, *"My love please calm down your scaring the children."* She felt the children crowded around their dad and calmed returning to her human form. The children saw their mom through the veil and cried, *"Is that momma?"* Teera seeing the children through the mystic veil smiled proudly at her babies and told Brenat to hug them and tell them she loved them. Sallem whispered, *"Daddy, was mommy mad at us for being bad?"* Brenat hugged her and said, *"No"* then relayed the question to Terra who smiled and shook her head, *"No."*

Brenat told the children, *"Your momma and I would never be that mad at you children, we love you too much. Each of you are our miracle children and very special to us. Momma was mad at those that hurt Joel and the rest of our family."*

Soon the children fell asleep in Brenat's bed as Teera and Brenat continued their visit as the moon shone on them. Finally, before they parted, Brenat asked Teera, *"Who are leaders of the four quivers? Who is your second in command?"* Teera answered, *"Eve is my second, Brian, Blane, Tom and Ryan lead the four quivers, we have one in each direction. Each had set up baths to aid in finding out if any red cloak spies try to sneak in. Dru and Reed are my betas in broken arrow town."* Brenat told her, *"I love you, Teera, and I will be so glad when we can be together again."* Teera told him, *"I'll be arriving soon love"* then she sent out an alpha promise that had both Kenny and Brian paling and Eve glad it was not directed at her.

The next morning after the children had settled back to their chores, Kenny and Rinette meet with Brenat in the kitchen as they waited on Brian and Rose to arrive. Kenny smiled and said, *"I hope you calmed her down."* Brenat laughed, *"Barely but seeing the effect her tigress's rage was having on the children did it faster than even I could."* Brian and Rose walked in hearing that, Brian shivered before commenting, *"The last time she was that mad she was just a cub and still killed two grown men before we could contain her."*

Brenat smiled, *"Yeah, my Teera is a powerful force to battle, if not for my training and our special friendship I would not have survived the battle we had when we bonded and she still drew first blood. Angered she is extremely dangerous and deadly."*

Brenat told them what Teera told him about the quivers, the baths, broken arrow town and her second Eve. Rose ran to her brother hugging him. Kenny and the others again went to apologize but Brenat stopped them, *"You did correctly and I understood the reason for it and agreed that it needed to be done and so does Teera now that she has calmed down."*

Joel sleepily walked in and went to his daddy looking like the four-year-old little boy he really was as everyone stared having never seen him in his true form. Rinette exclaimed, "He's only four!" Everyone looks from her to Joel and nods in realization at the power of the young boy. Brenat hugged him close as Joel climbed on his lap asking, *"Daddy, do they believe us now or are we still bad guys to them?"* Brenat kissed the top of Joel's head and said, *"They believe us baby boy."* Joel pressed close and whimpered, *"Daddy, I want momma,"* Brenat whispered, *"We both do son we both do."*

Brenat was still not allowed out of the house or courtyard as he was still being actively hunted by the red cloaks just as Teera and Joel were. So he continued to train his children in the walled garden when not training, he helped the children with their reading and writing, as well as taught them of the different people they could meet.

Teera arrives to claim her family

Teera's caravan passed through the town gates with little more than a cursory look over, when the tariff was paid. With people meeting various members of the caravan it begun splitting up. Teera's wagons with her spices, salts, carefully packed flowers and oils headed to the baths.

Ryan and his mounted two hundred red cloak trained warriors entered the city three hours behind Teera's caravan.

Brian had Teera's room available in the middle interior rooms, her guards surrounding her on all sides. After a private bath Rose came in to help Teera and introduced herself as Brenat's sister. Rose helped Teera with her hair while they talked about Brenat the children and how Teera had about three hours before they arrived. The children excited about being able to go to the pools today worked hard at getting their chores done. Brenat and Teera talked in their bond of the surprise they had for their children when they met their mother.

The orphanage emptied in a rush and as the children ran excitedly down to the pools with Rinette, Kenny and Brenat following the children. Brenat told Teera they were on their way when Rinette counting the children noticed seven were missing and walked back to the house to overhear Joel and the others talking. Sallem excited cried, *"Come on Joel, let's go, it will be so much fun."* Joel replied, *"It is until I show up and people see my back, then things change even if I keep my back covered or not it will still effect how people treat you. So if I stay back you can have fun."* Tyrone and Mike announced, *"We will stay with you."* Sallem and the rest sadly agreed to stay behind as well. Joel sighed feeling his sibling's sadness finally agreed to go.

Sallem happily hugged Joel as they skipped around the corner, saw Rinette clipping flowers. She handed them to Sallem and told her to take them to Rose as she followed the children to the pool.

Getting to the pools, all the children stripped down excitedly and jumped into the biggest pool laughing. Joel walked to the smallest pool with his back to the wall, stripped down and climbed into the almost uncomfortable hot pool, sinking into the water up to his chin. He watched everyone laughing and having fun, the joy they were having filled him with a powerful sense of blessed peace.

The red haired woman saw Joel off by himself, went over slipping into the pool with him Smiling, *"Hi Joel."* Joel looked towards her thinking feeling for her essence, suddenly smiled and hugged her saying, *"It's you, Solana. I never did say thank you for saving my life on the trip. It was you in the forest not long ago wasn't it?"* She smiled, *"Yes and it would be harder for me to do that again as I have been watching you train."* The quiet conversation was watched by a few distrustful adults but unheard as the children frolicked and laughed.

Brenat found Teera's room just as Rose was leaving, he hugged his sister before walking in and locking the door behind him. Brenat stood admiring his beautiful wife, her long flowing hair hung past her shoulders. The white silken dress barely restrained her ample bosom while hugging her hips and teased his eyes for wanting to see her strong shapely legs. His eyes noticed her red painted toes before coming up to rest upon her eyes and the mutual passion reflected there. He crossed the room and took her in his arms, his lips claiming hers once again after being separated for so long.

They glided across the room the dress fluttered to the floor with his shorts and shirt as they fell on the bed. Their hands explored each other's flesh while their tongues tasted each other. His arousal pressed against her moist warmth, she lifted her hips as he pressed his hip forward and the feeling of being whole once more encompassed them both. While Teera's long emptiness was filled and her heart filled at being once again in his arms. Her legs wrapped around his hips pulling him even closer. Their hips smacked together like the ocean crashing on a rocky shore line with bruising force, and the waves of passion meeting and flowing apart only to crash together again and again.

Their hearts beat a unified rhythm that their bodies rushed to meet with a final explosive clash. They clung to each other as the waves of passion continued to ebb and flow settling down to a gentle caress. Resting together they both said, *"I missed you so much"* smiling at the unified thought. Brenat said, *"Right now you are all mine, but soon I will have to share you with the children, then the rest of the broken arrows."*

With that thought Teera's yearning to see her children surfaced, with regret they separated and walked to the pool's hand in hand, dressed in light robes and feeling satisfied. Brenat whispered in her ear, *"I love you and you are beautiful with my scent all over you."*

At the pools a red cloak and twenty of his warriors walked in, starring at the people in the pools and an almost palpable inhale could be heard as everyone wondered at how fast they could get to their weapons. Brian walked in with fresh warm towels, went to the priest bowing, said *"Weapons and clothes over there, please rinse the dirt off your feet before going in. If anything else is needed, please let me know."*

The Priest pulled his hood back and Ryan with a huge grin asked, *"How about a hug from my little brother?"* Brian punched Ryan in the arm, as he handed the towels to one of his servants, *"You're earlier then the day you said you would be here."* Ryan motioned for the warriors to join the others in the pools before whispering to Brian, *"I got your message that the queen, her king and the prince were all to be here in the city, so I brought a large troop of my most trusted warriors as added protection, the rest of the force will be showing up at their designated times. Besides the score of men, I have here, I have several more scores scattered about the city."*

Brian smiled, *"Go relax we'll talk later. Oh, by the way, the Royal family is in the pools as we speak and there are six ROYAL princes and a ROYAL princess as well as the King and Queen."* Brian laughed at the look on his little brother's face. Ryan stammered, *"But I thought they only had one son."* Brian said, *"Go, relax, I'll join you shortly and explain."*

Ryan undressed looking around his eyes fell on the prettiest woman he had ever seen in a small pool, he walked over to stand at the edge of the pool looking down at her with a big smile, *"Hi, I am Ryan like what you see?"* Solana looked up, *"Not really, it looks like a penis only smaller, but I must admit I have never seen a smiling donkey before."* Ryan laughed then slipped in beside her before he looked over at Joel saying, *"Hey, kid."* Joel looked at him, *"Hello, that was a nice trick you played on everyone."* Ryan distracted by the red haired beauty asked, *"Trick?"* Joel said, *"Yes, pretending to be a red cloak."* Ryan replied, *"I am one."* Joel confused said, *"But you're not evil."* Ryan said, *"Not all are, but first and foremost, I am a broken arrow."*

Just then Teera and Brenat opened the door to enter the pools. Joel jumped from the hot pool and raced across the water of the big pool, pulling everybody's eyes to the fact that he was not even getting his feet wet. Teera and Brenat watched just as stunned as everyone else, until the children seeing their parents together hollered, *"MOMMA"* and all ran towards Teera.

Joel wrapped his mother in a hug that threatened to squeeze the air from her lungs. Tears of joy at seeing her oh so big son, filled her eyes as did the sadness of remembering when she could cuddle and hold him in just one arm. Her arms wrapped around him, until her fingers felt the scars upon his back. Her hair striped as her rage resurfaced at the thought of what her son had had to endure in his four no soon to be five short years, even though he currently looked ten. Everyone grew still, as they felt Teera's rage start to surface; Brenat hugged her whispered, *"Calm down, love, it's OK"* keeping her rage barely contained. Suddenly the rest of her children wrapped her in their arms and the love of her seven miracles replaced the rage from just seconds before. Teera's pack felt her overwhelming emotion as they changed, before Teera was able to regain control over them. The children started running questions at Teera, *"How was the trip? Was it long? Where were you? Why did it take you so long to get here?"*

Just as Teera started to answer she saw her little daughter who had seemed like such an angel moments before, suddenly turn into an angry spitfire at Joel. Sallem looked angrily at Joel with her hands on her hips stomped her foot and then poked his chest with her finger as she asked him, *"Just when did you learn to walk on water and how come you did not tell us you could do it before?"* Joel blushes and stammers, *"Ah, I did not know that I could, I was just so excited to see momma that I ran to her the quickest way I could, I did not notice the water."* Sallem gave a very loud *"Huff"* that caused everyone to start laughing.

Solana, mumbled, *"We have got to teach him to keep public displays of his powers hidden."* Ryan, *"Sighed, I completely agree. I just hope the other six are not as powerful, if they are we are in trouble trying to teach and protect them if word gets out."* Solana looked at Ryan, said, *"I feel they will be, they just have not grown into their powers yet. She will be a force of her own I fear."* She pointed towards Sallem

Ryan and Solana looked at each other as if they have always known one another and passions flared in a tongue filled kiss. Solana blushed as the heat of the water started to bother her and Ryan offered that perhaps they should go to his room to cool off. Smiling as she took his hand. Solana said, *"I'm not sure we'll cool off any."* Ryan replied, *"True, but think of the fun we'll have finding out."*

Brenat jumped high into the air curling into a ball as he splashed into the water drenching Teera and the children. Only to be joined by each child in turn as they imitated their daddy. Joel walked his drenched mother to the lounging pool where the other adults were relaxing then left at the urging of Teera, and for the first time frolicked with his siblings and father in the big pool.

Teera smiled as she watched the children and Brenat, before getting pulled into the conversation that the fall festival was only a couple of moon cycles away and plans needed to be made on taking Arena City and the castle. She sighed happily as she felt Brenat slipping behind, her in the lounging pool, pulling her onto his lap. As their duties were delayed as Brenat and Teera's passions rebuilt, the other adults went to search out their own mates.

Rose and Brian watched as Ryan left with Solana, Rose elbowed Brian, *"I think Ryan has found his mate."* Brian pulled Rose in for a passionate kiss whispered, *"Lets sneak away for a while, we are going to be busy later."*

The children sensing a change in the atmosphere got dressed and left to go check out all the new merchants that had arrived in the city. The adults paired off and separated to go to their individual rooms or started to frolic in the pool.

While two workers handed out towels, Lorraine looked over at her mate, *"You just had to add some passion salts to the water."* As she dragged him to the shower room with her own passionate kiss.

❊ ❊ ❊ ❊ ❊ ❊ ❊ ❊ ❊ ❊ ❊

Blane and Tom waited until the last minute to send their main body of troops planned to get there a few weeks before the fall harvest festival begun got held up by torrential downpours and thunderstorms. Roads were washed out in flash floods and lightning strikes sent burning trees in their path. The troops got divided, the fastest got sent on, while the slowest would catch up when they could.

Blane and Tom coming from different areas on the continent, threw their hands in the air, complained as yet another storm hindered the progress of their main body of troops, after the riders had already been sent on ahead. They both looked up and said, *"God, would you at least let us get there before the city is rebuilt."*

Blane climbed out of the wagon, helping his people douse the burning lightning struck tree then helped in pulling it out of the way so they could continue. Tom climbed from his wagon and helped his troops push out yet another wagon that had gotten stuck in the mud.

❊ ❊ ❊ ❊ ❊ ❊ ❊ ❊ ❊ ❊ ❊

When passions were spent, Brenat and Teera went looking for food, smiled at seeing all the children scarfing down pancakes and sausage with Rinette and Kenny. Before long Rose and Brian meandered in, followed by Ryan and Solana, along with many other paired adults that found their way to the dining hall. Eve arrived followed by two very worn out yet happy men and soon joined the rest of them at the table.

Kenny started talking between bites, *"Over a tenth of the castle troops and over half of the city troops are loyal to our cause. A quarter of what are left will be deciding which side to fight on when the battle encompasses them. The rest are absolutely loyal to Silfer and his like. He also has the witches, gargoyles, red cloaks, hell hounds, vampires and two wyverns."*

Ryan said, *"I have two hundred men here in the city and another couple hundred warriors and militia mixed in among the red cloaks, merchants, and peasants on the way."* Eve said, *"We have got a several hundred warriors arriving over the next few weeks."* Brian states, *"A quarter of all the merchants and trades people in the city, along with their guards and militia will join us when the fighting in the city starts. As well as several hundred each of Blane and Tom's troops shall arrive a couple of weeks before the festival. Right now we are just over half in total warriors and we are still waiting on Ryan, Blane and Tom's main bodies of warriors to arrive."*

Joel hearing the mention of hell hounds walked over and asked, *"Who has hell hounds?"* Kenny replied, *"Silfer, Keres and the bad guys control them, remember how they used them to search for your daddy?"* Joel stated, *"They don't control the hell hounds, I do."* As one the adults all stared at Joel trying to digest what he meant. Brenat asked, *"What do you mean, son?"* Joel replied seriously, *"I told the hell hounds that were sent to find daddy, to pretend like they couldn't. They all do what I say."* Looking at the expressions on the others faces he asked, *"Is that bad?"* Kenny said, *"No that's good, but what do you mean by ALL?"* Joel sensing the unease in the room moved to press close to his parents, while his pack as one surrounded him as if prepared to fight to protect their alpha. Solanna and Ryan suddenly found themselves joining the young pack to protect the young frightened alpha and was astounded as they saw they were followed by Ryan's lycan warriors.

Sallem piped up, *"We didn't know how to shift until Joel*

ordered us to shift, when he did we all turned into our animals; they obey Joel, he is, "The Alpha." Brenat asked, *"Joel, could you show us how you got the others to shift?"* Joel pressed closer suddenly scared of the emotions that was pouring off so many in the room. Teera pulled him close, a low rumble of warning issued from her and those protecting Joel. Brenat said, *"Its ok son, we just need to know what you can do, as it could help us destroy the bad people."* After looking around Joel felt for the animals in the room, gave the mental Alpha command *"Shift"* and suddenly every lycan and royal in the room, including Teera, Brenat and Kenny found themselves in their animal forms, unable to resist *"The Alpha's command"* then just as fast they found their selves back in their human forms at his command.

Kenny started laughing as he sat back down in his chair, *"Well, we sure found out what the children meant by he is "THE ALPHA". Now we have to get everyone in place and figure out how we can identify each other so the quivers don't kill each other."*

Meanwhile, all the adults suddenly paled, realizing that Keres, Silfer, Dukut and the red cloaks would stop at nothing if they found out about Joel's powers and his abilities. They all agreed that he must be protected at all cost and wondered what hidden powers, the other young royals might have. But they were very thankful that Joel and the royal family were on their side in the upcoming war.

❀ ❀ ❀ ❀ ❀ ❀ ❀ ❀ ❀ ❀

Once Tom and Blane arrived they joined the daily meetings with Teera, Brenat and the others as they each discussed their parts in the upcoming battle. Plans were made for a specially trained team to go after the red cloaks, and their elite warriors. They strategized over how best to take down Keres and Silfer, with minimum damage being done to the city. Plans for defeating

Dukut were agreed upon, but everyone agreed that they needed to wait, until after the battle at Area City and its Castle was over.

The group also discussed ways to keep the children safe and out of the enemy's clutches. Everyone knew they needed to protect the young royals, and were glad that Silfer, Dukut's and Keres had no idea of Joel's powers.

No one knew that Silfer and Keres had already heard rumors of the royals. While Keres was working on capturing the young Alpha for her own plans. Silfer was working on plans of his own. He planned to kill the young royals and Brenat, and capture Teera for himself.

Book 2

The Battle

The battle for Arena City was in its third day, fighting in the streets and within the castle walls, the death count piled up on both sides.

Keres and her coven summoned the tormented souls that they control, sending them into the city to possess the dead and to kill all they found.

Teera and Brenat believing the children safe in the orphanage, meet up to help Kenny by adding a hundred lycans to the battle through the castle halls. The very stones running with blood, as they fought for every inch gained in the vicious battle. Not knowing that Keres had learned that Joel was at the orphanage

Joel saw Tyrone gripped in battle with one of the possessed. Tyrone slipped just as the dead warrior starts to impale Tyrone with its sword, Joel yells, *"STOP"* stopping the possessed warrior in its tracks. Joel stared at the warrior holding it in his gaze, while he unravels the bonds that the witches were using to control the spirit. The spirit once freed was able to join the northern lights, as the body it had possessed crumpled to the ground. It let out a screeching wail before it was freed, that directed the other spirits to Joel. At its wail, two more come around the building, heading straight for Joel. Joel stops one as he did the first, while Mike and Tyrone fight off the other. While the battle raged on, the Raven squawks, Sallem ran to the front of the orphanage to investigate, where she saw forty more of the possessed making their way to the orphanage.

Sallem communicates, *"Forty more are coming."*

Joel concentration broken the possessed warrior advances again. Tyrone replies, "We cannot fight that many here, they'll kill everyone here at the orphanage." Joel orders his pack, "Lets lead them away from the orphanage and city." Mike asks, "Where to?" Joel answers, "Out the gates, into the wilderness." With his pack on his heels, Joel drawing the attention of the possessed warriors, headed out of the city gates, drawing them away from the orphanage, the fighting and the general populace, as the possessed attacked anyone within ten feet of them. The pack followed and guarded Joel, from the regular enemy warriors that he did not even realize were near, as he led, fought and freed, the tormented souls, that possessed the dead warriors.

❈ ❈ ❈ ❈ ❈ ❈ ❈ ❈ ❈ ❈ ❈

Silfer mustered his loyal troops for a counter offensive, after realizing the siege weapons were useless, with the enemy inside city and castle walls. Hand to hand combat had made the archers shoulder their bows as they could better fight with sword, shield, tooth and claw.

Keres giggled with glee at the wanton destruction and told Silfer, *"Use the siege engines on the city below. So what if it kills more peasants then warriors use the extra warriors to push the enemies back to the city."* Just as he went to give the order one of his generals reminded him, *"Sir, if you do that the warriors you have would join the other side for it is their families that live in the city you would be destroying and it's their families your threatening to kill."*

☒ ☒ ☒ ☒ ☒ ☒ ☒ ☒ ☒ ☒ ☒

Meanwhile elsewhere, Eon continued his hunt for the black panther bitch and the pup, she protected. Still fantasizing about converting her and how he would force her to service his needs, before together they ate the miserable pup she protected.

Characters

Brenat: Royal Multi Were ... Parents: Sid & Elsie ... Sister: Rose... Wife: Teera... Children: Joel, Sallem, Tyrone, Tye, Willie, Mike, Billy

Teera: Royal Multi Were ... Parents: King James & Queen Rizalle ... Husbands: Aslam, Brenat ... Children: Joel, Sallem, Tyrone, Tye, Willie, Mike, Billy

Joel: Royal Multi Were ... Parents: Brenat & Teera

Sallem: Royal Were Bear ... Parents: Brenat & Teera

Tyrone: Royal Were Wolf ... Parents: Brenat & Teera

Willie: Royal Were Jaguar... Parents: Brenat & Teera

Tye: Royal Were Panther ... Parents: Brenat & Teera

Billy: Royal Were Tiger... Parents: Brenat & Teera

Mike: Royal Were Lion ... Parents: Brenat & Teera

King James: Royal Lycan King ... wife: Rizalle ... Daughter: Teera

Queen Rizalle: Royal Lycan/ Hell hound Were, Queen ... Husband: James ... Daughter: Teera

Sid: Royal Were Polar Bear ... Brenat's dad ... Eon's older brother ... Elsie's husband ... Brenat & Rose's father

Elsie: Royal Were Panther ... Brenat's mother ... Sid's Wife ... Brenat & Rose's Mother

Rose: Lycan ... Brenat's sister ... Brian's wife

Silfer: Lycan Beta ... James's younger half-brother ... same mothers by her second marriage, Dukut's twin ... Teera's uncle

Dukut: Lycan Beta ... James's youngest half-brother ... same mothers by her second marriage, Silfer's twin ... Teera's uncle

Kenny: Royal Were Lion ... James's unknown half-brother only James, Rizalle, Kenny and Teera knew who he was ... same fathers ... Rinette's mate ... Teera's uncle

Arris: human ... Kenny's scribe

Rinette: Lycan ... Kenny's mate

Chris: Human - orphan

Chad: Human - orphan

Ken: Lycan- orphan

Larry: Lycan - orphan

Mary: Lycan - orphan

Eve: Lycan... Teera's second

Ryan: Lycan... Brian's brother

Tom: Lycan ... Blane's brother

Solana: Royal Were jaguar... Ryan's mate

Brian: Lycan ... Ryan's brother

Blane: Lycan... Tom's brother

Dru: human ... Reed's boyfriend

Reed: human ... Dru's boyfriend

Jason: Lycan ... Kenny's Sergeant

Walt: Lycan ... scout

Asslam: Vampire King ... Teera's first husband

Morley: vampire ... ex human gang leader

Keres: extremely evil witch ... sadist ... servant of Lucifer

Haroc: Redcoat ... aka Toe-less

Commander Rivek: red coat commander

Eon: Royal Were bear... Leader of Gaunts & Red coats, Lucifer's General... Sid's younger brother corrupted by Keres

Ranks

Lycan Clan Ranks

THE ALPHA: A legendary supreme alpha said to be able to command all Shifters and animals of all types

Alpha King: Male ruler of the clan

Alpha Queen: Female ruler of the clan

Alpha Prince: Next in line for the throne unless disputed

Alpha Princess: If they are the only child then they gain control of the throne otherwise is married to another leader or his son.

Beta: Second in command to the royal family

Knights: Takes care` of matters of war and protects the royal family

Captain: Lead warriors in times of war. Providing more input on the war

Scout / Warriors: A dangerous positions and important roles in the clan

Scholar: Handles most of the paper work that the clan must deal with

Epsilons: The elders of the clan

Zeltas: Lycan members of the clan that work with the human clan members

Kappas: Young Lycans

Sigmas: Human members of the clan

Omegas: clan members at the bottom of the ranking by either punishment or lack of experience that do the most work or jobs others don't

Red Cloaked Monk / Priest Ranks

The Chamberlain: Head of the council. Has final say in all matters

Second: A member of council   Acts as Chamberlain when Chamberlain is absent. Usually sent on the dangerous missions in place of the Chamberlain

Council: consist of four from the religious faction and four of the warrior faction

Inquisitors: direct council members wishes, command killers and priests

Elites: Only answers to the Inquisitors and does all spying and assignations.   They are Masters of disguise, stealth, weapons and magic.   They are all purpose Mercenaries

Killers: lead warriors into battle train warriors

Warriors: fight wars also train the militia to fight and protect their towns.

Militia: town defense

Priests / Monk: train, teach, handle the blessings of the general populace and testing the children taking the chosen ones as apprentices or sending them to the Militia

Vampire Coven Ranks

King: the undisputed Leader of all vampires, the eldest and most powerful

Coven Lords and Ladies: King's direct descendants; they are the ones who are entrusted to enforce the affairs of the coven and to its members

Death Dealers: trained by a Master Death Dealer, they are specifically chosen to hunt down and destroy their arch rivals, the Lycan

There is only One ***Master Death Dealer*** at any given time

Weapons Master: in charge of creating weapons and body armor specifically designed to kill Lycans they are chosen for their ingenuity and high intelligence

Aristocrats: vampires who no longer care for the mortal world and have little concern for the war between their species and that of the Lycan